THE
MADNESS
OF
ROBIN
RANDLE

THE MADNESS OF ROBIN RANDLE

a novel
by
WOOD DICKINSON

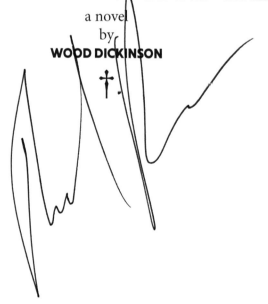

The Madness of Robin Randle

Copyright © 2018 by Glen Wood Dickinson

Taygete Press
644 W 61 st Ter
Kansas City, MO 64113

www.taygetepress.com
www.wooddickinson.com
www.10pastmidnight.com
www.robinrandle.com

Cover art by Liz Dickinson
Layout by Andrew Dickinson

ISBN: 9781728657790

First Edition

14 13 12 11 10 / 10 9 8 7 6 5 4 3 2 1

for
Patti Shea

TABLE OF CONTENTS – BOOK ONE
IN THE REGION WHERE MADNESS DWELLS

Prologue...11

The Nightcrawlers..**16**

   The Long Walk Home..17

   The Nightcrawlers..40

   Tattoo..46

Between Darkness and Wonder..........................51

   Station...52

   The Truth of Shadows...61

   The Return..70

Under the Stars of Madness...............................81

   I Am My Nightmare World..................................82

   Across the Hills of Damnation...........................88

   The Foundations of Heaven and Hell.................96

The Mystic Chords of Memory..........................102

   Arrival...103

   Sign of the Raven...108

   Reunion...117

The End of Reason..124

   The Passage Comes..125

   Between Wonder and the Sky............................134

   The Circle of Wind..141

The Legend of My Creation...............................148

   The Slow Melting Snow.....................................149

   The Tablet of Destiny..155

   The Gate of the Seven Stars.............................163

TABLE OF CONTENTS – BOOK TWO
DURING THE TIME OF SHADOWS

The Order of Eternity..171

Reclamation..172

The Binding Place..199

The Wind of Terror..215

In the Valley of Dying Stars............................226

The Black Tower...227

The Unfolding...233

The Lake of Murders...238

In the Place of the Unknowing

(The Place That Should Not Be).......................242

The Ending to All Things..243

Crossing the Gates of Dusk and Dawn...............248

Ask First The Holy

From the Journals of Macy Beas............................267

Notes on Mythology and Religion.....................280

Bibliography...282

Book One

IN THE REGION WHERE MADNESS DWELLS

Wood Dickinson

PROLOGUE

A madness filled my nights. Well not nights exactly. I worked nights so I guess I should say a madness filled my days. Regardless, I hoped maybe writing all of it down would help me gain some measure of control over my sleep. I was plagued by a recurring nightmare. I don't know how most people's recurring nightmares play out but in mine every detail seemed to happen in exactly the same way. Never varies.

This was how it started. I was outside and it was always late in the afternoon on a cloudless day. A warm summer like breeze blew my hair into my face, stinging my eyes. It does this every time. I reached up and pushed my hair back into some semblance of order. Listen, I was having this same wretched nightmare every day of my life and the timing was great, it always finished just before I would normally wake up and get ready for work. It's crazy silly, like getting lost in the fun house when all your friends had gone home. You realize you're alone and what was fun now is terrifying. In my nightmare, I find myself standing in this strange meadow that was sloping down and away from me. I'd never seen a meadow like this. It was filled with waist-high grass as green as new spring leaves and as the wind blew this grass started swaying like hula girls at a late afternoon luau on Waikiki.

Storm clouds rolled in from off the horizon, spinning and tumbling like a wicked ocean reaching out a warning just ahead of its hurricane. The clouds were always changing color from a steel-like gray to a boiling black with lightning flashing highlights into their creases. In my heart, I knew this storm carried an evil that only God and his angels could fight. I feel fear as it rides on the tips of the wind. This storm was bringing something wicked and it was coming on fast. The lightning flashed, budding from the clouds like small flowers then exploding into blossoms that grew across the length of the sky casting a searing white light that blinded me. Then there was the thunder. It was a thunder that could only have been born at the center of the earth. Everything shook. I stumbled backwards as the grass around me was blown as flat as a dirt road then I'm shaken to the ground as well.

Now on my back I opened my eyes and my vision cleared. I was looking up into this raging storm. I saw a horror torn from the pages of some ancient and forgotten manuscript not meant for the eyes of man. I was seeing a monster and I mean that literally. This was nothing like the movies I'd seen, it was a real horror being born from the violence and power of the storm. It had a bulbous shaped head that seemed to stretch out for miles across the sky as it pressed down out from the boiling clouds. A black face formed on the surface of the creature's head and what began to grow and hang from it looked like a hundred wild black snakes whipping around with a mass uncontrolled purpose. I struggled to my feet looking for some kind of shelter but there wasn't any. Not even a tree. With nowhere to run, I stood frozen in my terror as I realized it was me who had become their purpose. These wild black snakes began to resolve themselves into tentacle-like appendages dripping with some kind of heavy black oil that was beginning to rain down on me. Where this oil landed, it soaked through my clothes and started to burn my skin. The tentacles reached up toward the heavens, then turn back toward the ground, and me. They dropped from the sky like lightning. There wouldn't have been time to hide even if I could have found shelter. These tentacles are just there, reaching out toward me. They looked like long broken fingers bending in impossible and horrid ways. They stroked my face and then each probing finger splits in two, creating even more dripping black fingers for this monster to use as it began to caress my waist. The tentacles tighten, holding me captive so this monster could paint its sticky black oil over my entire body. Everywhere they touched there was pain like hot grease. The black oil penetrated into my skin causing blisters to rise and erupt oozing more of the black oil from my own body. It smelled like a hundred dead and decomposing rats left in the walls of an old house long abandoned.

The creature's face began to grow a deep-set pair of eyes that ignited and burned a red as red as a setting summer sun. I think that they could burn holes right through me, blazing from their black distorted sockets. These eyes spewed hate. That hate was all I could feel. A hate just because I was here and still alive to witness this monster's birth. A hate that let me know that this girl should have died years ago when my dad had tried to beat me to death. I began to feel remorse. I should have just let myself pass away at the hospital where I'd slept in a brain-dead coma just so this monster wouldn't have had to waste its time killing me today.

It was just when I think these thoughts that a deeper darkness opened in its face right below its eyes. Inside this new and growing darkness, I could see stars. Midnight had come to that one spot. An evil midnight for sure, full of dark matter and black star dust filling the space between dead angels and dying suns all born in a distant age. It was the age when creation had only happened a moment ago. I know this sounds crazy but it seemed as if these stars had been waiting for me. Waiting for me to see them since their birth just so I would know all was out of whack with both space and time. I felt these stars. They were watching me, knew me and now they had learned the truth. I was the one who'd cheated death once. Now I was being called upon to settle that debt. The tentacles encasing my body reached up and tightened around my throat choking me with their oily stench. I gasped for air but found I could no longer breathe. A sadness passed through me. I thought, I would never know the wonder of drawing a breath again. The light faded from my eyes and I could feel a distant pain somewhere in my body but I could no longer tell where it was coming from. My life was slipping away. I had only moments left. I wondered at how a life was nothing more than a collection of these moments and now mine were done. That's when I scream. Not in the dream but in real life. I would bolt awake at that exact moment every time. Never gentle.

A mist floated around in my head. I always hoped the memory of the nightmare's events would pass from me upon waking. Fat chance that. It seemed fate had already chosen for me that this will be the nightmare I will never forget.

So that's it. Now the world knows why an eighteen-year-old Robin Randle believed in monsters.

PART 1

THE NIGHTCRAWLERS

I look above
Into the failing sky
A cold dark silent blue.

Then beyond that and into the inky black place
Where death waits
Rolling and boiling like snakes in swamp water.
Then I see it reaching,
Reaching down.
Always reaching down
Just beyond the collapsing blue
Like smoke ahead of a fire with Halloween tree hands
Made of black ice so cold they will never melt
In this humid summer air that surrounds me.

I sigh as sweat drips down my face,
I look toward the lake yearning to forget
Yet knowing it is always reaching.
And I wait.
We wait.

Until that day.
The day it finds us,
As it has always found us.

Wood Dickinson

THE LONG WALK HOME

I was told once that there seems to be some of us that just stand ready to give everything we have for a cause no matter what the cost. I want you to know that when this started I knew I wasn't one of those kinds of people. I had a lot to learn if that was the kind of person I was going to be. That's if I even wanted to be that kind of person. So listen, this was how it started. I think maybe it's how all stories start. I mean the stories we live and the stories we tell each other. True or not they're important. Without sharing this part of ourselves, surely that which makes us human would fade and die. As it turned out, my story was going to be long and complicated yet the beginning was small and simple. Like the epics of old, events had been put in motion and out of the control of those who would pay the price. Nope, not a hint at what was coming. Especially for me. I'm Robin Randle, waitress extraordinaire at a dive on Mill Street, Mel's All Night Diner. Thankfully, or so I thought, on this particular night, my shift ended at midnight. With the chime from the grease-stained 1952 classic Coors clock watching over the bar, it was now the first day of October. My most-loved month. You know, it's good to get off at midnight. I mean I get to avoid the inevitable drunks who started arriving around two a.m. I never could understand how those men got up at seven in the morning and made it in to work on time. Four hours just doesn't sound like enough time to sleep it off. Well, not for me anyway. But shit, every night, there they were, the same drunks wandering in, eyes glazed and attitude sharp. Small town familiarity plus the alcohol prompted these men to take liberties they shouldn't. Especially with waitresses. To them, we were toys to play with and if you didn't take all their obscene shitty remarks along with endless bitching and the inevitable small tips, the job would simply evaporate much like the paycheck I got every week. At that time in my life I didn't feel like I deserved better.

Now listen, when I say familiarity it's because Mason wasn't a big city, just a punk town of about two thousand people nestled away in the Texas Hill Country. For anyone who stopped for gas as they were passing through or maybe visiting relations, they were sure to learn that it was the home of Fred Gipson, Mason's little claim to fame. For those who aren't literary types, he's the guy that wrote Old Yeller, which I can state, I'd never read. The facts were reading had never been my strong suit and for sure reading wasn't high on my to-do list now.

Now for the disadvantage of getting off at midnight. I'd have to walk home alone. Carrie who usually worked the same shift as I did wasn't a great friend or anything but we did live in the same wreck of a boarding house. The venerable Hartford Arms. An unlisted national historic landmark. Shit, it was probably built a hundred years ago but it sure wasn't on any preservation list I could find. I worried these days much more than since my event. To be honest I didn't know what I knew. I think I knew it might be time for the psych ward but know this I'd die before I'd let them drag me into that place. I had to get back into the moment. Right now, walking with Carrie just felt better. Sweat made a surprise appearance on my forehead. Not at all normal for my usually calm exterior. So then, and I mean right that very second, every damn thing around me felt wrong. After my event, I'd somehow become aware that there was a kind of balance in the world. Deep inside me it was like the feeling of the guilt you get when you think you've been caught doing something wrong. No reason for the guilt. You haven't done anything wrong but somewhere inside you know you really did do something wrong in the past but just didn't get caught. Now balance had to be restored. But for all I could tell there wasn't any real surprise where my life was concerned. These days I saw too much.

Mel broke my introspection and barked, "Robin you're out of here. You think I'm paying you to stand around?" Mel was a short fat and greasy little man with a bald head and piercing blue eyes. He rarely left his kitchen to help us. He liked to cook his chicken fried steak mashed potatoes and gravy and leave the drunks to us. His voice scratched in my ears.

I didn't answer just went to my locker in the kitchen. There I stopped and looked at the locker door that I claimed as my own. I examined the names scratched into its faded surface that was pock-marked with dirt, rust and faded white paint. Running my fingers over those names I had to wonder. A lot of years, a lot of women. I shuddered. What was the fate of these women? Were they even alive? My name was gouged into the door too, just to show I was here. Shit, I wouldn't know until I had joined them in their fate.

I opened the locker door and retrieved my travel-worn backpack then turned away from the kitchen and headed out the back door. These days I felt temporary. My thoughts weren't clear anymore and looking out into the future, my future, wasn't in my wheelhouse. To be honest each night I left work I didn't know if I'd ever return. The fact was after this night I'd never return to Mason again in my life. I could feel a high strangeness. Tonight, was peculiar. It was like the slamming of that rusted and stained dark red kitchen door sounded more like the closing of some part of my life. I became light-headed, wavered, and then slumped against the dirty brick wall. Then I slid down to the ground and sat amongst the empty beer cans and cigarette butts. Looking up the blind alley, the walls were covered in graffiti and the ground was littered with dirty needles scattered deep into the dark corners where nothing more could be seen. Wow, evidence that even Mason had a drug problem. I couldn't tell but I didn't think anyone else was in the alley with me. It was just me and the good old dumpster for Mel's. The smell of sweet and rotting food made me think of the putrid men inside the bar.

There had been one woman I'd waited on tonight that wasn't that way. I don't talk much to the women who frequent places like Mel's but this girl was different. She'd told me that I glowed. That was plain strange but the way she'd said it made me feel as if she cared. She asked me to sit for a moment and not being busy I did. I asked, "Where you from?"

She replied, "New England. Name's Macy." She reached out her hand. I took it and shook.

I said, "I'm Robin. I don't think I've ever met someone from New England. Far away from here."

She said, "Yes it is. I have a long way to go before I get home. If I get home." She reached into her pants pocket and pulled out her wallet. She opened it and took out a business card and handed it to me. "You never know where you might end up. Take it." I reached out and took the card. All that was printed on it was her first name and a telephone number. "Call if you ever need help."

I stuttered, "Why would you do this?" She smiled at me. Mel yelled my name and the moment was over. "Sorry have to go." I stood and said, "Thank you." I went to pick up an order and when I turned back toward the room Macy was gone. A pile of money rested near her empty plate. I stuffed the card into my jeans pocket. Maybe I would need it someday.

I fumbled around in my backpack and produced a cigarette then lit it, letting smoke envelop my head. That brought a gray haze to the already dim alley. I started coughing and felt pain in my chest. I coughed up some phlegm and spat it towards the black empty corners. At least I couldn't smell the dumpster any more.

Shit, dim alleys and smoky gray haze; my life. I shunned the daylight hours becoming a vampire that would be asleep before sunrise and wake after sunset so the world wouldn't notice she existed. This was what I'd come to. A life wasted by violence and confusion with no guide to show me the way out. If there was ever a person born without purpose, without hope, I'm the one. So far, my role in this world had been to be on the receiving end of hate. I mean I know I was never wanted. That's a no brainer, you think. I mean not from the very day I was born.

I took a final drag on my smoke and flicked it against the dumpster. It broke into pieces, hot ash scattering the alley. Looking down at my tattered jeans I noticed cigarette ashes had dropped onto my old white baggy sweatshirt. I brushed them off and stood, grabbed my pack and fished out my Nano. I put my ear buds on and started listening to Mogwai's "I'm Jim Morrison, I'm Dead" as I started out onto the street. Done. Smoking was done. I was a fool to even try it. Just one more desperate attempt to run from myself and seek my happiness in another substance. I used to drink. A lot. Drugs too, but only marijuana. No more. There wasn't anything in the world that could lift me from the darkness I was sinking into. Shit, every day it was the same old question, why had God bothered creating me? Some say we each have a purpose in life. That this great God had created each one of us for a reason. Maybe He was just having a bad day when my number was called. Maybe there just wasn't a God.

I came out onto Long Street and was greeted by a northern wind blowing through Mason bringing a chill to the air. Funny, I could feel the coming frost, the breath of the Snow Queen blowing a call to death as her dried leaves streamed down the street circling in crazy little tornados before blasting off into the alleys to carry on their antics in private. October is a fickle month. I still like it best. The imagination conjures witches and monsters, all nothing more than an extension of our own personal turmoil and evil. Leaves scattered everywhere painting the world in a palette of brown and reds. Unlike any other time of year. The loss of leaves from the trees allowed more moonlight to filter to the ground, making it easier to navigate the night. In the past, home was the last place I wanted to be. That was before my Mel's days.

I was still in high school then and thinking maybe I'd survive my dad long enough to graduate. I liked going out with Lucy and Jim, downing a fifth of Southern Comfort or smoking weed, sometimes both. All this made it so I could get home late. By then Dad was passed out and Mom would have had her nightly beating. I tried to miss the being beaten part. I was plain scared. I just knew one day Dad was going to hit me too hard, maybe it would only take just once to end my life. I'm not a big girl, just five four and barely a hundred pounds and I mean he was a very big man and did I say mean? His anger seethed out of his body like snakes out of flood waters. October was also the month all this started. It would be the month of endings too, but I can't jump ahead.

As I walked down Long Street the emptiness began to frighten me. I could feel the north wind trying to hold me back. I just stopped and standing very still I let the wind engulf me. I could feel the air blow softly around my face like a gentle piece of silk. I breathed in the smells of fall. The last vestiges of burnt leaves and dust. Then there was something else. Something buried deep inside the wind using the wind to carry its evil intent. Another wind, subtle and laced with ice. I got this crazy chill. Monsters. It was the wind that would bring the monsters. Not the monsters of Halloween that play and run from house to house collecting a treasure trove of candy. No, my monsters. Monsters hidden from the waking world only revealed to the few who had crossed that line between life and death and dared to return. This hidden part of the wind cut through me not gently but like a dull knife slicing slowly just to make the pain last longer.

I pulled my ear buds off. I needed to hear. Something was wrong.

I started walking with urgency. Now I had an unnatural fear of the dark. Darkness was something I used to love. I'd wander the streets at all hours of the night wanting to escape down to Fort Mason City Park. At the park, I'd take one of the paths into the deeper darkness of the woods. Alone and with no flashlight I would use the light of the moon to guide me. I never caught on a root or fell tripping over stones buried deep into the ground. Sometimes Lucy would come along, maybe Jim too. We'd go deep into the woods near the old Union Pacific mainline. Hiding off in the woods, we'd watch as trains would fly by like banshees in the night unaware of our presence. We'd put pennies on the tracks and if we could find them after the train's passage we'd consider them mystical objects. Back then the night was soft, friendly and concealing. The forest helped me step out of my wretched life. At least for a little while.

How times have changed. Now, darkness holds an evil power over me. A power that creeps like a tapeworm moving its way toward my gut. Slowly and methodically it cuts a trail deep into my body without me ever feeling a thing. That scares me; leaves me crippled. Being alone in the darkness was so frightening my anxiety would build to a point where I could hardly breathe. Last fall I'd spent what would become my final day walking far out into the country so when I'd made it back into town it was late. Night had stolen over Mason preparing to take me with it. I decided to cut through the park, walking in the woods that eventually formed a wall in my back yard. I could see just beyond the break in the trees toward the back of my house when the peace I had claimed from the night suddenly fled. Something grabbed me from behind, pulling me back into the darkness. I twisted and strained to see who it was, thinking maybe Jim was playing a joke. I'd let him have it but what I saw wasn't Jim. In fact, what I saw couldn't have been real. It wasn't a person even though it walked on two legs. Shit, I know a person when I see one and this was absolutely no person. It was something blacker than the shadows surrounding it and it smelled very old. Rotting. Its touch on my skin was cold as death. A monster, I could think of no other expression. It was breathing heavily as it pulled at my arm. I screamed and screamed but no sound came from my mouth. I pulled my arm with all my strength and it slipped from the monster's grip. It retreated into the darkness but I couldn't tell how far. How could such a thing be? I should have stayed to find out. I mean, where could such a thing come from? It was then that I felt it. Going home was going to be a horrible mistake. The night had suddenly become hostile. I was scared and where are you supposed to go at 16 to be safe? Home, just not my home. Not on this night. I barely remember what happened to me once I was inside the house. It just unraveled so fast and yet somehow, I always see it in slow motion. A thing I'd never seen except in the movies. That night I was beaten by my father. I can't remember much of it. I do remember what came before my beating. Murder. A brutal trauma that would live in me forever. I remember I woke up briefly in the emergency room at Hill Country Memorial Hospital. Everything was blurred and the words people were saying didn't make sense. Light then dark, I was fading. I was scared. I knew I was dying and struggled to come back from the black place I was fading to. I couldn't stop slipping into what felt like nothing. My last thought was death is the end. All I could sense was blackness all around. It felt completely empty. I pushed hard but I just couldn't hold it back so the black tide took me. I just faded away.

I stayed faded away for seven months. During that time, I traveled. In my head, I mean. I fell into emptiness. Then to my surprise I woke up on a beach. Ocean waves lapped at the shore and a dark forest loomed just past the sand. I would find out I'd landed in a place called The Region. A land of perpetual night. My memories of this place are dim. I searched many places and talked to anyone who would listen to me. I remember finally learning that if I wanted to get out of The Region and find my way back to life I would have to make a journey to a place where there were all these balls of light. One of them would be mine and I had to find it because only then could I dispel my darkness. I thought I had to shatter it on the ground. Most of this time was missing from my memory now. I do remember that there were things that tried to stop me. Dark things with snapping teeth and claws. Sometimes they'd keep to the shadows and other times meet me in the open. Fragments of terror ripped through my mind. I remember this girl. She'd come out of nowhere in my mind. She helped me. She fought with these monsters like a warrior and told me she could fly, but only sometimes. I just couldn't remember her look or voice, not even her name.

When I thought of her I felt an inordinate amount of sadness like you get when you think of old toys and comic books now lost in childhood. Those things that grounded us but now they're gone and only their shadows remain.

Day never came to The Region. Always a full moon up in the sky to illuminate the way through that darkness I feared. I lived what seemed like a lifetime hiding from things bent on my final death, while I kept trying my best to fight with my weak arms and small frame. I think I lost friends. Their names now buried in the darkness of The Region never to be remembered again.

Then it happened. I found my ball. This is so confused in my head now. I was in a place, a palace maybe. It was full of these balls. I know my warrior friend was dying. She'd just taken too many blows. The monsters were right on top of us and she had fought them as I took my glowing ball and broke it on the ground. Light flooded around me. I looked up and in her eyes I saw a century of sadness. Then I died.

In this world, the real world, I woke up. I found that I was in a large hospital room with tubes running riot all over my body. There were several other people sleeping on hospital beds in this room as well. You know not sleeping but in comas. At the moment, I didn't know better. What I tried to do was lift my hand and look at my arm but I felt so weak I just couldn't. It was like being weighed down. It felt as if something was pressing down on me and restraining me to the bed. I could rotate my head though, so I turned toward the windows at the far end of the room. All I could see were dark swirling clouds throwing sheets of rain at the glass.

I couldn't believe I'd woken up. I learned that I'd been in a coma. It took a while to realize all that I'd been experiencing the monsters, wars, even my special friend was all a dream. It had seemed so real. I ached for my lost friend with a true longing you can only have with certain loss, not a dream. Maybe the emptiness of a coma is another world, no dreams at all but a place where you live another kind of life. One thing's for certain, I've never told anyone about this world and over time most of my memories of The Region faded like dreams do upon waking.

Well, I'm eighteen now and on my own. That sounds funny. I'd been on my own for years. You see, the first monster I ever met was my father. He killed my mom. That was just before he almost killed me. He shot her dead right in the living room. The bullets went right through her spraying blood all over the living room wall. He did this right in front of me but I was lucky in a sadistic sort of way. He'd used up all his bullets, making sure mom was dead so when he turned to shoot me his gun just clicked. That made him furious. I turned and tried to run but he was a big man. He lunged for me and took me to the ground. Then I felt pain as his fist connected with my jaw. An explosion of light and that's all I remember until I woke up in the dream world of The Region.

I found out later the cops had busted the door down and shot him dead as he was beating me. Like everything else in that sick fuck's life, he couldn't even kill his family right. All he'd done well was drink, then get angry and beat my mom and try to beat me if I was around. I'll never understand why mom didn't leave him. Maybe even take me with her. She seemed resolved to stick it out. Until death do us part. She sure did that. No thought for me. I suppose the truth is neither of them cared much about whether I was alive or dead. Now it doesn't matter.

I shook my head to stop my incessant thinking and focus myself as I crossed 4th street at the edge of MacMillan Park. It was there that I saw a dark slithering worm trapped by the concrete sidewalk, unable to burrow back into the moist darkness of the earth. I stopped and looked down at it. There was a time. A time when I'd had grandparents. These memories were dim, buried in a past I spent most of my time trying to forget, but not lost. I do remember my grandfather calling these worms nightcrawlers. He said that's because they mostly came out of the ground at night. He raised them, if that's a thing you can do, in stacked boxes in the basement of his home. We'd go dig out a bunch and drop them in a coffee can to take on fishing expeditions. Bait! I remembered the pungent odor of those crates. A sweet mix of rotting vegetables and dirt floor along with mold growing on the old stone walls of the basement. I leaned down and picked up the worm. It twisted in my fingers wanting to escape the horror of a giant who possessed the power to rip him apart. I dropped him back out on the grass. Best I could do. Then something moved out in the darkness of the park. It sounded much bigger than the worm I just rescued. I decided to move on. The sound of irregular footsteps kept pace with me. When I'd stop there would be a scurrying sound like something shuffling a little deeper into the dark. It wasn't human. People just don't make a sound like that. There was this smell too. The stink of rotting flesh mixed with cinnamon and the smell of the ocean. In one moment, it intoxicated me and the next I wanted to throw up.

Adrenaline pumped, sharpening my senses. Standing still I yelled, "Hello? Somebody there?"

Silence answered. Then just like in those cheap horror movies the street light above my head grew bright then died, leaving me in the darkness I feared. I stared into the park, hoping to see something, anything that would explain the sounds. Turning my head, I looked down the empty street to see just how much further I needed to go. I felt stupid doing that but at the edge of my field of vision something large moved in the darkness of the park. It was moving toward me. I snapped my head around to find it but it hid from me somehow. Was that even possible? Of course not. There wasn't a chance in hell it was possible.

Knowing that, I took in slow deep breaths and tried to calm myself. There couldn't be anything out in the darkness except maybe a person walking in the night like me. I took a step and heard a loud scraping sound. It was like a large metal pipe being dragged along the concrete walkway in the park. I started back down the street then stopped. The sound didn't. It just got louder. Closer maybe. As I listened the memories of my dream world, the one inside my coma shivered through my mind. That's when I started running.

I only had two blocks to the boarding house. I felt stupid reacting this way but I wasn't brave enough to look behind me. I could still hear its foot falls and they didn't fall in pairs like a person's but more like the scurrying sound I think a crab would make. Click

click click and that dragging pipe sound. I was sure whatever was making that noise wasn't a pipe. I fished in the pocket of my jeans for the outside door key of the boarding house so I'd be ready to plunge right inside. Crossing 5th I left the park behind me. I could see the light over the boarding house door. Even with the park behind me now the sounds didn't stop after I'd crossed 5th. It was closer and more urgent. I reached the battered front door and rammed the key into the rusted lock. It took all my strength to turn the key in the lock and I hoped it wouldn't break off before I got the door open. The lock gave with a snap and turning the knob I risked a look back down Long. Nothing. Just the leaves blowing around in a midnight emptiness. I noticed the street light over the park entrance was working again. Figures. Just as I heaved a big sigh the bulb in the light over the door where I stood flickered out. Enough, at least for tonight. I stepped across the threshold and pulled the door closed. I locked it after me and stood for a moment listening to see if anything would challenge the locked door. It seemed silent outside but I couldn't be sure. I looked around the dirty entry hall and thought about checking my mailbox but decided this wasn't a good time. I don't get any real mail anyway. I turned and ran up the stairs to the second floor and ran down to the end of the hall where my room was. I stood looking at my unpainted apartment door and tried to catch my breath. This was crazy. I finally unlocked my door and went inside. I immediately turned and shut and bolted it. After a moment, I checked the door again like I was expecting it to have unlocked itself, but surprise, it hadn't.

I walked over to the kitchenette and pulled off my dirty sweatshirt. I dropped it on the floor then caught my reflection in the tattered mirror that had been glued to the wall of my room. I stopped and studied the girl on the other side of the mirror. She was too skinny with small breasts. She had dark red hair, long and tossed in an uncontrollable way. That girl had never worried about a bad hair day in her life. Slim waist and wide hips, I turned to look at my full ass and noticed my jeans were starting to wear through my butt. Time to hit the Salvation Army Store. I may be a mess of a person but at least I was standing straight. No slumped shoulders but confident ones daring the world to fuck with her.

I turned away and sat at the small table I'd pushed up against the wall. All I could do was put my head into my hands. There was something that would explain all this. I thought of my life before the coma. I was little then. Shit, I still am but it felt like another person's life all jumbled-up till the moment I was almost beat to death. My time in The Region was another person's life. A story told only in fragments. I closed my eyes and took some deep breaths to help calm down. I was having a hell of a life. Time had stopped for me when my coma ended. I didn't have anyone I could ask for help anymore. My old friends avoided me like I was a leper. I was the talk of the town even though I didn't do anything but survive. There had to be something wrong with me. Who has their dad try and kill her whole family? Sure, you hear about it on the news or a TV program but that's someplace else. Not Mason. Just maybe I could kill my whole family too, but I didn't have a family anymore. Just me. It'd always been just me. My eyes grew heavy and I nodded off. My dreams felt more like memories anymore. The event had left me with holes. That event being the witnessing of my mother's murder. The doctors told me I may never remember certain things clearly. I wonder if I'll ever remember anything clearly. So, when I do dream it all feels like memories I'd lost due to the event and the coma. As I drifted into sleep I dreamed of Lucy. I loved Lucy. She stuck with me, through my hard times. At least until the murder. Then even she scorned me. I had had two friends before the event. Lucy was my closest friend I think but memories of her are lost. Jim feels like a shadow. A name that was attached to a person I knew once but couldn't even picture in my mind. I didn't know where Lucy or Jim were now but back in the day we'd had good times. I remembered how we'd snuck down to Reading's Mill. We'd been drinking Southern Comfort all night and we were drunk and I mean slam drunk.

Reading's Mill was the town pool. It was on the edge of town and after dark no one goes out that way. It was Lucy's idea to go. We climbed the chain link fence. Straddling the top, Jim slipped and fell eight feet onto some lounge chairs. Lucy and I started laughing so hard we both almost fell too. Once inside we stripped for some skinny dipping. There was one small thing we didn't know. The pool manager actually lived at the pool.

Howard Beam. I'm not making this up. During the school year when the pool was closed Howard was the custodian of Hocker's Middle School. Since Mason only had one middle school Howard knew all the kids in town.

We all broke the surface at the same time, laughing, then the lights came on. Howard was sauntering toward us. "Well, if it isn't little Jimmy, Lucy and Robin Randle. You kids must be well along in high school by now."

There was no place to run and we were all naked anyway, which was okay when the lights were off but now the fact posed a serious problem. Howard continued, "Let's see, should I call your parents or call the cops? Got to think this over a minute."

Jim, always trying to be the suave one, was a guy with a cool exterior but he didn't have the goods. He spoke up, "Mr. Beam. How yah doing? Uh, listen, we've learned our lesson Mr. Beam. I mean, we're here on a dare and who could resist. We'll just go on home and never do anything like this again."

It sounded weak to me and Howard shook his head. "That's a good story boy but the bait is weak and I'm not biting. You kids naked?"

Embarrassed out of my sixteen-year-old mind even through the Southern Comfort haze I answered simply, "Yes." Always dreams about the past were hazy to me but tonight this dream seemed very clear. Things had shifted. That tilt in the world I'd felt earlier tonight left me suddenly feeling like an observer sitting outside my own life watching to see what damn fool thing I'd do next. I didn't know hell was about to pay us a visit. This memory was all wrong. We all started swimming toward the side where Mr. Beam was standing and Lucy was bringing up the rear as usual.

I made it to the edge of the pool first, just in time to hear Lucy scream. It was one of those, "I'm gonna die" kind of screams and to tell the truth, I'd never heard that kind of scream until that night. Then she did. Die that is. Something in the water grabbed her arms and lifted her naked body out of the pool. Huge black worms started to wrap themselves around her body. They oozed a black oil that seemed to be burning Lucy's skin. In just seconds she was completely covered. They reminded me of the nightcrawler I'd rescued earlier tonight but way too big to be real but this was a dream the worm I'd rescued had been real. Then a little squeeze and pop. Lucy was now all over the pool and us. Jim turned to me and said, "I'll never forget this day."

Looking into his eyes I said, "Neither will I."

As Lucy's screams drifted into the night Jim and I stood shoulder-to-shoulder waist deep in the now red tainted pool, ready for anything but what came next. I heard something like the rhythm of someone pounding a drum. The smell of ashes filled the air then I slipped away from that moment. I'd shut the entire world off so when the pounding on my door came I jumped awake.

Someone was pounding on my door. I fell out of my chair hitting the floor. Not moving I listened to what was in the hall like I had super hearing or something. Feet shuffled and again bang bang bang. This time someone said, "Robin Randle. Open the fucking door and let me in."

I screwed up some courage and screamed, "Go away you shit! I don't know you. I won't open shit to a stranger." Quiet again. I could feel the man in the hall, I was assuming a man, standing still, thinking. I wondered how he'd even gotten into the boarding house. I bet he picked the lock somehow.

Then he spoke in a much gentler voice, "Robin, please let me in. I have something important for you. To help you with the thing in the dark."

My breathing quickened. Maybe it was real. Here was a man saying so. Maybe my imagination wasn't playing havoc with my shattered brain. I was still too scared, "I have a gun and I know how to use it."

I could hear the man sigh, "That's fine Robin. You won't need it against me and I'm not sure it will help against what's coming." I didn't own a gun. I hated them after my event. I walked toward the door grabbing my sweatshirt and pulled it back on and removed the chain, like the fool I was, and let the man in.

"Who are you," I demanded. The man was not bothered a bit by my brusque tone and entered my room. He stopped and took a moment to smell some wild flowers I'd picked the day before.

I shifted my weight from one foot to the other. He looked up at me for a moment. Finally, I yelled, "This is bullshit. We need weapons, we need purging in our ranks." I had no idea where that had come from. I felt scared. These words coming out of my mouth made no sense.

The man walked over to me and looked me in the eyes, "Robin. Not doing too well tonight it would seem." I'd shocked myself into silence. The man was tall. I mean he towered over my five foot four inch frame. I looked up into his face and saw a hooked nose and pointy chin adorned by wrinkles. Lots of wrinkles, yet they didn't betray his age. It was hard to fix him but I could tell he'd been powerful once. A strong and deadly force from who knows where. He continued, "Robin, first we need ranks to purge."

I slumped down in my only living room chair. I don't even know where all that came from. All of a sudden, I was living two lives. The hopeless life of an eighteen-year-old near homeless wreck who hadn't even finished fucking high school and a life fixed in a coma. Dizzy. There was something else I couldn't see or maybe feel. Something I knew was left over from my coma days. Unfinished business leaking into my real life and maybe my dreams as well. Or maybe this was my real life. Shit. My sleep was a wreck, why not torture me with a half-remembered life lived now in my sleepless mind? Deep inside I knew this would happen someday. I just wouldn't walk away clean. Now I believed. As impossible as it was, the journey I took while in my coma had to have been real. It's just after waking up I'd never given myself a chance to believe it. I'd hoped from day to day it wouldn't come back to find me but shit, with my luck, today it did.

I blurted out, "I'm new to all this. Maybe that's good. My eyes are fresh and may see something you've missed. I could teach you a new way of living and seeing while you teach me the old ways. Together we can do it, brother." I reached out my hand. I felt a sudden kinship to this stranger and wanted, no, needed, his friendship. "Of course, I have no idea what needs fixing." All these feelings confused me. It seemed I'd known this man for a long time yet I didn't have any memories that included him. Sloan. His name was Sloan I was sure of that.

"Robin," he reached out and took my hand. His grip was firm and reassuring. His eyes were scanning the room. "My name is Sloan. How much in this place is yours?"

The question puzzled me, "What difference does it make?"

"Because you need to pack and we've got to move. Things are unsafe here. I shouldn't have to tell you that after your walk home from Mel's tonight."

Now that creeped me out. This guy had been keeping close tabs on me. What in the world do I matter to anyone? I looked him in the eyes, "I have a pack's worth of gear. The rest was here when I moved in. If we need to go I can be ready in five minutes."

Sloan said, "Do it."

As I packed I watched Sloan pick through some junk in the living room. He was at least six feet five and I'd guess two hundred forty pounds. He looked like an old man but I sensed he wasn't. He wore a long black duster made from the hide of some unknown creature and a flat rimmed cowboy hat. Funny how he smelled of honey and mint, which was pleasing, but he felt very strange. Like he wasn't there. I knew I had no choice in this matter. After my walk home tonight along with my attempts at fixing things in that other world I was left with no doubt in my mind I was in trouble. I had to find out why. Really it felt like somehow, we were all in trouble. I do mean all of us.

Sloan asked, "Get the tattoo yet?"

I stopped packing. Looking up I studied his eyes. How had he known I had been thinking about getting a tattoo? I hadn't told a soul.

Sloan said, "It's very important. The tattoo I mean. It won't be the last one but you need the star on your right shoulder now. The Star of David I mean. Time to reclaim what was taken from you. I know a good place we can go."

Was choice something that I had any more? I felt like the proverbial puppet on a string. Some puppet master was pulling and I jerked and moved where he wanted me to go. It was all happening too fast. I mumbled, "Great." Then from nowhere this overwhelming sorrow about the girl I'd known in The Region passed over me. She had stuck with me till the end. I'm sure she'd paid the ultimate price and she'd done it for me. Just what everyone needs you know, a dead girl trying to learn to fly and me just getting ready to fight the good fight about hell knows what. In the dim reaches of my memories I started to see the afternoon of the day of my mom's murder. I'd been walking in the country and I met someone. I think she said she was a witch. She told me to go home. That turned out to be the worst advice of my life.

THE NIGHTCRAWLERS

One thing was certain, Sloan wasn't a talker. He sat silent and almost motionless behind the wheel as we headed down old US 56 in his 1984 Cadillac. The car smelled of old vinyl mixed with cigarette smoke and whisky with a little pot thrown in for good measure. Years of use. Creating fear and doubt in my heart. Here I was heading away from Mason for the first time. Leaving all I'd ever known behind and with a perfect stranger. I knew my face would end up on a milk carton soon. I leaned my head against the passenger window and looked out into the black night. To think about it, there wasn't much to leave when it came to Mason, Texas. Just not much to leave I kept telling myself. I don't even know where those feelings were coming from. Sleep crept over me. That mixture of memories and dreams folded themselves together as I slipped to another place and I never even noticed.

Now I was standing alone on what seemed like an old two-lane highway. It was a narrow road without any stripes or shoulders and riddled with cracks. It seemed to go on forever. Just ahead was a crossroads. The land was flat like the high desert I'd seen in pictures so I could look up and down these roads forever. Nothing was moving. I recognized this place. I'd been here before. Was this part of the dream place I'd lived in while I was in the coma? Fear raised its head. I wasn't ever supposed to come back here but shit, here I was. Alone at night standing on a decaying blacktop road as a tepid wind blew and the full moon shined. The crossroads beckoned to me. I had a strange, almost uncontrollable urge to go stand in the middle of it and see what would happen next. It felt like a gun was being held to my head unsure of the fact that it was loaded or not but unable to stop myself from pulling the trigger. Then I sensed movement off to my right. I turned and about fifty yards away was an impossible abomination. A horror that couldn't exist. A creature that was over two stories tall. It had four long and spindly legs that merged under a squat box-like body. It was turning toward me so I didn't move. There was some kind of face on the box. It was smelling the air. Then it began to walk away in the same direction as the road I was standing on. Nightcrawlers. That's what they were called in this world. The sound was the same as what I'd heard in MacMillan Park when I was on my way home from Mel's.

Somehow, I knew these creatures. They are dangerous and best to avoid if possible. I watched as it moved rapidly away from me and I hoped they didn't travel in packs. I scanned the desert. It was lit by a full moon, I could see the rest of the land was empty. I looked back at the crossroads and felt danger there so I turned and started walking down the road in the opposite direction the Nightcrawler had gone. I found myself having these fleeting thoughts of the girl I traveled with in The Region. She felt like more than just a guide or protector to me. Could I have loved her? That seemed impossible. I was defiantly straight.

After about a half mile of walking I was stopped by the sudden movement of the ground around me. Just off the road to my left something was burrowing up out from the dirt. As a head emerged, I realized it was another Nightcrawler but this time only yards away.

I was unable to move. Fear had me nailed to this spot. There was nowhere to run anyway. The creature pushed itself up from the hole it was making. It seemed to be climbing now, the enormous legs extending higher and higher until it was completely out of the ground. I held my breath. The creature turned slowly toward me and stopped. I couldn't tell if it could see me but this was a dream anyway right? None of this was real. That didn't help as it walked toward me stopping directly over my head. Silence. The wind had stopped. With directed effort these worm like tentacles seeped from the bottom of the creature. They were dripping a kind of black oil. I couldn't tell if it was poison or the creature's own blood. Maybe the blood itself was the poison. Impossible tendrils, black like worms started to wrap around my legs, then worked its way upward reaching my waist. They burned me where they touched me. It was the oil that was burning me. Alarmed, I tried to back away. Another tendril slipped around my waist and pulled me forward. I was being drawn closer to the creature.

I knew this was just a dream. Maybe more a nightmare. It had to be. I was sleeping in Sloan's car heading east toward Abilene but strangely I knew I'd seen this before. A man walked out of the distance toward me. He was tall and gaunt. I couldn't see his face because where it should have been was filled with darkness. There was terrible power there. Power in his darkness but then I saw, there were also stars. Another place? Maybe another universe. It was bad power. For some reason, I thought of all the days I'd wasted drunk or drugged out on the front porch of my old house in town after my parents were gone. I just lost myself. No one checked on me. I couldn't find much reason for life to go on but seeing this man sparked something deep inside me.

I was wrong. Life is important, I thought. Even my life, wasted and beaten as it was. He called out, "Robin. Robin, you can't run away. I'm your destiny. All that you fear dwells within me."

I shouted back, "That's not true. Running is all I can do, you bastard. I won't be part of you!"

He kept walking toward me. I could see the stars swirl in the blackness of space. They were calling to me to enter. To just give up and hand over my life to this madness. That man was hard, old, dead. "You just don't understand yet. When you do you will be glad you came with me." He held out his hand. The urge to travel with him was strong. I wasn't worth the effort. Not even my own.

I was being held very still. The worm-like things from the creature above had embraced me fully. I thought of Lucy and how it must have felt to be squeezed to death. It happened so fast, did she even know? Wait. That was a dream too, wasn't it? Now everything was fucking confused.

Jesus, I was a kid no one wanted in a world that didn't give a shit if I was alive or dead and here I was worried about Lucy, who'd walked away from me in my darkest hour. What the hell was going on? Never and I mean never, had I felt loved, wanted, or anything like that. I'd always felt like the biggest piece of shit ever created. If I was about to be squeezed to death by a monster, who cared? Only me, and in my life, I was never enough.

The man had gotten nearer to me and was changing shape. He was screaming something at me over and over but it was like he was under the water. I couldn't make it out. Then I jolted awake.

Sloan was on top of me shaking me like crazy. My mind was swimming. Suddenly I was back in the car with this stranger. My eyes were open wide and I tried to move away from Sloan but he had me pinned to my seat. He said, "You were screaming in your sleep. Like to never gotten you awake." He slumped back into the driver's seat wiping sweat from his brow.

I was covered in sweat and breathing like I'd just run ten miles. "Where are we?"

Sloan answered, "Just outside Abilene. You were screaming so loud I had to pull over and shake you awake. I don't think there's enough screaming I could have done to wake you up."

The man in my dream. That's why he changed. It became Sloan trying to wake me up. Wow. It was still dark out so I opened the car door and stepped out into the colorless night. I had to see if the monster was there.

Sloan jumped out and walked over to me, "What the hell are you doing now?"

"Nightcrawlers. That's what they are. They're called Nightcrawlers!"

Sloan had a look of alarm cross his face, "Damn. I thought we'd lost 'em."

I reeled back looking at Sloan, "You mean they're real?"

Sloan took my arm and opened the car door. He pushed me back inside and slammed it. Then he was back behind the wheel and peeling out fast. "What do you think was in the park? What do you think followed you home? Shit. We've got to get to Rex's place for the tattoo."

I sat frozen in my seat. Now I didn't know which was the dream or what was real. Maybe it was all the same thing. I couldn't speak and Sloan didn't say a word as we sped down the black ribbon of the two-lane highway.

TATTOO

We hit the outskirts of Abilene at about two a.m. I remember thinking just a few hours ago how lucky I was to get out of Mel's at midnight. Now I had no idea if it was lucky or not. One thing was for sure, I'd never been so far from home. Unless you count the places I visited in my dreams. I watched the tired houses as we passed. Things looked much the same as in Mason. Hopeless houses full of darkness and violence. People holding on to the edge of life wondering where their humanity had gone. We pulled into an ancient strip of old shops. Half were boarded up. Spaces that would never see the light of day again. Poverty had blown over this place like a tornado leaving little in its wake. I could see a bar on the corner. A couple of cars and a motorcycle parked out front. I knew the men inside even never having seen them. I guess nothing changes. The only other place that was open had a neon sign in the window proclaiming it to be Rex's Tattoos. I could see through the window that the place was empty. Half the lights looked burned out.

Sloan pulled the car in a space right in front and switched the engine off. Then he said, "Nightcrawlers are the weakest ones. I don't know, kinda like the dogs of hell."

"Some dogs," I spat out. "That fucker was two stories tall! Really Sloan, have you ever seen one of those things up close?" He didn't respond so I continued, "I didn't think so. What are we doing at Rex's anyway? I've done some dumb shit but this is the worst. I've changed my mind. I want to go home."

Sloan sat in silence for a long time. I was starting to get uncomfortable with the silence when he finally said, "Look Robin, I know you didn't see this coming and that nothing makes any sense to you right now. When you were in your coma you traveled. Not just in a dream but to The Region. It's a place we aren't supposed to go until we die. But you broke the rules. It's like you leaked into it then used something to get back to here."

I said, "It was a glowing glass ball. That's all. I broke it and then I woke up. It felt right."

Sloan answered, "It wasn't right or we wouldn't be sitting in front of Rex's right now. Did you ever think just maybe you weren't supposed to wake up?"

I snapped my head up, "You've got to be shitting me? Would you just stay dead in a coma if you knew there was a way out? I don't think so. I don't remember even thinking what the consequences would be. Shit, I was living in a world full of monsters and all they wanted to do was kill me again. Where would that have sent me Sloan? Do you know that?"

"You have a point," Sloan said. "No I would have found a way out, same as you. Right or wrong. I don't have a clue where you go after the second death but I don't want to find out. You just didn't know the possibilities."

Sloan opened his car door and got out. I joined him at the door of Rex's place. Sloan said, "The tattoo will keep the Nightcrawlers away. They may be big but trust me they're weak. There's worse coming. We have to get you ready."

I just sighed and pushed the door open and walked into the dingy room where a man sat smoking a Lucky

Strike unfiltered cigarette that was creating a haze in the room mixed with the smell of rotting plaster walls and mold, along with that putrid smell that greets you in a gas station bathroom. That smell that reminds you that you'd never pee in a place like this except you have to pee so boundaries are broken and for a few seconds you suspend the reality around you as you sit and pee then instantly forget about it as you walk out the door. I assumed the seated fellow was Rex. He was reading an old L. Ron Hubbard paperback with the cover torn off. I could tell by the spine. Looking up he said, "About time you got here. It's two in the fucking morning. The damn bars are closing leaving me no place to go and forget this nightmare."

"We had a little trouble," Sloan replied. "Please shut up and just get it done."

Rex grunted and turned toward me, "Take your sweatshirt off honey."

I laughed, "You've got to be kidding me. I haven't worn a bra ever in my life."

Rex looked like he wasn't kidding. With a bite to his voice he said, "I got to get this on you 100% right or it don't work. I also want to get the fuck out of here. I've been here too long as it is."

Sloan turned toward me and said quietly, "Don't worry. He's gay anyway. He just wants to be done with us. With the trouble you're going to bring. Don't blame him, just cooperate."

I sighed. It was true. I mean my life wasn't mine any more. I crossed my arms and grabbed the hem of my dirty white sweatshirt and pulled it off over my head. The chill in the room hardened my nipples. Rex seemed very disinterested. Maybe he was gay.

Sloan had turned away. More a gentleman than I'd given him credit for. Rex took a pencil and found the perfect spot on my right shoulder. There he traced my star then took his tattoo gun to start. "Not to be fussy but do you clean your equipment after each client?"

Rex let out a rush of air and got even more irritated. "Look sister, you'll be fine. Now be still." In about ten minutes I had my first tattoo. It looked exactly like I'd imagined it when I'd first dreamed about it in Mason. I dressed and Sloan turned from the window. "You have reclaimed a bit of your life, Robin Randle. The start of a boundary between here and there."

Sloan started to reach for his wallet and Rex stopped him. "This one's on me brother. Hell is coming. Time for me to pack up and go far away."

Sloan said, "You know there's more."

"Hey man, have I ever let you down? I'll be there when you need me but I have to disappear for now."

Sloan nodded his head in agreement, "I understand. Thanks, brother." Sloan looked at me. "You're safe for the moment. The Nightcrawlers will leave you alone now. Time to find a place to rest then on to your new home in Lawton, Oklahoma."

I could tell by the tone in Sloan's voice there was not going to be any choice. Me wanting to just go back to Mason wasn't even up for discussion. It seemed suddenly, after a lifetime of being invisible to the world, I'd become important to everyone. But still I was treated like shit. Go here. Now go there. Oh, and by the way, don't let your dreams bother you.

Life had become a blur. It felt more like looking at a photo album. Not something I was living. One picture was of a Motel 6 where we spent the night the next was just black night then on the last page was my new life in Lawton. At least I'd survived the Nightcrawlers. Sloan had a parting piece of advice as he dumped me by a boarding house with some cash to get started. "Get two more tattoos around the star. A circle, then a larger circle. Writing needs to go between them. Don't let anyone touch the star. Now I have to leave but you will be safe for a while. I'll be back before the shit hits the fan. And don't and I mean don't befriend anyone. No strangers. Got it?"

I looked at this man. Was he a man or a creature? A friend or foe? Or just another monster in a hidden form? Maybe he was the thing that tried to grab me in the woods by my old home. Maybe a member of The Region. Just maybe Sloan had a true identity. Some link to my past or even my travels in The Region. Maybe he knew that girl that seemed to care about me. Maybe just because he cares, next time he'll explain. I sighed and said, "You're the boss."

PART 2

BETWEEN DARKNESS AND WONDER

Must all of worth be travailled for, and those
Life's brightest stars rise from a troubled sea?
Must years go by in sad uncertainty
Leaving us doubting whose the conquering blows,
Are we or Fate the victors? Time which shows
All inner meanings will reveal, but we
Shall never know the upshot. Ours to be
Wasted with longing, shattered in the throes,
The agonies of splendid dreams, which day
Dims from our vision, but each night brings back;
We strive to hold their grandeur, and essay
To be the thing we dream. Sudden we lack
The flash of insight, life grows drear and gray,
And hour follows hour, nerveless, slack.

-In Darkness
Amy Lowell

STATION

Never in my life have I had to hide from the world. Now I've been hiding out for six months. Robin Randle, on the lam.

I'm sure there had been a time when someone had touched my body, with her perfect mind. With all these fucking imperfections, there was this gnawing buried memory of true love. I couldn't even begin to think why. I'd never dated anyone in my life. Love was for the movies. Still, it felt that way. I mean, what deranged psychopath would love a loser like Robin Randle? After all that happened in Mason I felt my life was winding down. Think about it, there couldn't have been much reason for me to hang around too much longer. I shouldn't complain. I didn't think I'd ever get this period of peace. You know, in a way it was like a weight on my soul. Every night when I woke for work I wondered, when is this moment of grace going to end? I never wanted any of this. I didn't ask for a homicidal father. I never wanted to stand and watch as he shot my mother to death. I never wanted to have my dad beat me into a coma. Most of all I never wanted to find out the dreams I'd had while in my coma weren't dreams at all but real events and now they were back to seek revenge.

You know, there was this one thing this break had given me, time to think. Think about all that had come before the coma and then life after. I spent hours trying to remember The Region. Hard as I tried, I could only see fleeting glimpses while awake but when I went to sleep it was a different story. My sleep had become connected to the darkness in ways

I could never have imagined. Dark things moved around me, slipping behind me where I couldn't see them then I'd lose it when they touched my back. There were other things in the darkness too. Horrors lost to the memory of humanity. Those things screamed in the night, filling the air with the distinct smell of ozone. Those monsters screamed lightning, the flash so bright I was blinded by it, never able to see the monster making them. I feared these the most. I knew they were not from The Region still in a place that dwelled in my future.

One thing that was for sure, my new mysterious friend Sloan was right about the Nightcrawlers. None to be found after the tattoo of the Star of David was inscribed on my shoulder. None on the streets of Lawton or the dead roads of my dreams. Over the months I was spending in Lawton I'd found a decent tattoo parlor so I could add a few tattoos like Sloan had said. The first was just a swirling set of lines I had seen in one of my dreams and the second was a sword. They felt right but the sword needed something else. I just didn't know what that was. The Star certainly wasn't the focal point on my shoulder anymore. I couldn't figure out why it mattered if someone noticed it or not. Another piece of my out of control life. That's when I'd decided to create the Robin Randle's Unsolved Mysteries list. My questions with no answers.

What was disturbing me? I was just biding time. I know this time would end. It's just a matter of when and how. When I got dumped in the wonderful town of Lawton, I'd found Kelly's Bar and Grill. Mostly a bar. I offered to work the overnight shift and got a job. No one wanted to work the overnight shift. Again, I had condemned myself to the company of drunk men whose idea of how to treat a woman was just about any way they wanted to. Didn't matter if you knew her or not. Over the past six months I'd thought about quitting the bar. Maybe work at the McDonald's. But that would have me working days and daytime scared me now. Anymore, I was afraid of both darkness and light. That didn't leave me much choice except to maybe jump off a bridge and honestly that wasn't sounding as crazy as it did when it first occurred to me. Shit, there wasn't anything in the day worth doing anyway. I felt hidden by the night and death was only a deeper darkness. Right?

Tuesday was usually a light night, meaning fewer drunks, so less drama. Then in walked this woman. I couldn't remember ever seeing her before but there was something oddly familiar about her. One thing was for sure, she was striking. Her left arm was covered with what looked like tattoos from shoulder to wrist. No piercings I could see. She had short black hair with a whiff of pink on top. Just enough. Tall and slim she was pale with the most incredible silver shaded eyes that seemed to glow with moonlight tinted with mercury. What was funny was the way she was dressed. Brown leather pants combined with a brown bodice made her stand out when she entered the bar. Not the usual garb for a night out on the town here in Lawton but it suited her. I thought maybe she was a biker. Maybe not alone. She looked to be about five eleven. Her naked shoulders and arms were slight but muscular.

There was no doubt that this girl could take care

of herself. Unfortunately, I just felt she would have to prove it to these drunks in the bar. Billy had won the award for worst drunk of the evening. He was a big guy both tall and broad. His belly hung out over the front of his jeans hiding his belt. He dressed like a cowboy and smelled like he'd not seen a bar of soap in a week. He decided to make a pass at her as she walked by his table coming toward the bar. She politely asked to be left alone and that brought the other three drunks at Billy's table to their feet, ready to teach the little woman a lesson.

Billy tried to grab her shoulders from behind. She looked at the ceiling rolling her eyes. You could tell she'd been through this drill before. Bending her knees slightly she slipped out of Billy's hold while stomping his foot. I could hear the crunching and breaking of several toes. Billy screamed bringing another one of my favorite drunks, Charlie Criss, out of his chair. He wanted to move in and do some damage. Charlie was bad news. Most everyone in Lawton gave him a wide berth. Lawton's town bully. He just came straight on pulling back his hand ready to throw a haymaker. Charlie said, "You bitch. You're going to the ground."

She advanced toward him as he tried to punch. Her movements were graceful, like a dancer. She had reduced his ability to do the damage he wanted to. His forward inertia carried him right into her powerfully moving elbow. She had redirected all his energy right back into his nose. The crack was sickening. I'd never seen a nose break as badly as his. Blood was all over his face.

But she wasn't done. She moved past Charlie and sent out a low kick to his left knee. Another crack and he went down. Then, standing tall and silent looking at the other guys now stunned into silence she asked, "Anyone else?"

She waited. No reply. The boys started calling 911 and cleaning up the mess she'd left behind. It was over. She turned and approached the bar. Now I had a clear view of her face. High cheekbones accented with dimples (more when she laughed). Her lips were full and covered in deep red lipstick. And then there were her eyes. They seemed to glow with real moonlight. Silver, large and beautiful. It felt as if they were made for me. How silly was that? The curve of her waist along with the curve of her back begged a woman of near perfection. This girl wasn't from anywhere I could ever imagine. What the hell was she doing in Lawton?

Walking up to me she said, "Greetings."

"Hello," I managed.

"I've been on a quest. I'm trying to find a lost friend. I've been looking for her all over the state of Oklahoma. You wouldn't by any chance know of a Robin Randle living in this village?"

Her voice was earthy and rich like fertile soil. I felt comfort at her sound. I was overwhelmed with the feeling that I knew this woman. That she'd been special at some point in my wretched life. Sloan advised me to trust no one but I was falling under a kind of spell cast by this girl. I looked closer into her eyes and felt the ocean. In my mind, I could see an old house in a field. The memory was mixed up with sadness and loss along with the joy you have when someone you meet turns out to be an honest and faithful friend. The sounds of the ocean were distant but the smell was in the air mixed with faint wood smoke from distant watch fires. The place where I woke up while I slept in the death of a coma. To hell with Sloan, I didn't want to stop myself. I said, "It's me."

She smiled like she already knew the answer. I was amazed at the marked sexual attraction I had toward her. This was a new feeling. I'd never gone for girls. At least I don't think I had. Wow. Something was different here. Love? A love born over decades of friendship, shared experiences and loss. Confused, I couldn't imagine why I would feel this way. Something old was here.

She held out her hand, "Station. Station Cross. I'm so glad I found you. I've been searching a long time but something has kept us apart."

That name. Station Cross. It was familiar yet I'd never thought of it until right now. I reached out with my hand and she took it not to be shaken but kissed. When we touched I felt something strange. It felt like it does after a thunderstorm and she smelled of fresh rain on a spring day, bringing all the elements of life that I would need for the day ahead. She raised my hand to her lips and gently brushed them on the back of my hand. I stood motionless. Time itself had stopped around me and I found myself living in just this moment. A moment filled with wonder. I thought of God and the gifts He'd given me and then about Station. My faithful companion. I turned her hand over and kissed its pale and amazing back. She did taste of spring rains and she did smell of the ocean and ancient fires. I felt time pass. It was the first time since waking from the coma that I'd felt time. The passage of moments building one after another into a reality that becomes a life. My life? We parted and she asked, "Can a girl get a beer around here?"

I cleared my head. "I'm just a server but I don't think anyone would complain if I drew you a beer. It's not like I haven't done it before." I drew our best draft, "It's on the house." She turned to watch the last of the cowboys leave the bar then relaxed.

Turning back toward me she said, "So many guys with something to prove. I've even killed a few to make a point. They just don't get it when I say back off."

"Tell me about it. And this is a slow night."

"Robin, what are you doing in a dive like this?"

I stuttered feeling oddly embarrassed. I gave the true answer but it felt so wrong, "There isn't much else I can do. High School dropout. Not a lot of options. It's my fault. I quit. I didn't have to but at the time it was all I could do."

"And why was that? You appear intelligent."

"Oh, that's never been the problem. Where I lived my dad shot and killed my mom then tried to kill me. Spent seven months in a coma so that kind of fucked up my senior year; and the rest of my life."

Station looked sad and for a moment seemed to become distant. Was it my language? Then she leaned in close and whispered, "Then you've been to The Region. Any memories of it?"

This was the last thing I'd expected on a Tuesday night in Lawton. A toxic chill passed through me. The time of change, I feared, was coming.

I said, "Yes I've been there. Came back too and now all hell is breaking loose."

"That's what I've heard," Station said.

I couldn't stop looking into her silver eyes. The beauty this woman radiated was beyond the physical realm. Something much deeper than a human love of maybe thirty years. No. It felt like a love thousands of years so rooted in my soul that eternity itself wouldn't be long enough.

I'd been so careful to keep people at a distance since coming to Lawton but now I couldn't help myself. I asked, "Do you have a place to stay tonight?"

"No. Hadn't gotten that far. Just finding you was a task and I guess that's not all bad."

I glanced at the Budweiser wall clock over the front door. "I get off at midnight. Maybe you could crash at my place." I caught Station stealing a look at me. I knew this woman. Maybe she was from The Region. I felt certain she had been very important to me. No, more than that. She had been my friend. My champion. The one who stuck with me to the bitter end. Unbelievable as it seems, and with sexual confusion I knew she must be my lover. Then words just formed and spilled like tears from my mouth, "I thought you died."

She looked into my eyes with hopefulness, "It takes a lot more to put me down than a gaggle of monsters. Being stuck in The Region has been the most difficult task I've ever done. Not being able to be with you has been much worse than the damage any creature from hell could cause. Aching to pick up the sword and finish what we started." She looked down and a sadness crossed her face. She whispered, "Maybe to love you a little while longer. Until this ends."

"That scares me."

"As it should. Frankly it scares me too." She took a

long pull on her beer. I could tell she was suddenly scared to say what she wanted to. It was hard to imagine this girl scared of anything. "You know," she hesitated as resolve washed over her face, "It may be hard to believe but we were lovers once. Tonight, we could be lovers again. Maybe have one night of rest?" She quickly added, "That's if you want to?"

I didn't even think before I said, "Yes. More than anything. I've known so little love in my life." I thought, Sloan's going to kill me but I'm not his. "When I saw you, I knew I remembered you. You were my right hand. No, you were my whole heart. I can't remember the full story but right now it doesn't matter. It's time for me to clock out. We'll go to my place. I want to get to know you again."

Station laughed and stood up from her stool and finished her beer.

An odd thought crossed my mind. I asked, "Did you get that flying thing down?"

She grinned, "You'd be amazed."

THE TRUTH OF SHADOWS

We arrived at my apartment and a feeling of shame overwhelmed me. Walking down the hallway to my apartment door I noticed the filth of years; walls splashed with gang signs and obscene words, the floor littered with the trash of booze, drugs and sex. I'd never thought about how I lived in such squalor. For some reason, I hated Station seeing this. I wondered at that. Since when did I care enough to worry about how I looked or where I lived? Station seemed to pick up on my shame. Unlocking my door, I held if for her so she could walk ahead of me into my apartment. It was dark and well-worn but at least orderly. I followed, stopping to flip the light switch. Station said, "You live under a roof. I have no home. At least not right now."

"Then where do you sleep at night?"

"Under the stars Robin. I like it. I think you'd like it too."

I sighed, "I'll probably get a chance to find out before I'm done." I forced a weak smile. Station walked toward me and stopping close in front of me she reached out and turned the lights back off. Then she took the hem of my sweatshirt and began to pull it up. I raised my arms letting her finish the task and stood nude from the waist up. Tears welled up in my eyes. "I'm sorry Station. I know I'm not very attractive."

Station laughed, "And who is to be the judge of that? Me, I think!" She looked into my eyes, hers so large and glowing with silver moonlight and asked, "Will you unlace me? I should have changed before I came." My tears had streaked my face. Station reached up and wiped them away as I reached for the laces on the front of her bodice. Her breasts swelled under its pressure. She looked so soft and warm. I couldn't remember ever feeling the warmth of another human body. No, there was some other memory there but different. Her bare shoulders were straight. I stopped and rested my hands on them and massaged. Her skin was soft and warm to the touch. I dug my fingers into her muscles and felt strength under her gentle skin. She stretched her neck obviously enjoying my impromptu massage. "It's been so long since I've felt your hands on my body. Too long. Lord, thank you for these moments of peace."

I reached down to finish unlacing her top. My feelings were conflicted yet this felt both right and wonderful. Soon her top was loose and she pulled it off dropping it to the floor. I reached out toward her and became lost in her breasts. My hands just knew the roadmap of Station's body. It felt like wonder to me, an amazing mixture of suppleness and warmth laced with a hint of firmness. I sensed her growing excitement as she took me in her arms pressing her breasts against mine. She was right, we fit together as if we'd been flaked and honed with great skill for this very moment. Station kissed my lips like morning dew on grass and I opened my mouth to receive her. Our tongues touched and I wasn't ready for that. It produced a jolt like electricity was passing into me. Station pulled away saying, "I'm so sorry Robin. I'm sorry. I'll be gentle. I promise."

"I'm fine Station. You have no need to be sorry but do be gentle. This is so new to me. Well, maybe not.

Maybe we were lovers long ago. In The Region. I just don't remember."

"I'll be gentle, my Robin." Her hands explored me as well until my body made a clear statement that Station and I had been lovers for ages unremembered to me. I felt limp lying in the bed breathing like I'd just run the Boston Marathon. She laughed, "You've missed me. Now Robin, return my love."

The rest of the night was wonderful. I didn't think I would ever feel intense passion nor the rekindling of love. I became lost in her. I realized that Station had loved me more than anyone in my whole wretched life. No one had ever loved me. I found that out in Mason. Since then I thought I was just one of God's failures. Made unlovable. Never would I know love's heart pounding bliss. I was wrong. Now I did. I knew she would die for me. I knew Sloan wouldn't even begin to approve. He'd told me not to trust anyone and never get close. He'd wanted me ready to travel when the time came. So much for his advice.

During an intermission, I noticed dawn was breaking. I could see the deep blue of the morning sky. I couldn't remember the last time I'd seen the sun rise. Station rolled onto her back, pulling the blankets up to her neck to fight off the chill. I couldn't know what she was thinking. We'd loved all night and in-between I told her about my life in Mason. All the loneliness and abuse. How I was beaten by my father and my mother, never lifting a hand to save me. No one saved me. It felt like I was whining. Like I should just grow up and get over all the past horrors. So, I switched to the escape I'd made with Sloan. Then at last my frail mind couldn't hold together any longer. I had to know, "Why did you wait to come until now? Station, I needed you by my side all the way from Mason. Maybe even before. It seemed like you were there for me in The Region." I turned away from her. I felt guilty. I was judging her and it seemed wrong. "I'm sorry I said that. It's just things are all jumbled up in my head but I know you helped me."

Station was quiet. I turned to see if she'd maybe fallen asleep. She hadn't but now there was a sadness in her eyes. A sadness that echoed like summer's memories in a fall wind. She said, "I couldn't, Robin. You don't seem to have remembered much of what happened before all this started. I pray you will. You need to remember why you're here. Just telling you won't help you. It has to come from inside you. I can tell you this, that your coming back to this life, your human life, has messed with your mind." Tears started streaking her cheeks. She reached up to wipe them away but I stopped her.

I said, "I didn't mean to upset you." I leaned in and wiped her tears away with my cheeks.

She wrapped her arms around me and held me tight then whispered, "There are rules. I'm not sure I understand them anymore but it's important that we try and work inside of them. This is the hardest thing I've ever done." She let go and pulled away. "After you left, I needed time to heal. There are these creatures called the Seers of Sand. It's hard to explain but they can see me when I'm injured, then they come and take me to a realm called Elysium. It's like your hospitals I guess, but better. I had sustained grave injuries. I hurt Robin. I was in a lot of pain so the Seers put me to sleep. I slept there until I was healed. When I woke there was other work to be done."

The Seers of Sand, Elysium these names sounded vaguely familiar but elusive like so many of my memories of The Region. It's like trying to hold water in your cupped hands. You can sip a moments worth then you look and the rest is gone. I was silent. Station continued, "I had to go to Thessaly to fool with The Gypsy and her Dust Witches. It was the only way I could think of to find a passage for your key."

"My key?" I said. The Dust Witch sounded so familiar like I had met one in this world. The damn haze that filled my memories just blocked my mind. I reached up and touched my key. Station got quiet. I had prodded too much. I didn't even know what questions to ask. "What happened after I died?"

Station heaved a big sigh. A sure sign I was asking too many questions. "Robin, I shouldn't say anymore. I just don't know what it'll do. You know you found your starlight and somehow you opened it up. No human is ever supposed to be able to do that but here you are, this kid that arrived on the shores of the Southern Ocean wanting to find the Palace of Starlight. No one has ever done that. Every form of hideous creature was after you. There were abominations I'd never known existed unleashed just to stop you. Least of which was the Queen of Starlight herself. The Prince of the Power of the Air isn't pleased with us."

I asked, "Who is The Prince of the Power of the Air? I've heard that name before."

Station gathered the sheets and blankets around her naked form and sat up. "Satan, Lucifer, take your pick. You don't remember or at least not yet. You had left the ocean and entered the Great Forest. You asked everyone you met for a guide. I mean you'd say that you needed someone to guide you because you were going to the Palace of Starlight. No one goes there. No one even knows where it is. You get that? People started to think maybe you were dangerous. I had to find you and that took a while and when I did you were so," Station paused she was searching for the words to express the sorrow written on her face, "broken."

I said, "Broken? How?"

Station ignored my question, "At last I did find you and offered to be your guide. You don't remember much do you? I offered to guide you there but you had to tell me why you needed to go."

I'd stopped breathing, "I needed to go and take my star from the Queen of the Palace. She has no right to hold so many of us in her power. I do remember being very angry when I learned the truth. I just don't remember what truth I learned"

Station looked at her hands, "I know. This is painful, but we'll make it Robin. I love you. The Palace of Starlight is a creation of The Prince of the Power of the Air. All the stars of every human are being held there and guarded by the so-called Queen of Starlight. I knew if you got your star you would leave me but I also knew it was what you wanted most in the world. You told me you needed to know where the Palace was. Needed me to guide you there. Acutely Robin, it was you who found it. How could I have held you back from claiming your prize? The last fight was brutal. Horrors I'd never seen before started slipping from folds in the sky. You were hurt and failing. I'd flown into the Palace not knowing really where I was but I saw you and interceded. It was then that I struck the Queen."

"My God. How could you do that? I mean she seemed full of all the wickedness that's ever been."

"Yes, she was and I decided it was time to end her. She had hurt you with her knives and that angered me. I struck her across the neck and her head fell to the bloody ground. Then there was silence in The Region. The Balance had changed and I had no idea to what, but prayed I was following the plan. You're wrong, Robin. There is one much worse than the Queen waiting for you. I was just beat to hell and needed time. Time to heal. Since that day no one in The Region has messed with me. I can tell you this, that the evil beings of The Region have a name for you. They call you 'The Storm Bringer.'"

I could almost see that last fight. It was close in my mind. Station was covered in blood. Much of it hers. I remembered slipping away. Leaving her behind. She cried out in pain but nothing could stop things. I think I was with the Queen inside her palace. She was angry and slashing at me with knives covered in blood. My blood. Then somehow Station was there. It was like she'd been created from a flock of birds. That couldn't be right. Station stood between the Queen and me stopping her attack. Then Station struck the Queen down. It all ended and I woke up back here where I thought I belonged. Now I wondered, was this truly where I belonged? I remembered how I felt empty at first. Now I know why. "I'm sorry. I should have never left you."

Station smiled, "Robin, you couldn't help it. This

was all set in motion by the unseen hand long ago. I thought I knew how things were supposed to happen but nothing had quite worked as simply as was planned. I can say no more but know change had come to The Region and it was long overdue. Now, we just have to make sure it stays that way until we finish this to save the two worlds."

I stood from the bedside and looked out the dirty window of my bedroom. A poor and most would say, useless human being. Not much of a future. I'd refused the drugging and whoring route. No porn, exotic dancing or peep shows. No. I'd stopped the drugs and drinking. I was clean and I was going to stay that way. What hope that left me I couldn't know. I just knew I was tangled back up with a place and time, with people and monsters that folks in this world weren't even supposed to know existed. It was the truth lurking in the shadows waiting for its time. "How is it that we are supposed to finish this?"

Station said, "Robin, it's time. All time is caught between the darkness and the wonder. We have to keep fighting until the wonder overwhelms us."

I said, "What if the wonder isn't something I want?"

"A bit late for that my friend. I love you, Robin. That I can promise you." Station stood and took my hand and pulled me back into the bed. Back to her. She whispered, "For now anyway, we can have that simple love we've been denied. Then we wait for Sloan and all hell to break loose."

I fell back into her arms and we kissed. She was all I ever wanted. Her hands exploring my naked body and I doing the same. Life could stay this way forever but I knew it wouldn't. Another change was on the doorstep. For now, for this moment, I felt what I thought the wonder should feel like. The softness of her skin and the heat from her breasts. Even more the pull of her heart. I had never experienced another person's love for me. I took these moments and was glad for them when they'd passed.

THE RETURN

Sleep had taken most of the day. My internal clock woke me up, as it always did. I turned toward Station but she was gone. Suddenly an ill feeling crept over me. I reached over to where she'd been sleeping and the sheets were cold. I knew I hadn't imagined her.

I got out of bed and stumbled around my apartment looking for my underwear. It was on the floor in front of the window, which looked out on Fort Sill Road. My sweatshirt lay there as well. I gazed out on Fort Sill Road. Shades of late afternoon sunlight were streaking through the air. I thought for a moment and dredged up the fact that it was Wednesday. I worked from seven tonight to three tomorrow morning. I felt like I was out of sync, like I was living inside a déjà vu event. I raised my eyes to Highlands Cemetery across the street and fear got hold of my mind. I could feel an ancient horror building under the graves. Something was decidedly wrong. I turned away and slammed my fist into the wall shattering the plaster. I didn't know I had that in me.

"Holy shit. It's starting again. I don't want it to start again," I yelled, "I want to be left alone!" Looking back out my window I could see a mist forming over Highlands. It was coming up from the ground but not like steam, more like fog just seeping out of the earth. "No. No no no no!"

Something was moving in the mist. Something large and ancient. A creature not born of Earth but from the space between. It moved suddenly then stopped, its form still hidden from me as a low rumbling started.

It sounded like nothing I'd ever heard. Low, almost subsonic, but loud. The glass in the window started to vibrate. I backed away, still watching the monster.

The windows rattled with greater intensity until they exploded into the room. I was thrown to the ground and most of the glass blew past me. Some small shards found a home in my body. I got on all fours and picked at the shards trying to get them out. Blood oozed from each spot. My jeans and shoes were where I fell so I finished dressing. It seemed a trivial matter about the glass as a large crack started down the front wall of the apartment. This was it. Left alone without a clue about this horror. Left alone to die some horrible death. All those who said they'd protect me were gone. No, I needed to learn. I had to learn how to protect myself. All my life a victim of violence and rarely did I fight back. I never tried to stop the cycle. Maybe all this was as much my fault as anyone else's.

The entire building began to vibrate then shifted suddenly. I looked for my backpack. I kept everything I own in it always expecting to have to escape. It was under the bed so I grabbed it and started toward the door. A loud pulse came from Highlands and the ceiling started crumbling; pieces of plaster raining down and I fell to the floor again. I had to find the strength to get back up. Then my door exploded open and in walked Sloan. He put out his hand to help me, "Time to go."

I had never been in a war zone, but this was what they looked like on TV. Something had exploded behind me. I didn't look, only stumbled down the stairs, Sloan pulling my arm. Pieces of the building were falling all around me. I was aware of screams. A lot of screams coming from somewhere and that awful low-pitched rumble that seemed to strike me in the very pit of my stomach.

I stumbled down the last three steps falling face down on the dirty linoleum floor. Raising my head, I saw what looked like a small square of deer skin. Picking it up I glanced at it. It was familiar but this wasn't the time. I slipped it into my pocket as I got to my feet and started running down the alley between the two buildings behind what was left of my apartment building.

We'd come out on 13th Street where Sloan had parked his car. "Get in quick, Robin," he said.

In a matter of moments, we were racing down Williams Avenue at about 100 miles an hour. I looked behind us and the creature of darkness had risen above the buildings. Searching. I felt it looking for me. Sloan braked hard swinging left onto Sheridan Road heading toward US Highway 62. I slammed against the door window with my head and nearly passed out. The only reason I didn't was that Sloan started yelling at me not to. I could hear him somewhere saying, "Don't you dare pass out! We may have to ditch the car." I felt sick to my stomach. Then from behind us I heard the horror that had risen from the graveyard. Looking back down the road I could see the huge form not a block away. It was still hidden in a dark cloud that traveled with it. The ground shook as it got closer like the monster was walking, not gliding in the air. The whole town shook. Sloan tried to coax a little more speed out of the old Cadillac he was driving but it had seen better days.

Then something happened I was totally not expecting. The car just died. We started to slow so Sloan took a hard right saving my head from more injury. We were traveling east on Irwin Avenue as the car came to a stop. I looked behind us and the black horror that had been there was gone. "The monster is gone."

Sloan laughed a dry laugh, "Sweetheart, it is coming over those buildings on your left. Get out. Time to hide for a bit."

Sloan took off down Irwin heading for what looked like an auto repair garage. All the buildings were brick but that hadn't saved my apartment. I threw my door open, grabbed my backpack and ran after Sloan. As soon as I left the car I could hear the evidence of Sloan's assessment. The monster was making a tremendous pounding noise that competed only with the sound of buildings being crushed. It was almost here. Sloan slammed into the door of the auto shop breaking it open. He disappeared and I followed behind. He kept running until he found the stair down into a basement storage area. He pulled a flash light out and leaped down the stairs and was holding the light on the steps as I turned to go down.

Once in the basement I threw my pack down and sat against the cold concrete wall. Sloan said, "Don't get too comfortable."

"Don't worry. Concrete walls and floors along with the smell of oil and gas permeating the air, ah." I said, "What could be less comfortable? So, what the hell do we do now?" The pounding had passed over the building we were in and there was no telling how much of it was left or if we were buried beneath tons of rubble.

I pulled the leather square I'd found out of my pocket and studied its strange image. A raven. Sloan turned his light on it and said, "Where did you get that?" He bent down to get a better look.

"It was at the bottom of the stairs at my apartment house. Why?"

"That's a calling card for the nastiest bitch I know. If we have her on our trail as well as monsters in the air we are in deep shit," he spat. "That could be some kind of talisman set to hurt you."

"Oh. What's her name?" I asked idly just trying not to think about what was going on outside.

Sloan stood, "Station. Station Cross."

I gasped so loud Sloan looked back at me.

"Don't tell me you met her?" Sloan approached me with anger in his eyes.

I was sheepish not wanting to talk about it. I had to say something, "I met her at the bar I worked at. We had a few drinks after my shift and we talked," I lied.

"Damn it," Sloan yelled, "What part of NO STRANGERS don't you understand?"

My eyes welled with tears, "She seemed very nice. Beautiful too. I can't believe she had anything to do with all this."

"Oh, I see. She appears and the next thing that happens is a monster seeps up from the cemetery that is right across from your apartment. You think that was coincidence?"

I shook my head. Stunned I turned away from Sloan. Station had felt so right. Perfect in my arms. She helped me. I know she had fought for me at the end of the world. That's what she said. I felt love for her and now Sloan tells me she is an evil bitch. I started crying. Why was I always betrayed by people I trusted and loved? That's been my life starting with my mother. I screamed, "You don't know what you're talking about!"

Sloan moved closer, "Look, I'm sorry I yelled. I'm a bit worked up. I'm not saying she did or didn't bring this monster, I just don't know her to be a good person. I don't know her at all. Just her reputation. She has killed."

I turned toward him, "And maybe you just don't know everything Sloan. She was there with me when I was at the end of the world. You're right, she kills. She killed the wicked Queen of Starlight. And I'll tell you, the Queen was a much more horrible monster than that thing outside." I remember as I faded away I saw Station all bloody just standing looking incredibly sad. Then my memory of her faded away as I woke up. A sad expression flashed on Sloan's face.

Sloan answered, "Ok, Robin. Damn all this. This has to wait. Right now, we need to live through the next ten minutes or none of it will matter."

I said, "Can't the military hear this? I mean can't they drop a bomb or something?"

"Robin, these creatures don't walk. They fly and the damage they do is through their use of sound. Looks just like an earthquake to everyone else. They can't see it."

There was the sound of rock shards hitting the stair filling them up with stones and bricks blocking our escape. I mumbled, "This is it. I can't believe it. I lived through the beating from hell courtesy of my dad then all the way through The Region and now in the little punk city of Lawton, I'm going to buy the farm."

Sloan listened to the crashing sounds as they retreated for the moment. "Don't be so quick to give up. I know you are young, but patience is a discipline you must learn. Relax and breathe slowly and deeply. Center your mind far away from here. See your world without these horrors. They will only devour you then with free rein destroy this planet!"

Sloan ran over to a bunch of 44 gallon barrels pushed into the far corner of the basement. Figuring the operation being run from this place was really a chop shop he wasn't surprised to find five barrels of gasoline and one of motor oil. Sloan said, "The problem as I see it is, we are in a basement with one way out that is now blocked. There are hostile forces cruising overhead with a lot of firepower. The only way out is to blow the room up and hope that opens a door to the ground level that might give us a chance to escape, steal a new car."

I went with him to look at the barrels, "You think we'll live through this?"

"Better than the alternative, don't you think?"

I shrugged. What did it matter? It looked like my life was going to hell, live or die. I could hear the beast coming closer again and this time huge crashes accompanied its fly over.

"Great." Sloan mumbled. "Time to go. Get behind the support piers at the far end of the room. Plug your ears. I'll join you shortly."

Sloan pulled rags out from his bag of tricks backpack and shoved a piece into one of the barrels at its pump connection. Hoping this one barrel would give a kick and explode the rest. He set the rag on fire and dashed back to the peers where I was and screamed, "Cover your ears!"

I wasn't ready for this. The explosion was devastating. Even with my ears covered I found myself deaf from the blast. Smoked filled the basement and debris had flown everywhere. It was at that moment that I knew this wasn't like a war zone, it was a war zone with me caught in the middle and not even a solider.

Unbelievably the blast had opened a hole in the floor above our heads. Choking on the smoke I stumbled toward the opening to meet Sloan and maybe get out of this death trap.

As I reached Sloan an incredible explosion happened above us. Unable to see what was happening Sloan jumped grabbing the edge of the hole and started to pull himself up. After a moment, he stuck his head down and screamed, "Come on, we got to go. Now!"

He grabbed my arms and pulled me up through the hole and onto what was left of the floor. The entire building was gone. Just rubble piled all around me. I wasn't naive enough to think our little explosion caused all this damage. This was done by something much bigger. Sloan picked his way through the rubble and I followed. Now for sure The Region had spilled out into the world and the results weren't pretty.

Ahead a partial wall still stood and when we reached it Sloan stopped. "I don't know what we'll find on the other side of this wall but let's hope it is more rubble. We have to make it across the street and down the alley toward 14th Street. We'll find a car there to jack."

My breathing was labored. The smoke and dust combined with the effort needed to negotiate my way through the rubble was all taking its toll. Sloan peeked around the wall and motioned for me to follow. As we moved away from the auto repair shop the rubble thinned out dramatically. The road was passable so we made a break for the alley. Running between the blocks it seemed too quiet. This running reminded me of the day I met a woman who looked like a witch. A Dust Witch? Her name, I blanked my mind trying to let the name float up from the darkness. Erictho. That was it. I'd met her at the crossroads near my old home. I'd forgotten that meeting. That was the day I ran home to hell. I do remember my dad's explosion that brought an end to my mother's life. He had seemed so calm when he'd walked in from work. I remember thinking that it might actually be a peaceful evening. I was wrong. After about five minutes he screamed at the top of his lungs. It was like I imagined a banshee's wail would sound. My mom screamed. I couldn't understand why she was so frightened until she had crossed the room running away from him, a large handgun pointing at her. Then there was an explosion. The sound of the gunshot was loud. I'd never heard one up close. I turned and looked at my mom. She'd almost made it. Standing in the doorway, she just looked down at her stomach and watched the blood erupt from her. She was crying. My dad yelled, "I'm gonna put you down, woman. For the last time, I'm putting you down. Then I'll fix that damn daughter of yours."

He fired the gun over and over. My ears were totally deaf. My mother was just a pile of bloody meat on the floor. Her face was gone and brains were spilling out onto the floor. I looked up at dad and he was looking at me with such hate. The gun came up and he pulled the trigger. I couldn't hear anything but the gun wasn't working anymore. He threw it to the ground and stormed toward me. I couldn't hear anything he was saying but when he reached me, his fist in a ball, the pain from his blow knocked me to the floor. I hit the back of my head on the floor and that's the last thing I remember. If I was still conscious, my mind had blocked all memory of the events past the first blow.

Sloan was approaching the end of the alley and I followed him out and we were immediately stopped. Before us was a massive boiling cloud. It rose up three stories from the ground. You could distinctly see a dark body of some unspeakable horror moving inside the cloud. I turned around and looked down the street. Retreat was impossible with all the devastation blocking the road.

A low moaning sound started coming from the monster. The sound reverberated in my soul taking me back to primal times before we'd developed language or discovered fire. A distant past oozed from this creature. It was ancient. What chance did we have against something that has lived a million years?

There was nothing to do but face the beast. It raised its head, or at least I think it was a head, like it was a snake ready to strike. I was glad it would be over quick. Sloan was backing up still facing the monster with his arm out. He yelled, "Stay behind me." The moaning grew to that rumbling I heard in my apartment. The ground was shaking and I couldn't stay on my feet. I fell and Sloan fell on top of me trying to still protect me. Old habits die hard. Then the rumbling just stopped. The sound turned into a high-pitched screaming sound as the creature turned away from us. Something behind it had struck a blow. I have no idea how unless you had a rocket launcher.

The black fog thinned and I could see what looked like a person floating about twenty feet off the ground. This had been another day of impossibilities. Slowly the person lowered to the ground and stood in the middle of the street facing off with this ancient monster. A giant shudder passed through the ground as the beast collapsed. We watched in amazement as the black fog thinned and sank back into the ground. Now I could see who had come to our rescue. It was Station Cross.

She waved so Sloan couldn't deny what she had done. Then she was gone. Sloan said, "Well we live to fight another day and I don't have a fucking clue what that was all about."

I said, "Maybe I was right in trusting her. Sloan, people change."

"Not that bitch. She was handy though."

"Now what? More running and hiding until the next monster finds me? I don't think this is working."

Sloan looked at me, "You're right. It's time to change plans."

I said, "I hope so. The next monster will be as big as all of Lawton!"

Sloan laughed. I joined him and for a moment the thrill of having survived the impossible coursed through me. Sloan looked down the street and said, "Time to get another ride. We have someplace to be."

PART 3

UNDER THE STARS OF MADNESS

They worshipped, so they said, the Great Old Ones who lived ages before there were any men, and who came to the young world out of the sky.

-The Call of Cthulhu
H.P. Lovecraft

I AM MY
NIGHTMARE WORLD

We were heading east on US-24. Sloan said we were north of Columbia, Missouri. It was nighttime so it didn't matter to me. Sloan wanted to keep off the major highways and out of big cities. We were sure doing that. Where we were heading I did not know, but it seemed like we were never going to get there.

All our traveling had been at night. During the day, we'd stop at some rundown motel and sleep. In between we'd eat. Wasn't much different from my usual schedule except each night was filled with the black of the night. Open lands with no detail or texture. A darkness hiding all. We'd always stop at daybreak, so the world had become dim and wasted to me. By the time we'd get up to travel it would be night again. I felt like I was living in a room with no windows or doors, no lights to guide my way. My sense of place in the world was gone. Was this my new life? If so, did I want to keep living? That was a scary and new feeling. I'd fought so hard for life and now I wondered if it wasn't a mistake. Something was changing inside of me. It was in my mind and I realized I didn't know where my mind was or anyone's for that matter. Sloan rarely talked as we moved along old and broken highways, through small towns devastated by the creation of the interstate highway system. Few people traveled here. It seemed that most were called scenic byways now. I could only guess at what lurked in the dark, just beyond the reach of the headlights.

I was becoming obsessed with how my brain had shut off for seven months and machines had kept me breathing and my heart beating. The nurses tried to gossip quietly but I think sometimes I could still hear them talk about how I was brain dead and how this was wrong. I shouldn't be alive. It was true, I had no awareness of my place in the world or what was changing around me. Time was passing and I wasn't part of it. I remembered that when I was in The Region my real world seemed shrouded in mist. I couldn't remember a sunny summer day with open fields to run through picking wildflowers for no good reason except they were pretty. No recollection of summer breezes and the blaze of stars in the night sky. Before the coma I'd spent as much time away from home as I could. I would explore the forests around Mason and walked the dirt roads out into the country. It was my freedom. Back then I had no fear of the night. I loved the night. I loved lonely places and would seek them out.

Out of the crumbling wreck I still called my mind, I remembered. One day, it was outside Mason—the last day of my old life, I know now—I was wandering the lonely country roads. I approached the crossroads of Olden Road and Puckett. I'd been to this crossroads countless times. I especially loved visiting at night. I'd walk to the center and just sit for an hour. It brought peace to my chaotic mind filled with my father's violence. Now it was dusk and a woman dressed in bulky, black clothes was walking up Olden Road. She looked like a witch straight out of a Halloween postcard, minus the broomstick. She was coming right toward me as I came up Olden Road toward the crossroads.

Stopping, I looked at her but couldn't place her face with any name in my database. I started into the crossroads and she yelled, "Stop!" I did and stood still looking at the face of this woman. She was as old as the dirt road I was standing on. Wrinkles and lines were burned into her face from what I guessed had been years of living off the land. Time had left her a shadow of who she had been. She looked weak. No, frail, like a china doll riddled with spider-cracks just waiting for the right moment to collapse.

I took a few steps toward her. She seemed harmless enough, "Can I help you?"

"Yes, you can. Stop. You can't enter the crossroads."

I grinned, "Really? I've walked these roads and hills all my life and never had a lick of trouble."

She moved closer to me, blocking my progress. I could see a grim affect plaguing her face. Something had her deeply disturbed. "You don't know today do you? Do you think every day is the same? Do you think that changes won't come?"

She was starting to spook me out. It seemed I was in the presence of a certifiable nut case and what that meant I could only guess. I said, "I don't think anything is different today than yesterday. I walked these roads last week and just enjoyed the peace of the country. That's kind of what I need right now."

She said, "Much happens in a week. There's no comfort here. Especially for you," she paused then continued, "I've been waiting for you. You are the one. The one who walks two worlds."

I had no idea what she was talking about. The wind came up blowing dust off the road and into the air where it spun and danced, pushing me towards the crossroad. The woman began coughing as the wind blew harder.

Finally, she got control and stopped me again by holding both my shoulders and putting her face nose to nose with mine. In a whisper she said to me, "Be the fool you want to be, but I was sent against all odds. I almost died on my journey to this very spot so I could give you a gift and a warning. That may mean nothing to you but by the God that dwells in Heaven and Satan who sits below I tell you for your own life, no your very soul, journey no further this day. Return home. You will take a long trip Robin, but I think you should already know that. You'll need all your strength."

I looked hard at this wizened old woman, "How the fuck do you know my name? Who the hell are you?"

With this the woman showed lightness for the first time. "Oh, my sweet Robin. You know so little for the journey ahead. That's always the way, though. Never enough answers and always too many questions. Time never favors us."

Confused and convinced this lady was mad I took a step back and thought heading home wasn't such a bad idea. "Ok. I think I'll head home now but you really don't know the kind of home I have. Maybe I'm safer here."

"Robin, my name is Erictho. I am a Dust Witch from the realm of Thessaly. Not the Thessaly of this world. I hold great power. The power to draw down the moon. Enough power to raise the dead and learn the future. I know what your family is. Both families. Cursed in violence unto death I fear. What I can't see, none of us can see, is what difference you could possibly make."

Stunned by her rudeness I shouted, "You and every other fucking son of a bitch in Mason! I'm nothing more than a waste of DNA according to my dad. My mom never disagreed with him. I have no friends, well maybe two, the rest of the town shuns me. They talk behind my back. Their gossip is meant to be cruel and I promise you if I died today no one would mourn the loss. I wonder if I'd even get buried and what do you mean both?"

Erictho grew silent. Looking deeply into my eyes I seemed to become transfixed to the spot where I stood. She moved close to me again and whispered, "Robin, trust me on this, a waste of DNA, no. Important, yes. I just can't see why. An angel maybe. Listen, great change has come to the two worlds you walk. You will be called the Storm Bringer. Death will ride at your heels and follow your command. I have been told the days of the Shadow Tales are at hand and you are the one hoped to claim the power to set things right. Only a few know the meaning of the Shadow Tales and I'm not one. To me they are like whispers woven into the fabric of reality a smoky mist that obscures my visions. I can tell that they are as old as time just like you. You are one of those whispers. It's I who am scared. I know not my place in the new order of things."

This was just way too weird. I was living in a story right out of Fate magazine. Time to go home. I turned away from Erictho and started back down the road. She said, "Tonight it starts. I'm so sorry for what you will bear. Before you go I have a gift for you. It's from before time and from the hand of God."

I stopped. Turning back, I started to ask her what the hell she meant but she was gone. The wind was still and the world silent. Then I knew someone was buried at the crossroads. Someone from years ago. A woman I had met in The Region. I could almost see her name. A shiver passed through me. I would meet this woman one day and it wouldn't be pretty. I just knew this. I was scared. Very scared. I noticed on the ground where the witch had stood was a necklace. The chain was made of finely worked gold and hanging from it was a small key. I went to pick it up knowing this was the gift Erictho had been sent to give me. I lifted it from the ground and it shocked me at how heavy it was. It didn't make sense seeing such a small object that seemed to weigh twenty pounds or more. As I lifted it its weight seemed to lessen. It looked old and was covered with what looked like tarnish. The key was unlike any I'd ever seen before. It was sort of like an old skeleton key but I could tell by holding it that it was older than any door that's been created. The bow was shaped like the Star of David with ornate markings along the stars edge. I couldn't read the markings but they looked like words of some kind. I slipped the chain around my neck expecting to feel the weight but I didn't. A chill passed through my body like someone walking across my grave. I didn't even have a grave yet. I started running back to town. To what would be the worst night of my life.

ACROSS THE HILLS
OF DAMNATION

I was startled awake. Sloan had left US 20 and we were on an old and dark road. At last I could see a bit out the window. I asked, "Where are we?"

Sloan replied, "Lake Erie outside North Tonawanda."

A deserted wasteland surrounded us. To our left was a lonely beach that hadn't heard the laughter of children or the quiet breath of lovers in years. Beyond the beach lay Lake Erie. A mass of darkness in an already dark world. The dream I was having remained fresh in my mind now like a memory. Maybe it was. To tell the truth I was getting confused about what's real and what isn't.

Sloan looked over at me and asked, "How can you sleep all day then sleep all night as well?"

It wasn't a sarcastic question. He seemed to be wondering.

I hadn't thought about it much. I hesitated then said, "I don't know. It isn't like I sleep all the time. It's more like I'm in a trance where I remember things. It feels like real memories not like dreams. When I dream I usually can't remember much when I wake up. Now when I sleep I don't dream, I think I'm remembering things because I wake up and all the dreams feel more like pieces of me that seem to be fitting together somehow."

Sloan had a look of concern on his face. He looked me up and down then turned back toward the road, "That worries me."

"Why should it worry you!"

"Because, I don't know what you might be remembering."

I laughed, "And what the hell does it matter to you what I remember. Sloan, you don't get it. After the coma, it seems I'm living two lives. I just can't piece them together or maybe it's more like I can't take them apart and put them in the right order. For sure it's none of your business."

Sloan said, "Maybe it is my business Robin. Haven't you ever wondered where I came from or how the hell I got here. You haven't even asked about who I am?"

I frowned, "In fact I have Sloan. You think my lack of questions means I don't care? It seems everyone around me knows everything about what's going on in my life except me. That has me distracted. You see Sloan, I can't comprehend even for one solitary second what has happened to me. My life growing up, my dad trying to kill me not to mention a seven-month stint in a coma. Then there's the surprise flight from Mason, that incredible monster in Lawton. Fuck, I have no idea what has gone wrong inside my head. You see, I don't know if any of this is real or if I'm suffering delusional trauma from the brain damage most certainly caused by my father when he hit me over and OVER! Shit, for all I know I'm still in a coma or dead."

"Oh, I see." Sloan said, "It's all about you. Your poor life. You listen to me, this isn't a coma or a dream. This is deadly real. All of it. Didn't you learn anything when you were in The Region or were you so focused on getting out you missed the point? You know what I think? I think you're slipping."

I sat silent. No one in the whole fucking world would believe any of this. I felt anger well up inside me. There was no place to go, no life to live, no friend to talk to or lover to hold. I wondered why Station had left me. It was a thought filled with pain and great longing. I remembered how she smelled of the ocean. I wanted to hold her. Maybe there would be a day we could just be together without this wretched experience. Too many questions. This was madness. I climbed between the seats to the back. There was no more to say. With my head against the window I looked up at the night sky. I could see the stars blazing out from their eternal resting places. The stars of madness. What secrets did they hold? All that had come before? I thought about my recurring nightmare. I remembered how those stars seemed to be watching me. What had they seen? Nothing I could remember. To me all was madness. I was certainly living in the region where madness dwelled. It didn't matter if I was here or there it'd all become the same and now mixed together, it had become my reality. My mind was lost and I needed a drink. Bad. I yelled up to the front seat, "Sloan, so you think I am like what, slipping between two different worlds? So, like when I was being attacked by the Nightcrawlers in that flat desolate place you're saying I might have really been there? I had somehow slipped into The Region?"

Sloan sighed, "That's what I'm afraid of. Except you never left the car. You see, once you travel to The Region you're not supposed to come back. You either stay in a coma until you die or you are already dead. Robin, I'm not trying to be harsh but you fucked up when you went after your starlight then used it to return to Earth. It wasn't yours to reclaim. That light pays the tolls for each of your sinful acts. The tolls keep you from entering the Binding Place. Now yours are gone. That leaves you between."

I asked, "Between what?"

"Heaven and Hell, Robin. No one gets it here. There is most certainly a Heaven and a Hell but there is also the place between. It's a place of preparation. All souls pass through The Region. You must justify yourself there to move on to Heaven or you can be cursed by evil and dragged to the Binding Place. What you call Hell. It is a constant war. There was a story once. It's one of the stories from ancient times. These stories are called the Shadow Tales. They are told only in hushed voices, whispers really. It's a story about a woman who is called The Storm Bringer. A person who really exists. A person who threatens us all." With these words, my heart froze with terror. It's what the Dust Witch had called me. That had been a memory, not a dream. It made me wonder, when was the last time I'd slept.

I leaned over the seat, "What story?"

Sloan said, "No one knows if it's true. I've been around a very long time and I've never heard that this person really exists. It's someone always cast as a woman. Those who know her call her the one who walks two worlds." I sat back in my seat wondering if there was a chance I was that person and if I was what the hell it meant. What was I supposed to do? Was I good or evil? I started to cry. I just don't want to walk around feeling sorry for myself but I just don't know what else to do.

So, I said, "Sloan, what if I tell you that I'm that person?"

Sloan chuckled, "That would be a surprise. You don't strike me as one who brings storms. More like one who runs away from them."

"So then tell me Sloan, why are you here? I mean you are putting yourself at risk protecting me. Why? Did someone tell you to do this?"

Sloan was silent for a while. "I just am. I had to leave The Region. When I'd come over here, I found out you were here so I decided to protect you. I can never return."

"How did you know I'd needed protecting? Tell me Sloan!"

Sloan shifted in his seat, "I don't know. Robin, I just help where I can."

I could hear the lie in his voice, "If I slip you are saying I go into The Region but my body is staying here. Like when I was in the coma. What I need to do is be able to take my body with me."

Sloan laughed, "Robin, now you are losing it. No one from here ever slips. You die. That's why it scares me. We born of The Region can't move between worlds except with exceptional need, and people from here only make a one-way trip. So, you see, I don't know what all this means." Sloan fell silent.

This was all too much. I tried to empty my racing mind. I looked out the window over the great expanse of blackness where the waters of Erie lay. Then I noticed something moved under the surface of the water causing the water to swell. I was frightened. Trouble was coming. The size of the swell was growing in the lake but it ran parallel to the shore.

It was pacing us. Sloan didn't seem to notice. I sat up and poked my head through the space between the seats and said, "I have a bad feeling something is in the lake. Something big."

Sloan jerked his head around in time to see a black form rise up from the water. It broke the surface and plunged into the lake. "Oh shit. No kidding we have problems." Sloan hit the gas. "We're on State 531 and it moves closer to the lake where it becomes Old Lake Road. Not far from there the road bends back toward US 20 and away from the lake but I'm not sure we're going to make it."

The car bounced, throwing me around the back seat. I grabbed the front passenger seat and pulled myself back into it. Strapping the seatbelt on I looked out the windshield and saw a horror that must be the Leviathan from the Bible. It rose up out of the water stretching toward the stars. It made the Nightcrawlers look like ants. It just kept climbing, maybe eight stories. It was flat but its mouth was ringed with row after row of teeth. Then suddenly it came crashing down across the road.

Sloan yelled, "Oh shit." He slammed on the brakes and we came to a sudden stop. Putting it in reverse he swung the car around and we headed back the way we'd come.

I looked at Sloan, "You've got to be kidding me. What the hell is that thing and why is it trying to kill me?"

Sloan didn't answer. He was focused on the task at hand. I look out the rear window and could see the mass of the beast rising then falling ever closer as a wretched moan escaped its mouth. It was louder than the noise the car was making.

Sloan screamed, "I'm sorry! I should have told you more. Maybe taught you some things. I just didn't want to expose you to more than you needed to know. I thought maybe knowing more might make things worse for you. Robin, there is only one world and we're in it. Apart from that is Heaven and Hell. Like I said you can't leave those places once you're there but The Region is the middle place." The car shook violently and the tip of the monster's mouth brushed the bumper. Sloan cut left to counter the move. "Once you enter you aren't supposed to leave but you did. Great powers are at war in The Region. At stake are all the souls of mankind, both those destined for Heaven and Hell." The creature slammed into my side of the car taking us up on two wheels. Sloan fought to bring the car back to earth. "I think I was wrong. Maybe you can slip but you can't slip all the way. Take your body with you I mean. This monster is going to chase us and there will be no stopping it. Something or someone must have sent it here. It's coming for you."

The road dipped under a small bridge built to span the marshland and give passage to a dock. Sloan slammed on the brakes stopping the car in the middle of this small space. He opened his door and climbed out of the car. I didn't have much choice. The monster slammed against the bridge shaking the earth. It couldn't reach us but the bridge wouldn't last long. I opened my door and slid out onto the damp ground. The creature was lying before us but it had become still. It wasn't making a sound. It wasn't moving at all. Sloan rounded the car and took my hand to guide me away from it. Sloan whispered, "You need to run. When this monster regains its strength, there will be no stopping it. It is one of the ancient ones and it wants to claim you for its own and it will."

THE FOUNDATIONS OF HEAVEN AND HELL

I was angry. No one was claiming me. All my miserable life I had suffered at the hands of others. No, I should say I've allowed others to set the rules. I've allowed others to define who I was or maybe more like, who I should be. Now it was Sloan. He tells me where to live. Drags me on a car trip to who knows where. So, I'm not to run and now I am supposed to run.

When I was a little kid I felt helpless. I can remember when I was nine. It was the first time I was beat. Before that I'd lived in a fantasy world where kids were safe. Then one night my dad rolled in drunk. I knew at the time it was bad. I'd always heard the arguing between my mom and Dad. Sometimes he'd slap her. Those moments scared me. I did all I could to push them away. I could never have a sleepover because my dad might come in drunker than hell and bitch and scream and hit my mom, scaring the shit out of me. I think that's what made me such a solitary person. Hell, everyone seemed to know about my family life so no one wanted to be my friend anyway.

On that night things were different. He had come home drunk as hell and the yelling and screaming ensued but then he didn't slap her. He slammed his fist into mom's face breaking her cheekbone and knocking her out.

So, she wasn't there to protect me. Really, she never was there to protect me. I guess Dad didn't know what to do with his rage, so he pounded down the hall to my room. As he approached my door I became frightened. This was new. I'd been left alone. Not this night. My door flew open and in walked the first monster I'd ever encountered. He entered my room and stopped and just looked at me. He mumbled something I couldn't understand, then shook himself. After that he said, "You damn bitch! All you are is a knock off of your shit-filled mother. I can't stand the sight of you!" Then he said something he never said again. I've never forgotten it though, "By The Prince of the Power of the Air and the rage of the ages, I claim you."

I cowered in the corner of my room. Tears started to flow from my eyes. I had nowhere to hide. All his rage was now focused on me. I whimpered. "Dad? What's wrong? Did I do something wrong?"

He yelled, "You got born, you bitch." I didn't know what this all meant but I picked up on the disgust. "I should put you out of your misery. The world doesn't need a bitch named Robin." With that he walked toward me and grabbed me by the hair and pulled me to my feet. It hurt but that was nothing compared to what was to come. He lifted me off my feet and then struck me in the head. The blow was so hard it knocked me out. What happened next was I woke up with a bitchin' headache and the house was dark and silent.

Slowly I stood up and immediately fell to the ground, my head swimming. So I crawled toward my bed. I was crying uncontrollably but I dared not make a sound. I can remember still, thinking he was passed out someplace so things were ok, but I didn't trust myself. Suddenly, I didn't trust anything. When

I reached my bed, I crawled in and wondered if my mom was ok. I was just too scared to go into the hall and see. I fell asleep and next thing I knew the police and paramedics were lifting me onto a gurney. An EMT saw I was waking and said, "I'm Emma. You are safe now. We'll take you to the hospital and away from this horror." There were tears in her eyes.

I noticed a burning pain in my privates and tried to raise up to see why. I caught sight of blood on my nightgown but Emma gently pushed me back down fixing the restraints. "Don't want you falling off the cart."

"Why do I hurt so bad? He hit me in the head. I don't understand."

Emma was at a loss of words. What do you say to a 10-year-old who just got raped? Emma seemed to finish up and turned toward me saying, "I'm not a doc but in a few minutes, we'll have all the answers."

"My mom? Is she dead?"

Emma jumped at the change of subject, "No. Broken cheekbone but that's easy to fix. She'll be fine."

"And my dad?" I could see the cloud pass over Emma's face. She was emotionally involved in this incident.

"Don't know where he is darling but the locals along with Highway Patrol are looking. If he gets as far as Grange, the State Police will get involved. Past that, he crosses state lines and the FBI takes over. He won't get far." She sighed, "I'm so sorry. I have a little girl your age. It's inconceivable to me that anyone could do this. If I can, I'll come by and check up on you. Maybe introduce you to my daughter Lucy."

A low moaning sound brought me back into the

moment. It was emanating from the ancient creature now lying very still at the mouth of the underpass. Sloan was scared but it didn't look like he was scared of the monster, but something else. I thought maybe he was afraid of me. Afraid of what choices I might make. Choices he didn't want to be made. I was no detective but something seemed wrong. I was never supposed to leave The Region. But I did. Maybe I had it all backwards. Sloan didn't like Station but maybe it was only because she wanted me to return. She'd said, "Pick up the sword and finish what we started."

I loved Station Cross. That I knew. The seeds of doubt Sloan had sown hadn't taken. I had no life here. If I went to The Region maybe I could come back but then maybe not. Amazingly I didn't seem to care. It was then that I realized the Dust Witch had been right. I am the one who walks two worlds. The storm bringer! Shit, I was going to bring the fucking storm of a lifetime. Now I had to do the most incredibly stupid thing I've ever done.

I turned to Sloan and got in his face, "No Sloan. I've got it all wrong. You're not protecting me from these monsters. I understand your real plan now. All you've ever cared about was making sure I never get back to The Region!"

Sloan stuttered, clearly caught off guard. I got even closer.

"Listen Sloan, news flash, it's me! I am the one who walks two worlds. Don't you get it? I am The Storm Bringer and you can damn well bet that death will ride at these heels. You know Sloan, it just might seem like a Ripley's Believe It or Not thing, but I'm a lot tougher than I look. I have lived a brutal life and now all you want to do is make sure I stay stuck in it."

Sloan stepped back, "You can't go back! It will be the end of the balance. You might be found then who knows what will happen?"

I waved at the ancient monster, a god of the old world, "That's from the place between, yet it's here. There is no balance. You know I feel like I'm the only one that can restore the balance and you and whoever you work for are afraid. Well, this is done. No more running. No more being told what to do." And with that I walked out of the underpass and directly toward the god.

"I'm Robin Randle. I'm the one who walks two worlds. The Storm Bringer. Open beast and give me passage to The Region.

The beast reared up its full eight stories. It seemed as if it had no end. I turned to look at Sloan. He was gone. It didn't matter. I looked up and saw the glistening teeth as the head of the beast rushed toward me. Then darkness and I was falling.

PART 4

THE MYSTIC CHORDS OF MEMORY

Deep into that darkness peering, long I stood there, wondering, fearing,

Doubting, dreaming dreams no mortal ever dared to dream before;

-The Raven
Edgar Allen Poe

ARRIVAL

Falling. It felt as if I was falling but there was no feeling of air rushing around my body. It seemed as if I was wrapped in midnight. No stars to guide me. No moon to light my way. Only the sensation of falling. Endless. Timeless. Maybe this was death. Had I made a mistake? Even though blackness surrounded me, I decided to try my relaxation exercise. Closing my eyes, I slowed my breathing and tried to let my muscles fully relax one by one. I thought the last time I made this trip I was in a coma.

Then music began to play. These mystic chords weren't like any music I'd ever heard. It felt ancient - older than the gods themselves. I felt this hum had traveled from the beginning of time. Each strike echoed in my head. No. My mind. That's where this was now. With every strike of the chord a door opened in my memory. Suddenly I recognized the impossibly low pulsing. It was from my dream that I'd had in Sloan's car. I was back at Redding's Mill. Memories were becoming clearer. My life on Earth was opening up to me like I'd never known it to.

Then with utter horror I knew I was a victim of my own delusions. The events that took place at Redding's Mill weren't a dream. They were memories. I'd just compartmentalized them and locked them away telling myself Jim and Lucy had just abandoned me like everyone else. That wasn't true. Before the pool I was still living in the house where my mother was murdered. I didn't know what else to do. No one bothered me, so Jim and Lucy would come over and we'd sit on the front porch drinking and smoking pot. We were very drunk when we started off to the pool but who could have known what was coming.

A lot like my dream, Mr. Beam turned the pool deck lights on and we were surprised. Mr. Beam did know us by name and Jim did try to talk us out of the situation. Then the horror started. Just like the dream I swam to the side of the pool with Jim at my side. We reached the pool deck at the same time. Jim stood in the four feet of water but I stayed submerged to hide my naked breasts.

Then the scream. I remembered now, exactly how it sounded. Pure madness. Her throat sounded as if it were ripping out of her body. We all turned as she struggled in the water like she was drowning. Then she started to rise from the pool. Screams. Lucy could see something we couldn't. Her terror was like I've never seen. My friend. My first and only friend. I had to do something. Black shiny tentacles slithered out of the water and started wrapping themselves around her legs. More reached up winding their way around her waist. There were larger ones twisting around her torso. Everywhere they touched they burned her flesh. Mr. Beam started backing away from the edge of the pool no longer thinking up ways to make us the most embarrassed three teenagers in Mason. More of the black wormlike tentacles started to encase Lucy's body. Impossibly, she screamed harder. Blood started to stream from her nose. When she was totally out of the water she was encased in the black tentacles. It reminded me of my recurring nightmare and how it always ended with me in this same place. Her screaming stopped. The tentacles pulsed, squeezing her over and over. A little harder each time.

I realized I was screaming. I pulled myself up out of the pool, my nakedness forgotten. The pool water started to churn and this horror lifted Lucy about twenty feet into the air. An evil god of The Region had come to claim me. Poor Lucy just got in the way. The tentacles all came from the creature's mouth. The head of this god was round with two deep red bulging eyes. The skin was smooth and gray with multiple holes opening and closing as if breathing. Earth hadn't seen this kind of creature for millions of years. It felt like this monster was born from the wasted byproduct of creation grabbed up by evil and fashioned into a god before there were gods. Just to kill.

The monster crushed Lucy into a mush of blood. Unrecognizable red matter rained down on us. I started crying. These bits and pieces were a person. My friend. And now she just exploded over the pool. My screaming never stopped, mixed with tears. I realized Jim was screaming too. He turned and ran to the farthest corner of the pool deck where darkness hid all. His screaming had changed into whimpers and cries. He was broken. This being had driven all sanity from his mind. I kept moving backwards watching this god. It was looking right at me. A piercing sound came from its misshaped mouth. It turned into a rumbling sound deep as the ocean canyons. As old as the sun. The shower building behind me was shaking itself apart.

Mr. Beam walked out of the building just before it started to collapse, shotgun in his hands. Pointing the weapon at the monster he pulled the trigger, cocked the gun with a new shell and fired again. The explosion of sound was shocking. Over and over he fired until the gun had no more rounds in it. I thought I'd never be able to hear again. Mr. Beam didn't know this monster was a god. He looked confused that it was totally unfazed by his violent attack. Mr. Beam just threw the weapon down on the pool deck and watched as tentacles reached out for him.

Unlike Lucy, the creature held Beams arms and burned into his body. Then it lifted him high into the air. Eye-level with the creature. Light grew in the monster's chest and a pulse of white light moved into Mr. Beam. Then he burned up. He was just ashes now floating down on me like black snow on a winter's day. It was just so surreal to see the blood-tainted pool, my blood-covered body now with the ashes of Mr. Beam slowly floating all around sticking to my skin. Remains of two human beings now reduced to nothing. The violence was serenaded by the weeping from Jim.

I heaved a large breath and turned toward the wrecked bath house and ran right over the remains and out into the parking lot. Turning around wasn't an option. I've never run so hard in all my life. Naked and shoeless, I reached the line of trees at the end of the parking lot. Before plunging into its total darkness, I dared a look. The impossible horror grew white with light and suddenly all the water in the pool just exploded. In a moment, the pool was empty. The god raised in the air and I was sure it would follow me.

I disappeared into the blackness of the forest. No longer was the forest my friend. I stumbled and fell tripping over old tree roots and cutting my hands and feet on sharp rocks. Bleeding and filthy my naked body burst from the trees and into my back yard. I thought the little house, the house I'd grown up in, the house I was almost killed in, looked very fragile. The back door is always unlocked so I slipped into the house, locked the door and slumped to the kitchen floor crying uncontrollably.

I'd just abandoned my friends. I had just run away. I knew Lucy was gone but maybe I could have saved Jim. I sobbed for over an hour waiting for the monster to find me and rend my body to pulp. When nothing came I just fell asleep on the linoleum floor, naked, bloody and crusted with mud.

All that had happened. My mind was clear. When I woke the next morning, I sat up caked mud cracking from my naked form. I needed to create a new reality. One that explained the disappearance of Lucy and Jim as fallout from all that was wrong with my life. To me they became alive again but never called or came over. At night as I would fall asleep I'd wonder what happened to Jim. Maybe he was evaporated by the explosion or is sitting in a cell at an asylum. The Region had broken into our world and my mind wouldn't accept it. We had seen the impossible and only I survived. Why? From that night on, my fear of the dark grew until just walking through my dark house caused me to become frightened. My love of wandering nights was over.

SIGN OF THE RAVEN

I felt overwhelmed by this experience. I guessed this was why memories are clouded in this place. My rotating came to a lazy stop and the space I was now in felt solid. I even stamped my feet to kick up some real dust. A small comfort. At least I was on the ground now and still alive from the attack of that beast. I'd mentally survived the reinstatement of my Earthly memories.

And I mean what great memories they were. So few were happy. No child should ever have to grow up in a home like mine but I know it happens every day. Our top-notch social system grinds with persistent slowness. If you didn't fit in with the grinding, things seemed even slower.

I looked around and noticed the utter darkness was giving way to some kind of bluish light just forming on the horizon. It was in all direction with no apparent source. I'd never seen the sun the whole time I was in The Region. Just an endless full moon shone down on me as if I was lucky to have even that.

My mind slipped sideways a bit. I started wondering if I was in a psychiatric hospital. I mean how would you ever know? I might be schizophrenic. Everything just a grand illusion in my mind. When you think about it how could I ever tell what was real or what wasn't? My greatest fear. Locked away without hope of ever returning to the outside world. I would become one more forgotten child.

With that lovely thought a searing pain shot through my head. I doubled over. I could sense movement all around me but I couldn't open my eyes. I fell to my knees sobbing. The pain grew. I was about to go completely insane. It just wouldn't stop. Finally, I toppled over on my side and curled into a ball.

Then silence. It felt amazing. A gentle breeze had kicked up bringing with it the promise of untold adventure and amazing discoveries. This wasn't the killing wind I'd felt before. I stumbled getting to my feet. On the ground at my feet was a staff and an old travelers backpack. I wiped my eyes; and for the first time I could survey the land in which I stood. Directions were impossible so I just made up north for reference and plotted out my land.

To the north, great mountains stood. Steep and ragged; covered in snow. They looked impassible at least this time of year. To my west was a flat land that was the desert from my dream. Now I know it wasn't a dream either. A long road stretched forever to someplace. Looking east it seemed to be gently rolling hills dotted with what might have been farms at one time. I turned around and looked south. I just knew there was no help down there. The Great Forest was there, dense with underbrush. But I felt the weirdest feeling that just didn't make sense at all. Home. What is home here? South of the Great Forest is the sea. I've been there the first time I traveled to The Region. I woke up soaked with sweat. I was in my jeans and sweatshirt. I could sense the encroachment of the incoming tide. The boundary between two different worlds colliding and struggling to gain a foothold on each other.

Robin was one confused kid right then. My instincts told me The Region was real. If it was the integration of both worlds, no wonder I was psychotic. How could one kid hold all this long enough to get a chance to ask? I noticed I was standing alone at the crossroads and that brought back the memory of Erictho. Maybe not a good place to be. I took several steps to the east. It seemed the most hospitable.

I sighed and started east. After a mile, the pain retuned and I went down again. I tried my relaxation exercise and almost fell into a trance state. There were memories here too. Almost lost to me in the world of sunlight. Complete silence caressed me. The pain subsided to a gentle awareness of my whole mind.

I could remember the ER. It was the moment I woke briefly. I closed my eyes and all connection to my world melted away. I was on a beach. As I walked toward the shore, the edge of The Great Forest directly ahead and the full moon lighting my way, that fear of the dark dug its claws into me and I couldn't move. Directly ahead a path was leading into The Great Forest and I knew it would be safer in there so I took a deep breath and walked. The dark was everywhere, so standing in the dark seemed dumb compared to moving in it.

Then time compressed. All the memories were there but now I could fast forward at will. Of all people, Erictho stepped out into the road to stop me. I screamed at her sudden appearance. Erictho laughed making her wrinkled and cracked face even uglier. She said, "Look who's here. I see you took my advice. You went off to your happy Earth home filled with violence and murder to watch your mother die..."

I interrupted her, "What's your problem? Is this what you get off on? I have no idea what the hell is going on, where I am, where I need to go or why.

You show up to shame me because I don't remember everything."

"You know more than you think. You walk two worlds. This is the first. The Region. You won't be welcome here. Forces at work want you dead, so beware. So now it's time for you to become the Storm Bringer. Only then can you return to the second world or what you erroneously call home."

I looked her right in the eyes, "Now just hold it right there. I will not be a storm, killing as I go. I refuse to follow in my father's footsteps. Evil and destruction was his way. He killed an innocent then tried to kill me."

"Fear not, my little Robin. You know not which father you truly follow. Your purpose is much different. Remember, Robin. Remember those last moments before you passed back to Earth. It was then that you confronted the Queen of Starlight. Do you even remember why? What mission did you fulfill? Go back to that place and see the truth."

I closed my eyes and reached back to those final moments. A dizzy wave passed through me and I was there. Opening my eyes, I saw Station fighting off a horrible monster. It looked like a man slightly taller than Station but its head was all wrong. Where the face should have been was a large mouth ringed with teeth and different sizes of tentacles protruded from inside the mouth. Several small slits surrounded the mouth. Maybe they were eyes. I couldn't tell. These tentacles reached out at her as the creature swung a large broadsword toward her head. She moved much faster than the monster and swung her sword cutting off most of the flailing tentacles then thrust the creature through its heart. I could see other monsters her size with long pincer like claws and razor-sharp teeth to fend off her advances. Some creatures were huge, at least twice her size with hundreds of legs, all moving together and others looked like small versions of the worm that had eaten me. I turned away and when I turned back I realized I was now far away from Station. I was in a hidden place. A place I was not to know about, but now I did. It was an enormous palace. I'd found it. The Palace of Starlight. I pushed the two enormous doors open and walked into the Hall of Stars.

The room was circular and looked to have no end to its height. Little nooks covered the walls, each slot holding a clear glass ball with a star inside. I thought they were the souls of those in The Region. The Queen was here as well. She was splendidly dressed in a Victorian dress that was glowing a soft blue. The dress was tight at her small waist. She was tall and stood very straight. Her deep red hair was pinned neatly up on her head exposing a long and elegant neck. Her face was as pale as mine with high cheekbones, her eyes stark green. I wasn't expecting a tall, beautiful woman. She smiled graciously and welcomed me. She motioned for me to come and sit at a small table in the center of the hall for tea. Waving her arms at the walls she said, "The Hall of Stars, Robin Randle. Come have tea and rest awhile."

Oddly the sound of battle was gone, along with all sense of urgency. I moved toward the table as if in a spell. The Queen said, "Robin, my poor Robin. You have been so misled by those you think are your friends." I slowly finished looking around the entire room. "You think I horde these stars, don't you? That I keep them away from their owners. Now, tell me why would I do that?" Her voice so sweet.

I stuttered, "To keep them safe?"

The Queen smiled, "Yes my dear girl. This is a dangerous land. When someone is ready to move on, they come here and I give them their star. Very simple."

"Oh." For a moment, all seemed right. I mean it all seemed so simple. The Queen walked to the table and poured me a cup of tea. Then floating like fall leaves on a frozen wind came thoughts of misery. Misery is all I'd found in The Region. Those I'd met so badly wanted to rise through the Ariel realm to fight for their fate. Heaven or Hell waited but life here was empty and all those I'd met felt hollow inside. It would make her story seem more credible if she'd let some go. This couldn't be right.

I stood, and in my most commanding voice demanded, "I want my star and I'll be on my way." As I said this I took a step toward the Queen. She was much bigger than me and I didn't know if she had a weapon. This was a bad idea but not my first.

I lifted my staff and was ready to strike, "Please sit Robin, and I'll tell you a little story." I felt drained so I sat at the tea table but the Queen kept standing. "You see the stars in these globes are not the souls of those trapped in The Region. They are the tolls that must be paid to pass to Heaven. Time was, each person was responsible for their star but that seemed such a large responsibility. The chance of breaking the globe before the time was right would have eternal consequences."

I stammered, "No. This is a lie. I just know something else wants to hold these objects."

She continued as if I'd not spoken, "It was decided they would all be kept in one place and I would take care of them. I've dedicated thousands of years protecting them. No one appreciates my sacrifice!"

I interrupted, "No you decided to keep them all for yourself just to drive people into despair. Everyone is so afraid of you, no one would dare challenge you." The Queen smiled. There was something more here. She was keeping the truth from me. It was about the use of the globes. I knew I'd never get it out of her but just knowing was a help. A thought did cross my mind, "So you became the puppet of some greater power that keeps you here never to travel The Region again."

Looking at her face I could tell I'd hit a nerve. A look of disgust flashed across it. Shame as well. I think she didn't want to do this but had no choice now. She was done with tea. She produced two short swords moving them with impressive speed. She spit, "All I wanted was Sloan. I never wanted you, but you had to come. The forbidden revealed." It was miracle time. I didn't even have a weapon to defend myself with except for an old staff. She circled me. "I was a fool not to kill you from the start. You should have died at birth but Sloan promised me he had a plan that would keep us safe. That was a mistake. One I will now correct."

She started to attack me just as a raven entered the Hall from a far window. It cawed over and over distracting the Queen. I couldn't believe the size of the bird. A dozen more entered the Hall just after the first, all aiming for the Queen. I grabbed one of the small chairs for defense as she turned and began to beat on me. The chair gave out almost immediately and one of her swords pierced my side. I used my staff to prop myself up and was surprised I could do it. Blood was freely flowing from my wound. I pressed hard at the wound but was starting to feel faint.

The ravens screamed then dived at her scratching and pecking at her eyes trying to keep her away from me. I backed up toward the shelves of stars. She lunged at me again and I was just too slow. She gouged out a part of my upper arm. I was growing weaker from the blood loss. Things seemed to be getting dark. I stumbled backward hitting a shelf of stars and then I saw it. My star. When you get close to your star it glows blue and mine was radiant. The ravens pulled together, circling insanely, making a massive black cloud. The birds fell away like dry leaves, leaving Station Cross in their wake. Station, seeing my injury, turned on the Queen.

The Queen yelled, "You bitch. You think you can even touch me with your blade?"

Station moved in, "Yeah, I think I can. You are pure evil. Stealing peoples' globes so there was no chance of making it to Heaven. You never wanted to let them move on. You're one of the most hideous monsters I have ever seen. I lived all this suffering to find you and end this."

The Queen tried to dance around with Station hoping for a lucky shot but that doesn't happen with Station Cross. Bleeding, I went to get my star but it was too high for me to reach. I turned toward Station as she drove her sword through the Queen's chest.

She pulled it out and the Queen staggered, "You will pay for this. A greater evil stands in the shadows. One even God should fear and now it is unbound."

Station walked up to the Queen and said, "Shut up, bitch. I know where you're going star or no." Station raised her sword and with a single blow took off the Queen's head. It became silent in The Region.

I was crying with pain. I turned towards Station and asked in a timid voice, "Station. Please. I can't reach my star!" She started laughing and walked over to me and boosted me up so I could grab it. For the first time, I felt regret. Inside my heart I knew our plan wasn't finished. "I love you Station. I'm sorry if I failed you."

Station said, "It's not our time. We will meet again to finish this. Get well my love." I threw my arms around her and held on harder than I've ever held somebody. I kissed her, and then pulled away.

"I know these aren't to be broken. Maybe they can't be broken." I held it above my head and it radiated down on me and through my tears and pain I saw Station for the last time and the music played on.

REUNION

Darkness lifted. My memories had healed enough that I could wrestle control of my mind away from the music that was surrounding me. When I did the music faded into the wind and now I could feel the wind blowing against my skin, the world around me still dark but with night, not blackness. I could see shadows from the light of a full moon shining overhead.

I seemed to be in a meadow, sloping downhill toward a tree line. I couldn't tell the density of the forest. Looking back up the gently sloping meadow I could see a set of Corinthian columns built in a circle. They held up an ornate roof giving some cover to the stone floor. I started toward this ancient gazebo and could tell it was old beyond reason. Dead vines clung to the columns and the stone floor looked as if it had been polished with a millennium of rain and wind. Once there had been a statue in the center. It had been a building with a purpose but now it was a ruin. I'd seen this place before. I couldn't imagine anything in The Region being so old it now was a ruin. But I'd been away awhile. How much time had passed here? I didn't even know if time was relevant in this place. Down the long gullet of that towering monster I'd fallen out of my world into this one. Frankly I didn't know which I belonged to. Maybe neither. Maybe both.

I could also see what looked like a campfire burning near the center of the floor. A person was lying next to it. Maybe sleeping. Maybe a trap. I wasn't in Kansas anymore. This was The Region. I didn't know the rules. The time I'd spent here before wasn't spent learning the history and geography of this place. Just how to survive. The vague familiarity Earth presented felt like a backdrop of normalcy. Here there was none.

I approached the campfire slowly watching for any signs of a trap. Stopping, I knelt down and studied the sleeping form by the fire. It was a woman. She was lying on her side facing the fire motionless and wrapped in a thick blanket that obscured her details. What I could see was jet-black hair, short and smartly cut with a whiff of pink on top, just enough. Station? It must be, but it was unusual for her not to have heard my approach. Then she spoke, "I hear you, whoever you are. Show yourself."

Her voice wasn't the same strong girl I'd known but weak and tainted with fear. Station afraid? Something was wrong. I stood and walked around the fire, keeping my distance so as not to frighten her. "It's me, Station. Robin." She raised her head looking past the fire into my eyes. Tears welled in my eyes and to my utter surprise tears flowed down her cheeks as well.

"Thank God you finally made it. I was getting worried." She sat up and the blanket fell away from her chest, exposing her naked breasts. I couldn't help but look at her freckled chest and the pale softness of her breasts. Looking at me with a weak smile she said, "Well? Come here." I rushed to her and knelt by her, wrapping my arms around her. I hugged and she hugged back but not with the same strength I was used to from this girl.

Pulling away I asked, "What happened?"

Station smiled, "Oh, sending that monster over to bring you here was a bit more than I'd bargained for.

There were some who didn't want that to happen. I couldn't cross anymore or I would have come myself. There's only one who walks two worlds," she managed a weak smile, "The rest of us are pushing our luck each time we try to. Mine ran out."

My tears stealing across my cheeks. "I'm sorry. This is my fault. I just couldn't figure out the puzzle fast enough."

Station laid back down leaving her breasts uncovered. Looking up at me she said, "Not your fault. Robin, not all that's bad in creation comes from you. You've had such a hard role to play in a story bigger than you know. Now, come sleep with me. That will give me the healing strength I need. Love. There is little love in this land and your love is the wellspring."

I stripped off my clothes and for a moment stood still closing my eyes and letting the cool night breeze envelop me like water from an ocean that held creatures that lived ages ago. I had never seen this ocean, but it existed in this world, not mine. Wondering if the images of me leaving the beach and diving into the forest were memories, not dreams. Standing a moment longer I felt danger in the wind. It was October once again and even here in The Region the smooth comfort of the breeze was gone, replaced by icy needles piercing every part of my body.

Opening my eyes, I looked at my lover and said, "I do love you, Station."

I got under the blankets with her and I brushed my lips against hers opening my mouth and with gentleness touched the tip of my tongue to hers telling her all I knew. Pulling away I held her as she slid back into a sleep as deep as death. I caressed her arm with the tattoos running from shoulder to wrist. I must have studied them before, but now I felt as if I'd never examined them in detail. I pulled back a bit so the firelight could dispel the shadows.

On her arm, I saw a winding trail. At the start was a glowing field. It's where we'd started this journey. Following up the trail I saw my old house in Mason. Confused, I turned her arm to see the trail running to a hospital and then back to the Palace of Starlight. The palace was covered with monsters and a blue light glowed from its windows. Then there was Mel's and next came the Mason boarding house. A Nightcrawler was there. I couldn't understand what this meant. A man was walking into a boarding house. He wore a duster and cowboy hat. Down the trail was Lawton and my escape and Station floating in the air killing a beast. Then Lake Erie with the trail running alongside. The worm rearing up and striking me, then I was gone. It seemed like it was all in motion. Then the trail disappeared into a dark forest that opened up on a meadow with this very building where I lay. Then the trail wandered around her arm up through steep mountains to a castle of some kind. As I gazed at it, fear gripped me and my breathing quickened. There was a young girl at a window waving to me. I knew her but just couldn't quite remember her name. Something about the tower and the girl scared me. I looked as closely as I could at the little girl and noticed she was waving her arms and screaming, like she was trying to get someone's attention. The arms were actually moving. I put my ear next to the image but couldn't hear her. At the base of the tower a woman stood looking as if she was going to enter this tower. Station? No, it couldn't be. This creature had wings. Around her head flew ravens. From there the trail went into the woods located on her shoulder. The trail was obscured by trees. My future? I sighed wondering why the hell it was all about me. I didn't want that. I just wanted to love Station and feel her love for me. That feeling was so unlike the rest of my life.

More mysteries. Me, Robin Randle, chosen from all the people in the world to fight for our very existence. What made me such a good choice? The life I'd had up to now seemed hardly worth it. What should be saved? I was cold inside. I pulled close to Station again and could feel the warmth radiating from her breasts. I could feel her heart beating and love overwhelmed me. As tears slid from my eyes I knew Station was worth saving but she frightened me as well. The story on her arm was like a movie. She was keeping something from me. For my own good, I knew. Enough. Station was my lover but more than that, my friend. That would never change.

I closed my eyes and reveled in the smell of her. Wonderful. The smell of wood smoke, reminding me of fires made in the deep woods and pine mixed with spray from the ocean. As I drifted toward the oblivion of sleep I saw the ocean fighting the boundary of the shore. Then I was falling again as my body moved toward sleep. Final fleeting thoughts pressed my mind. Where was I? This was all so impossible. The only thing I was sure of was my love for Station. That rang true. She felt like wonder in my arms. I cuddled close to her body creating a comforting warmth. So little of my life was spent loving someone and to feel the love from her was amazing. It lit my soul. For the first time I thought, where's my star, then I slid off the edge into my dreams, or was it my reality?

PART 5

THE END OF REASON

And you were dead in your trespasses and sins, in which you formerly walked according to the course of this world, according to the prince of the power of the air, of the spirit that is now working in the sons of disobedience. Among them we too all formerly lived in the lusts of our flesh, indulging the desires of the flesh and of the mind, and were by nature children of wrath, even as the rest.

Ephesians 2:1-2:3

A PASSAGE COMES

Maybe years had passed. Maybe just a single night. How could I tell? My mind started to clear from the sleep I'd been sharing with Station. She still rested in my arms breathing gently, reminding me there was life here and a most wonderful life too. I gently pulled away so I could sit up. What greeted me was the last thing I expected in The Region. Blue sky spotted with striking white clouds. The air was so clear that the vividness of the blue sky was overwhelming. I scanned the horizon. Things were just as I found them last night or whenever it was that I fell asleep. This small shelter was in the center of a meadow surrounded by old growth redwoods that towered above us. Up the meadow stood the ruins of an ancient house that looked as if it had been an elegant manor house at one time. I had no idea where I was. My journey to this place had been too confusing for me to be able to separate what was real and what was not I felt like it all was real. The ruins of the ancient house were made of stone. The smell of the ocean filled the air. I felt a sudden pull of déjà vu. I closed my eyes and thought of home for a moment. Home was not the horror where'd I'd grown up. I couldn't understand. Then I opened them and I looked down at Station and couldn't help but wonder about the story written on her arm. We are the sum of the stories we live. We might just live to tell these stories someday, but if we don't, well I guess then we never existed. There are choices we make that change these stories. Even the ones in the past. We are in much more control than

I'd ever known.

Up to this point in my life I'd lived in hopeless fear of the future. Nothing in my past would support the idea of a bright and wonderful life. I felt like the trash God forgot to take to the curb. Today a balance deep inside of me was pushing in new directions. Directions unknown to me because I was always too afraid. Maybe I didn't belong to the Earth. How could I ever find out?

The morning chill brought goose bumps all over my body. Looking for my clothes I found them where I'd dumped them the night before. They had all changed. My tight raggedy jeans and oversized white sweatshirt were gone along with my thong and shoes. In their place were a conservative pair of panties and a rather tight-fitting dress. No bra. Long socks and dark leather English style riding boots. It looked like a walking stick or staff was lying next to my backpack. My backpack had changed as well. Leather tooled with drawings. It looked very old. Stained and worn from years of travel. Once I was dressed I felt very medieval and somewhat comfortable. This hadn't happened the last time I ventured into The Region. One more mystery to add to my growing list. Station began to rustle around struggling to open her eyes. The sound of her voice filled me with gladness. When I turned she was sitting up hugging the blanket around her body. She said, "Nice look."

I glanced at the dress, "Well there wasn't a lot to choose from. Seems my old clothes have gone missing."

"That happens here." Station stood then dropped the blanket exposing her perfect body to the whole world. She seemed healed again. Cuts and bruises gone. For the very first time I was struck by the feeling that she wasn't human. That thought just poked out from some far corner of my mind and I wondered if she wasn't human, then what was she? What was I for that matter? The one who walks two worlds. Station dressed in silence.

"Station," I said, "I just traveled some kind of pipe or creature from Earth to The Region. Many of my faded and smoky memories have been cleared up and put in order, I've ended up with you here, whereever here is." I couldn't stop. The emotions were washing over me like a waterfall. "That tattoo on your arm, it's a story, isn't it? My story." Tears were streaming down my face. Station walked over to me and held me in her arms. I sobbed, "What am I?"

She stroked my hair, "You are the most wonderful creature in the two worlds." She became quiet. A large disturbance started in the trees down the slope of the meadow. Station pulled away and drew her sword. Trees were cracking and the air was filled with a sudden scream of a beast ready to jump its prey. Station said, "Grab that staff. It's yours. I know you don't remember but maybe you'll remember how to use it if you just hold it." I couldn't imagine what she meant but I followed her command. Picking up the staff from the ground gave me a rush of electrical power. Everything got brighter and sharper. It was as if the staff had just plugged into my mind. It was reaching into me searching for a key to unlock its power. No, my power.

Then the trees on the edge of the meadow broke open and we could see the monster that was upon us. The creature was an impossibility. Something that hadn't seen the light of day since the time of creation. It came out of the forest on its hands and feet, then broke from the trees and stood its full height. Taller than the giant redwood trees, the abomination screamed again such a scream that the very ground trembled. The head of this beast was unbelievable. How could something like this even exist? It was shaped in an elliptical fashion with a single eye in the center of its forehead. Two holes below the eye appeared to be the nose but the mouth was most of the face. The mouth was ringed with three rows of jagged teeth and a stalk was coming out of its mouth and that mouth had another mouth that opened showing small teeth, all extremely pointed and razor sharp.

The stalk seemed to be more the olfactory organ than the rudimentary nose. It searched the air like it was smelling for something it would know when it found it. It took two awkward steps forward. The body was very human-like. Smooth and hairless. The arms had hands more like appendages and each finger was like a snake in its movements. They seemed to curl and uncurl, then whip from side to side feeling for something. I'm sure it was searching for me. I thought why, just why can't I have a moment of peace? This was my life now. Hurtling from one monster to another. Station said, "I think maybe this is too much for us to handle alone. Let's go back to the tree line and into the forest. It looks like it might have trouble in tight places."

Why was it here? This just seemed too incredible. Why would such a horror be created just to kill me?

Amazingly the horror spoke. A soft subtle tone filled my ears. I couldn't believe such a hideous creature would sound so seductive. It said, "Robin, listen. Your sin must bind you to me. That is my purpose. I'm here to take you away to your proper home, not kill you."

"What sin? I've been tortured all my life. All I could do is run and hide or get beaten or worse. There wasn't time for sin." Station stopped and looked at me.

"Who are you talking to?"

"That monster right in front of us. Can't you hear it?"

"Not if it's speaking to you. Don't listen Robin. It lies. Aerial demons prey on some weakness of yours to convince you that you aren't worthy of Heaven."

"But we aren't going to Heaven. Are we?"

"Not now. There's still work to do. You need to remember why we did all this."

We were backing toward the tree line keeping the monster in front of us. Station said, "Robin, use your staff to shake the thing up. I know you don't remember how but just clear your mind and let the staff teach you." That was crazier than the words coming from that thing in front of me. What on earth could a walking stick do against this perfection of horror? I held it out in front of me and nothing happened. What I expected.

The demon whispered, "Don't bother with the staff. It's useless to you being in such a state of sin. You love to escape, Robin. Love to drink and use drugs. I will give you an eternity of escape. Just come with me."

Station stepped slightly in front of me blocking my view of the creature and guided me back toward the trees. Again, that scream. It sounded like two beasts locked together in combat. The ground shook and for the first time the abomination looked right at me. I was found. Slowly it struggled to move its convoluted body toward me. It dropped to all fours and the fingers extended out from the hands searching for me.

It said, "Robin you can't escape your destiny. You must pay the price for your sin. Come now and Station will be safe. I only want you." The soft sound of the words were incredible to hear. I couldn't reconcile the horror of the thing against its voice. I was drawn to it. Yes, I did run. I did escape. All my life. I even left Lucy and Jim and that was before all this started. Booze and drugs starting at 15. That was sinful.

I started to walk back toward the creature. I had to give myself up. I couldn't hide behind the violence of my father.

Station called out, "Robin. No! You can't believe that demon. It will drag you to the Binding Place." I heard her words but they seemed distant and of little consequence.

I stopped again and looked at Station, "Station, this demon is right. I'm a sinful person. I have lived such a withdrawn life, never giving to anyone just making sure I was ok. I've done nothing but run even when my friends were being killed." I turned back to the demon and started toward it. Station grabbed my arm. Her strength surprised me. The grip she had on me was too tight to escape.

I said, "Station, let go of me."

She replied, "Never. You have given everything for your humanity. The price you've paid far exceeds any wrong you might have done." She pulled me behind her and turned toward the horror. Then a most amazing thing happened. It couldn't be real. Station's bodice dipped toward her waist leaving most of her amazing back naked. Suddenly up by her shoulders folds of skin opened and large wings sprouted from them.

The wings were as wide as she was tall and arched upward. They were beautiful. I felt they were so natural on her even though that confirmed she wasn't human. She looked back at me, I think to judge my reaction, and then turned toward the horror that had stopped advancing.

"I am the angel Station Cross. I'm the one who carries Robin Randle through The Region. I tell you demon, she has not run away from life and responsibility. Quite the opposite. She's embraced death to be reborn to the Earth and to The Region. She has given everything that is hers, for the salvation of all humans. What more could you want?"

The demon stopped advancing. Looking at Station I could hear it say, "So is the truth, you wretch of an angel. You deprive me of her soul but I can still rend her body to dust."

Station started backing up again and we were getting close to the tree line, "Robin, you don't have your star. I'm not sure how this part works. You need to zap that thing with your staff. It just may be too much for me alone."

"Zap it? The demon says I'm too sinful to use this staff. I should just drop it. I don't believe in magic sticks anyway." If there was magic here, I couldn't wield it. It was God's power, not mine.

She turned toward me glaring, "It's not magic!

There is no magic. Just the power God has granted us each to our own position. Now listen, clear your mind and just think protection. Hold the staff in both of your hands, out in front of you."

"You've got to be kidding me. Now I'm a wizard? This is too much."

Station said, "What's too much is that monster that's about to attack you. I have no idea what it plans to do with you and I don't want to find out. You aren't a wizard, Robin. That I promise you. Don't get confused. This is part of who you are."

Another scream came from the monster. The ground shook to the point that we almost fell. I could smell a putrid stench coming from the horror's mouth. I walked around Station and looked at the beast. For God's sake, it was going to destroy me. I turned back toward Station, "If I'm about to die please tell me, what's the deal with your tattoo. Is it alive?"

Station looked confused, "Robin, we don't have time for this."

I looked deep into Station's beautiful silver eyes, "And when will we? I love you. I need some answers so I can put all these fractured pieces of my life together." I could feel the heat from the creature. It was close. I didn't care, "At least tell me who created that tattoo."

Station looked up at the horror then back at me, "God damn it Robin," Station stopped herself and looking heartbroken continued, "I'm very sorry for saying that. Forgive me. I love you so much. This has been so hard. Harder than I'd ever imagined. You did it Robin. You created the tattoo. Now you have the staff, please; try and stop that demon."

That was the last answer I expected. I was overcome with light. I turned back toward the monster and raising my staff, words formed from a dark and incomplete memory.

"When darkness unfolds, its arms rise up a source of light and clean Thy land." A blast of light expelled from the staff directed toward the meadow. Engulfing the beast. When my vision cleared, I saw the monster was gone. I stumbled and Station caught me and helped me sit down. I managed a meek, "What just happened?"

Station dug in her pack and pulled out water and I drank. Inside of me was power. Power I never knew I had. Something wasn't right. I looked up into Station's eyes as my head lay in her lap. There was pain in her eyes. I said, "There's more here than I know. Something you can't tell me. Station, it's ok. Don't be sad. What I did, I did to myself. I'm into something that runs deep. Just ride with me."

Station's tears slid down her cheeks. Amazing. Such a strong and magnificent woman with wings spread yet still she cries. Station whispered, "I love you, my little Robin. I have for longer than all of time. I will always ride with you."

I closed my eyes. I felt tears fall onto my face. Blackness surrounded me. I was swimming in it. Swimming away from now. I didn't want to go but there was no stopping the tendrils of night that engulfed me. It seemed as if a Nightcrawler had returned. It grasped me and I slipped away.

BETWEEN WONDER AND THE SKY

When I opened my eyes, I was lying in wet grass. I could hear the lapping of water on a nearby shore. Night. Again. Earth. I could tell by the very smell of the air. I was back. I could hear Sloan from a distance. He was shouting something. I stayed very still, letting the coolness of the wet grass soak into my clothes and my soul. I thought that just a moment ago I'd been with Station. She was getting me some water and then I just slipped back here. Earth. I didn't want to be back on Earth. I needed to control this. I closed my eyes and let the coolness of the wet grass soak in deeper while I slowed my breathing. A memory floated up from the darkness.

When I was a child I would run through a wet meadow laughing at the warm sun. A forest bound me on all sides. I wasn't far from home. This was before the beatings started. No, that's not right. It was a different place altogether. It wasn't my childhood yet it was. No wonder I was confused. I was remembering being a different child. It was a much more distant childhood. Distant in time as well as place. I relaxed and let myself move deeper into the memory. Somewhere I could hear Sloan yelling but it was very far off and finally faded all together as I seemed to live in the memory. I turned round and round in the meadow until I was so dizzy I fell on to my back. I lay still, looking up at the bright dabs of white that punctuated the blue of the sky. The

Region's sky. I blinked and was looking up into the starlit night sky above Lake Erie. I said to the stars, "I'm Robin Randle. The one who walks two worlds. I am the Storm Bringer and death rides at my heels."

I started laughing. The world swam around my head making me feel as if I was falling even though I was on the ground. I still held my staff in my hand and my ancient pack was by my side. Using the staff, I stood, my dress wet with dew. The breeze off the water sent a chill through my body. I looked at my hands, then my arms as if I was seeing them for the first time then finally I looked at Sloan who stood before me.

"Shit. You went back."

"I can go whereever I wish, Sloan. Whatever your game is, it's over. You've failed."

Sloan shook his head, "Damn that Station Cross. She did this. She's going to pay for this."

"And are you going to be the one who settles that debt?" Sloan looked wearily at my staff. He knew things had changed. I had changed.

"Despite this turn of events you are stuck here on Earth now, in the middle of nowhere. I'll give you a ride to North Tonawanda. You need your last tattoo anyway." This seemed reasonable. Sloan didn't strike me as the violent kind but I knew he could be taking me to a trap. I felt sure that's what he was planning. Some end to this whatever it was; war maybe, just didn't seem clear. Wherever that left me, or Station, I had no idea. I know from what Station had said, there was more at stake here than my life.

Back in Sloan's car we headed down the I-90. I guessed stealth wasn't an issue anymore. Traffic picked up and we changed to I-290 and exited at

Sheridan Drive. Once again, I found myself in a seedy part of town. I'd grown so accustomed to these types of surroundings. All poverty looked pretty much the same. I could be anywhere but tonight I was in North Tonawanda. I watched the street signs. Sloan turned up Parker Boulevard and at the corner of Parker and Dufferin Street was the familiar Rex Tattoo sign right next to the Happy Land Discount Store. Once again, we pulled into a parking space. Getting out of the car I grabbed my pack and staff. I didn't trust Sloan any more. Sloan had been silent the entire ride, so determining what side he was on was impossible. I just felt it wasn't my side.

A bell rang as we pushed through the door. There was Rex sitting in his chair sipping on a pint of whisky. Rex was exasperated. He didn't even need to speak to send that message. Rex said, "God damn it, Sloan! You are eight hours late. Shit, you think I have that much time here? Things are falling apart and you know it."

Sloan glanced back at me, "I'm sorry Rex. Miss Robin here took a detour I wasn't expecting." Rex looked wearily at my staff and noted the dress I was wearing.

"Shit, Sloan. She's got her staff back? This is bad and I don't want this grief."

"Look Rex, it's not your problem. Just do the job and I'm out of here. You can disappear. No one will look for you. Why should they?"

Rex snorted. "Shit. I don't like this. Not at all. Ok girlie, lift your sleeve." I walked over to the chair and lifted my sleeve. I guess asking me to take my dress off was over Rex's limit. He took a pencil and sketched an image. I could see it in the mirror in front of the chair. The image of the raven inside my sword tattoo. That surprised me. How did he know?

Sloan looked at Rex and shouted, "You dumb shit. You're supposed to add the binding circle."

Rex seemed calmer, "I'm not getting any deeper Sloan. The bitch will kill me as sure as I'm standing here." Sloan was full of rage. He slammed out the door.

I said, "Guess he doesn't like your choice."

"Look Robin, I don't want Station Cross in my life. She'll just kill me. If I add a binding circle you wouldn't live two days. I wouldn't live three. The game has changed." He took his tattoo gun and used black ink to create an outline of the raven, then filled it in.

He cleaned off the last bit of blood and stood. "Look Robin, remember I did this for you. I'm not the bad guy here." With that he was out the back door. Brave man.

I stood and turned my arm toward a mirror and looked at the raven. Seeing it finished for the first time my head felt light. The next thing I remembered was waking up in the front seat of Sloan's car. The passing street sign said Sodus Road. Ahead there was only black. We were heading back to the lake. My hands were bound behind my back and my feet were bound together. "Where are you taking me?"

Sloan sat silent, a look of resolution on his face. I said, "Let me go, Sloan."

"I'm sorry about how this turned out Robin. I have to do this."

I didn't like his tone of voice, "Why am I tied up, Sloan?" No answer. "Stop this car right now!"

Sloan looked over at me as if determining how much trouble I was going to be. I hated being so small at times like this. Just like my dad. He'd tie me up, both hands and feet then beat Mom senseless with me as the audience. When he was done he'd untie me and grab my arms. Shaking me, he'd say if I told a soul I'd die. Then he'd hit me in the gut just to make the point. Usually I'd stumble to the bathroom to throw up. Sometimes I just couldn't make it. I'd have to clean it all up after he rubbed my face in my own vomit. That's the reason I stayed away from the house. No more. I didn't care how small I was, no man was going to hurt me again.

We turned onto Lake Street End and drove until the road ran out. The headlights illuminated a grassy area. Abandoned. Sloan killed the lights and pulled me across the seat and out of the car onto the dirt road. "Get up. I'm not dragging you to your grave." Sloan pulled me to my feet and cut the bindings on my feet and hands. "You just couldn't leave this alone." He shoved me out into the darkness. I couldn't see well at all. He shoved me again and I stumbled forward and stopped myself from falling.

Standing I turned toward Sloan and said, "Do you know who I am? I mean really know?" Sloan stopped in front of me.

"Yes, I do. You are the biggest mistake of my life. The question is, do you know who you really are? I think not. Now walk. I'll tell you when to stop." I turned back toward the darkness. I realized even with part of my memory restored I still couldn't make sense of this. The raven on my arm began to throb and my back was struck with pain in my shoulders. "Stop."

Sloan pushed me to the ground. From under his duster he produced a large and fantastical dagger. He reached inside his coat again, producing a leather pouch filled with a white powder. Maybe salt. I thought about my father. He had so much anger. He was repulsed by his wife and daughter. In the end killing us was all he could do. Then it dawned on me. These demons or gods from The Region had invaded my life before he put me in the coma. That had to be true because I met the Dust Witch before I took my trip and it was just before his murdering mom that the dark creature grabbed me in the woods.

Sloan was walking in a circle around me sprinkling the salt on the ground and whispered words I couldn't hear. I closed my eyes and thought back. I thought that it was never going to be right again. Suddenly something snapped into place. I remembered the events at Redding's Mill happened before I was knocked into a coma. Mason, yes, that's why everyone avoided me. My father hated me for that. No one could understand what'd happened that night. I'd run from the pool into the forest but not toward home. I'd gone to a small cave Lucy and I had found a year before. We kept pot in there when we had some. I crawled into the cave, just a hole in the ground, filthy and naked. I struggled to the very back. There I shivered as the night cooled. I waited for the monster. Waited to die. But instead I drifted into sleep. Why would a creature from The Region try and stop me from my journey there?

Pain shot through my shoulders again. I cried out and Sloan stopped his circle making and looked at me with fear. Tears started flowing from my eyes. Old.

That's what I was. As old as time itself. I recognized the ancients that had attacked me. I was part of their world, not this one. Sloan came over to me with his dagger raised. On the handle was a strange marking.

What could that mean? I didn't have long to think about it. Sloan said, "That will have to do. Now, my angel, you must die to this place. I have to undo my mistake to be released." Sloan raised the dagger and spoke, "In nomine Dei Patris, Dei Filij, Dei Spiritus Sancti" then drove it deep into my chest.

THE CIRCLE OF
THE WINDS

I screamed, but only in my mind. A warm pain spread from my heart, and then faded. I opened my eyes and sat upright. I was in a bed, not in the dark field where Sloan had hoped to kill me. I wasn't ready for where the bed was. There had been so many impossibilities over the last year. The people I've met and places I've been. Trying to piece together my fractured memories only to find out I wrote my life in pictures on the arm of the woman I loved. Then to see her wings. I had remembered early on she was working on flying. But real wings? Angel's wings I'm sure. Station could be nothing less than an angel. I just knew now I had known her all my life. It seemed too long a life. That felt odd. How could my life feel any longer than it was? This thought worried me. My fear of being insane and locked away in a mental institution grew.

My dad had put me in that place. Tried to convince everyone I was going crazy. He guessed I was using and got me tested. Of course, I was positive for marijuana. That stuff stays in your body forever. He lied to the doctors about how I'd scream and throw fits breaking things and threatening him and Mom. He had me believing it too. I was locked up for six months. Drugged and basically dead to the world. Then Lucy's mom showed up. It was hard to remember because I was so drugged. All I know is I left the hospital and went home with her for about six weeks. That was a wonderful six weeks.

I'd been scared that I was crazy. That I'd seen things and heard things that weren't there. My imagination was now my enemy. I was worried again.

I looked around my crappy apartment. Mason, Texas. I was back to where all this had started. I saw my staff and pack. The rest of the room was dim, full of haze as if it was more a shadow of a memory not the real place. One thing I knew for sure: I was alone. Nobody would come to help me out of this mess. Silence embalmed the moments holding me to wherever here was. If I was back in Mason it must be for a reason. Sloan was going to kill me with that strange dagger but it didn't work. Or at least I don't think it did. Somehow, I'd moved myself to the farthest place I knew of that was away from him. I bent down to pick up my pack from the floor and a leather-tooled sheath was under it. I snatched it up. Standing, I pulled the knife from its sheath and to my surprise it was the very knife Sloan had used when he tried to kill me. No, it wasn't a battle-ready knife, it was more a dagger, I thought, as my memory just stumbled across it. It had belonged to me. Sloan had stolen it sometime in my past but I just couldn't remember it. I looked at the markings on the handle trying to place what they meant. The marks looked like two overlapping sixes, one slightly below and offset to the other.

This had been one crazy trip. I mean I'd never taken LSD or anything like it but this had to be what it was like. Right? How else could I frame things. Well, this wasn't home now so it was time to leave. Shit, all hanging around would do was probably get me killed. Again. I mean, that's if I wasn't already dead from Sloan's attack. I looked around. This version of my apartment felt completely wrong. I decided I wasn't waiting for help. It was time. My time to be my own help. Ok. With the dagger stuffed in my belt, I donned the dark cloak that I'd taken from my pack, then grabbed my staff. It was time to open the fucking door to my apartment. My hands were trembling as I turned the knob in silence.

I eased into the hallway. It too was silent. Too damn silent. The usual racket of music, screaming and yelling serenaded by loud televisions just wasn't there. Something wasn't right. I eased down the stairs to the first-floor hall and on toward the front door. I grabbed the front door knob and started to turn it, then hesitated. I wondered if I was ready for the creation on the other side. I sighed and thought no and slowly opened the door anyway.

I stepped into the mist surrounding the building. Then I felt the mass of the building disappear behind me. Here I was once again. The crossroads. The flat lands where Nightcrawlers lived. Something else lived here too. In the crossroad, Erictho had warned me I'd face it someday. Now was that day. I walked toward the center of the crossroads in the gloom of the night. The haze of memory lifting. I realized I had a lot of memories that hadn't surfaced yet but they were about to. I hoped I was ready. Better than last time.

Dirt and dust twisted up from the center of the crossroad. I waited to see what new horror was lurking for me. The dust and dirt spun faster like a whirlwind growing from the inside out. It reached higher and suddenly the dust just settled and before me was the head of the already executed Queen of Starlight. She smiled, "Thought you'd never see me again, my daughter?"

I stammered, "You're dead. I saw it myself. Station cut your wretched head off your body."

"It would seem she didn't do a very good job. But maybe I'm harder to kill. Or maybe Station just lacks follow through. Finish the job, I say. None of that matters because here I am. You too."

"And what could I possibly have to do with you? You were just in my way."

The Queen smiled, "You're so sure when half your memories aren't even in your head! Ha! There's more here, my little Robin. You tricked me, you bitch, and you don't even remember. I was Queen. Anointed by The Prince of the Power of the Air. It took me a century but I convinced all the dead humans waiting in The Region to give me their wretched toll boxes. Those globes that you stupidly called starlight. It was then that my poor Robin came to me. After you'd grown up you thought you needed a star. You wanted it so badly. So, there I was. I faced my life's most wretched mistake. You just came knocking at my door." Sloan had made a similar statement. I was the biggest mistake of his life. A very creepy feeling came over me. It couldn't be.

The Queen saw the idea dawn in my eyes, "Oh now you understand. Only now you understand who I gave birth to and should have killed the moment you were born. But no. Sloan wouldn't have it. Even though it would expose the forbidden love we shared. Sloan tried to hide you but nothing can be hidden from The Prince of the Power of the Air. I was chained to the castle and Sloan was forbidden to return and banished to Earth. "

The Queen said, "We loved each other and you, you wretched creature, destroyed that. You took from me the only thing I cared about."

"Oh, I see, because you weren't supposed to have a lover you took one anyway and I was the product. An inconvenience. You know I'm so fucking sick and tired of being everyone's excuse for violence and hate. I didn't ask you to get pregnant. I'm shocked to finally find out who my real mother is or was. Of all the horrific choices, you're the worst. And Sloan. One day I'll settle that score."

As the Queen started to settle back into the earth she said, "All is lost you know. You're just a trick of the light. Once an angel I think and now reduced to a powerless shadow. Those 'stars' you seek are still locked away in the castle. Even though you found it once, I promise you, you'll never find it now. Ha. Your plan almost worked. But now all those souls are lost. They will forever wander in the Region and all because of your selfishness." Finally, the earth closed around her leaving the crossroad looking undisturbed. This was crazy. I was crazy. I realized I couldn't have all my memories no matter what part of me they were. Somehow, I had to find them. I needed those memories to go on. No matter what the cost. I was part of a plan and it sounds like it might still work if I could just remember what that plan was. How was it I was born in The Region to Sloan and the Queen? I couldn't remember that life if it really happened. I know I was born on Earth. Really, what the hell am I?

I stepped into the center of the crossroad. Erictho said great power was there. I thought, let's find out. Standing still I raised my staff and words formed in my mind. Words not of my creation but of my ownership. I spoke, "Alone to be no more. I trust that it is the will of God that I am to be as I am. If I'm to be one true angel, then I freely give my own self to God's unending service. I know I was born of Earth, not created yet I feel as if I was first created when all the angels were created. If this is so, then I alone of all the angels of the lower realms can walk both worlds. Both the heavens and the earths. Just like the angels upon high. If for this one purpose I was created then it matters not to me if the memories of my life be given and forgot, so be it if I complete my task. But please, let me see, dear Lord, all the life, that is truly me."

I fell to the ground and a crushing weight came down upon me. I thought this was my end. I truly did seem to be born without purpose. Death would relieve me of the pain. But that was not to be. A great circle of winds embraced me holding me down. Then I slipped away.

PART 6

THE LEGEND OF MY CREATION

I felt the monsters move under me. Demons when they die have nothing else to lose and that's the truth all plain and simple.

-Ask First the Holy
Macy Beas

THE SLOW MELTING SNOW

Back to the field where Sloan had dragged me, the dagger thrust into my chest. I reached up and pulled it out and screamed, "This is mine Sloan." I sat up, dagger ready. "Listen you SOB why are you trying so hard to kill me?" Sloan stood stunned, just looking at me. Then he found his voice.

"I'm not trying to kill you. Don't you get it? I'm trying to hide you." He started crying and knelt next to me. Before I knew it, he held me in his arms, hugging me, "Will you ever forgive me? I was trying to help."

I shoved him away and standing said, "I see, and the circle tattoo wasn't going to hurt me?"

"No! It should have helped hide you."

"That's not what Rex told me. He was too scared to even put it on me."

"Shit. None of this has worked the way I'd planned. I thought if I put your dagger, really, it's called an Athame, if I'd put it in your heart, it would become part of you and combined with a ring tattooed on your shoulder you'd become hidden. Hidden from the Queen I mean. At least that's what was written in an old book I stole called, The Clavis of Twelve Rings. I was scared I might kill you. I didn't do this right. Shit, I just waited too long."

I looked at the dagger in my hand. A memory floated up. Athame. Yes. Looks like a dagger but it is more. Not magic. Station told me there is no such thing as magic. I looked at Sloan, "I have no idea what you're talking about."

"Robin, listen, I know this sounds crazy and there seems to be no way to convince you, but you are my daughter." Sloan looked exhausted, "How could I risk killing you?"

Suddenly all of these events started to feel very real and the thought of this truth was overwhelming.

I said, "This is such a mess. Now I know my parents are two of the most hated people in The Region." I turned back to Sloan, "I met my mother, she was hoping I was already dead." Sloan groaned and just sat down in the wet grass.

"Robin, please listen to me. I know this looks bad but it's not what it seems." He stumbled to his feet and I took a step back. "What we did was wrong. Your mother and I were not allowed to be together. There were these rules we agreed to. At the start, at least. You really can't remember?" I shook my head no. "I guess it doesn't matter anymore. Robin, I'm just a shell of what I was. I was played from the start. I thought I had some control over my life. Please, take my hand and let me show you. I promise I will only show you the truth." Sloan reached out his hand to me.

I stood looking at his waiting hand. Like I said, I've done some stupid things, but for once this wasn't one of them. As our hands touched it became black as pitch. I woke in a crib crying out and a woman, my mother, came in to comfort me. It was like watching a movie but I could hear her and feel her. She was a kind and loving woman unlike the two previous ones I'd met. My crying stopped and I felt loved. Wanted. This wasn't just a vision Sloan was giving me. He'd opened some kind of door in my mind and beyond that door were memories that felt like mine yet my connections to them were like looking at a life through a shadow. I felt as if smoke from distant watch fires had lifted in the wind, blown down upon me and now drifted between these memories and what I thought of as my real life. I focused on these new memories trying to gain a clearer view.

Then it was day. I was about 10 and running around the meadow Station and I had spent the night in. The ancient gazebo where we had slept was new. Turning back toward the ruins I saw a beautiful manor house built of stone. My true home. My mother was calling me for dinner and I ran to the back door. Free and at peace. Loved and wanted. Sloan had hidden me in this home.

Then I was 21 and it all changed. I was standing outside the house in slow melting snow. The day was bright and sun warm and patches of grass were revealed. Green between snow-covered plots. Another awful day. I went for an early morning ride. I knew when I started back I was going to be in trouble. I could see mom's face scrunched up trying to be mean. Never worked.

As I approached the house something was wrong. Too much smoke. I hopped off the horse and ran to my house. Mom and Dad were on the floor. I felt out of control and out of my time and place. I ran to my mom and knelt down next to her. She had an arrow in her heart. No breathing, just an emptiness in her eyes. She wasn't in this body anymore. Both of my parents were dead but I knew they were still here somehow. I pulled the arrow from my mother's body. I had to track the killer. At least find out why. It was time to move on. Alone. I raced to my room and got my staff, cloak and dagger. Shoving some clothes into my pack, I ran back out of the house and moved away as it burned. Now I know how the house became a ruin.

I turned and looked at the beautiful gazebo. It was torched and the angel gone. Who would have done this and why? I was helpless, and the immense feeling of loss was overwhelming. I sat in the meadow and watched as the house and all that I knew burned to the ground. It finally looked as if only ashes remained so I stood ready to start my journey. It was then I saw a woman emerge from the trees. She was walking toward me from across the meadow.

I wondered if she had anything to do with this. I pulled my dagger from its sheath ready to meet her. As she got closer I could see she was beautiful. I couldn't imagine such a beautiful creature involved with the horrible act of killing two old people and burning their home. My home. She stopped right in front of me and in an earthy voice simply said, "I was raised from creation to be yours." She shyly looked me up and down then she looked at her own body like maybe she wasn't worthy of me. "I'm so sorry we meet on such a horrible day but I promise we'll find the ones who did this." I instantly liked her. I never experienced these kinds of feelings this woman elicited from me.

I stepped back unsure of what was happening. I realized my dagger was in my hand. Looking at this woman I could see a brutish sword hanging at her waist. Little good my dagger would do. I put it away. She said, "I know this is sudden. To have such a tragedy on a day like any other and with obvious reason. Then I just show up. I'm so sorry." Tears were slipping down her cheeks even though she was trying to maintain such a hard exterior.

I said, "Please, can you tell me your name?"

"Station Cross."

"And where have you come from, Station Cross?"

"I was created before the Earth. Before time, same as you but you became the product of an evil that seeped into The Region. That evil doesn't reside inside you but now that you are grown you must learn the ways of the angels and take your place in all this."

What she said didn't make a lot of sense to me but it didn't seem to matter. I knew we were going to leave my home, maybe never to return. I turned away from Station and looked at the old manor house. I'd grown up there. I'd been loved and kept safe there and now the fire had taken it. My parents gone. The house too. When they needed me, I wasn't there.

Station said as if reading my mind, "You couldn't have stopped whoever did this. You'd probably be in there burning up as well if you had been around. I know that doesn't help right now but remember. It will as time heals your wounds."

"Can we go? I would like to find the evil that did this."

Station said, "Of course. I've been waiting so very long to be with you Robin."

"How do you know my name?"

She said, "Because I've known you since before time. You don't remember yet but you will."

I looked deep into her eyes. Silver and full of warmth. I couldn't help myself. I said, "You're beautiful, Station Cross. If you think I'm destined to be yours then I'm sorry. I think you drew the short stick." That was the first time I remember hearing Station's wonderful laugh. A joy of naiveté and irony perfectly mixed. Her brown leather bodice left her shoulders bare and it plunged to her lower back. The sculpting of her muscles left me no doubt she could defend herself. Maybe me too. Brown tight leather pants protected her legs. I loved her jet-black hair, cut short and sensible, with a slight hint of pink highlighting the top of her head.

More than anything I felt this warmth emanating from her. It felt strange, like we'd been together before. Maybe since the start of time. Which seemed crazy in the context of all that was happening but somewhere, in an elusive, but deeper part of my mind were other memories stirring. Having no reason to stay in the meadow I took Station's hand and walked away from the manor house not knowing the truth of how deeply I loved Station Cross.

THE TABLET OF DESTINY

Sloan let go of my hand and I was standing next to Lake Erie once again. "You hid me with that family? You saved my life?" Then I remembered how Station looked. It was her arm. There'd been no tattoos on it. I guess I hadn't done them yet. I wasn't sure if this excursion to my past had confused me rather than enlighten me.

Sloan said, "You can't die, Robin. Don't you remember that angels can't die? Neither can I. Die that is. It has become my curse. I was sent to Earth with no way of reaching back to Heaven. I'm just a shade of who I was. Now all I wanted to do was save you from the Queen and die. Looks like none of that's happening. You can't remember who you are."

This was just all too much. I mean, really, how could I have lived in The Region and on Earth. And now this talk again of angels? I clamped my eyes shut to block the tears that wanted to go streaming from them. So lonely in this world. Kept in hell by pathetic parents who neither cared if I lived or if I died. How different from the family I'd had in The Region. It was impossible, but I guess that I'd been born twice and that means I grew up twice, but somehow, I'm still one person. I guess I was part of both worlds.

A plan had been created and I was part of it but all the pieces were not in my head or maybe they were but I couldn't put them together. That thought gave me pause. How could you put them together? So, it seemed that Station and I had hatched a scheme. It had to be about these toll boxes I had found in the Palace of Starlight. I must have allowed myself to be born into this world, the Earth, so I could die, but that seemed crazy. Maybe I needed to learn the location of these boxes. Whoever hid them made the transition to Heaven for all of mankind impossible. But, I didn't die. I was cast into the abyss of a coma. Somehow that had messed things up. It was time to end all this.

I opened my eyes, "Sloan, thank you for the efforts you've made, but hiding is no longer an option. You know that. You say I can't die, but you're wrong. I know there is a power that can kill me. I've met it before and I must go meet it again and seek my fate."

"Robin, no. I can't let that happen. I can't stand by and know that evil will consume you."

I didn't answer. Sloan looked defeated. He turned away and walked back to his car. He pulled my staff and pack from the back seat. Walking back to me he said, "You'll need these. Robin, if there's one thing I want you to remember, it's that I did all this because I love you. There's nothing left I can say or do to help you. Remember this, God is Love. So, love is where the real power can be found. That power you'll need to finish this. I never wanted to be part of this evil. I just loved your mother and that was my sin. I can see you're so much more than just my daughter. I just didn't know before." Sloan's voice became weak as he trailed off he whispered, "Love is where real power lives."

I took my pack and slung it over my shoulder, grabbed my staff and closed my eyes. Now it was time to return to The Region. I didn't need monsters or dreams. I never did. If I was truly the one who can walk in two worlds then all I had to do is just think - go.

The air around me changed. It smelled of the ancient dust of the endless road where the Nightcrawlers lived. Opening my eyes, I saw the crossroads. My next stop, I guessed. No. Deep in my head was a memory just forming. One about crossroads. Somehow, they belonged to me. That seemed silly. How could a crossroads belong to me? Still, I did feel like I was home. I was at a place that warmed my heart. Deepened my soul.

It was night and not a breeze to be felt. In the center of the crossroad lay a small clay tablet. I walked over and picked it up. The writing wasn't English but somehow, I could still read it. It was more in my head than before my eyes. It said, "Now is your time, Robin Randle. Reach to the bottom of your heart and feel who you are. Remember I love you always." At the bottom of the tablet was the symbol of the Raven. Station had left this for me. As I finished reading, the tablet turned to dust and the wind blew it away. What was the raven thing all about? I just didn't know or maybe remember Station as well as I should.

Looking up I was shocked to see the dark man I'd only caught in glimpses before. He was walking toward me. The worst sense of evil came over me. I was afraid of this creature. I watched as he stopped in front of me and I wished for any other monster to face but this one.

A voice as deep as the Well of Souls filled the air. I remembered that the Well of Souls lay under a rock called the Foundation Stone. I think maybe it's also called the Dome of the Rock. I thought that it was there you could hear the voices of the dead and sometimes a place called the River of Paradise.

This voice surrounded me and permeated my very being. I didn't hear the voice as much as I was able to understand what was being said.

"My angel Robin. This is the time of your ending."

Boy, this was far away from the River of Paradise.

I thought, why does everyone keep calling me an angel? I'd been all but that. In actual fact, I felt sinful and hopeless. There was nothing I could do against such evil. As I stared at this man, I just couldn't see any detail of his body or his face. What I did see were stars. Another night fighting to replace the night around me. I noticed now I was floating in those same stars, no ground below me. Space. It was the darkness of all time and space and as I was floating among the stars I started to lose my grip on all that was real about me.

It was then I knew my greatest fear was true. Since all this started I felt as if I was someone else. With each revelation came a deeper sense I couldn't be sane. These things that were happening could only happen in the mind of someone who had been badly damaged or born with an incurable mental illness. Now out of the darkness emerged the walls of my tiny cell. Dull and filthy gray concrete with words and symbols scratched all over them. The ammonia-like smell of piss was all I could smell. There were screams of anguish coming from all directions. Some sounded far away and others right in my own cell. Maybe me. I was in the hospital I feared the most. A place filled with more horror than any forest or empty place. It was as dark here as it was in The Region. If only there was a Region I could escape to. There seemed to be a dim glow from someplace but it barely turned the dark back. The insane asylum. My head pounded as the cell became clearer to my eyes. Maybe I was having a small lucid moment. I was almost naked; my clothes mostly torn from my body and lying in a corner like discarded rags. I wondered if I'd torn them off. The only other thing in my cell was a sleeping mat on the floor in front of me. I crawled to it on hands and knees. Sleep, I thought, would stop this evil dream for a little while. I was hopelessly delusional. I had no sense of anything real and all that had come before seemed like a fractured waking dream. Even my life growing up in Mason. I had no sense of the reality of it. No coma. No Region. No Earth. My mind was bleeding out and all I could see was total darkness ahead, coming toward me to finally consume my last bit of consciousness.

So tired. I was lying on my mat wishing the screams around me would stop. I couldn't remember coming here. I couldn't remember any of what had come before. I didn't even know my name. A life of illusion populated by primal fear and memories of all our distant pasts.

Sleep was pulling me under and that felt wrong. I couldn't sleep now or I'd never wake up. Scared, I tried to push the darkness back with my mind. It was still coming for me. Steady and relentless. The end of time wanting to envelop me in total darkness. Pain shot through my shoulders. The shock of that pain sparked like a match in the darkness. It seemed enough. I pushed again and the darkness stopped. I felt a hand touch my shoulder. Turning to look, no one was there. Still I felt it. Warmth and the hope of love poured from that touch and that love began pulling me away from this darkness. What was it that Sloan had said? "Love is where the real power is." If that was true, I gave into love and let it take me.

My name. I'd had another name before but I couldn't remember what the before was. I just knew I had a name that was born with the stars made at the time of God's creation of all things. What was my name? With unexpected force a mighty wind blew pushing me to the ground. Dust clouded my eyes. I squeezed them shut and rubbed them trying to stop the pain. Everything went white like the heart of a sun pouring into me. I struggled to open my eyes. I had to see or surely this intense light would burn me alive. I pressed fingers on my eyelids and forced them open. That didn't work. I thought of my ridiculous relaxation exercises. How long ago that was. I took a deep breath and relaxed. My panic abated. Again, I breathed. Then I remembered what this battle was all about. Not to get stars, or orbs or toll boxes. It was just to remember. That's what this hideous dark man didn't want me to do. Again, I tried to force my eyes open. Still unable to do it, I thought about the tablet left to me by the most wonderful creature ever created by God. Real or not, I imagined it was her hand resting on my shoulder letting her eternal love flow into me. Persephone. It was my greatest and only love. And her ancient name was Persephone. I remembered I had to go into Hell once to bring her back. So long ago, before the loss of the toll boxes. I'd sworn never to leave her and this evil that stands before me is the one who took her from me.

I remembered. Before the time of man this war had started. I focused my mind completely on my lost name and it rose from the darkness. As it should. Darkness was mine. Not the evil darkness of demons but the gentle darkness of a warm summer night. I could see my name burning like a torch. Hekate; the Night Wanderer. I remembered. I loved the night because I was the Night Mother. There was a time when they called me The Distant One. That was before the ascent of man. The monsters of old, the ancient gods called me Propylaea, The One Before the Gate. I have been alive since before the birth of the world.

Memories flooded back into my mind. When man was created, he was slow to learn of the one true God. The creator of all things. Men remembered me as a goddess even unto this very day. Now I'm thought of as the Lady of Shadows. I still love the night, my fear of it gone. I was an angel created by God to fight this war and release the toll boxes.

Before, there were no tolls to be paid but now the need was great and The Prince of the Power of the Air has stolen all since the beginning so he could hold man ransom as a payment to God for his release from final judgment. He hates me so because I wear the key to Hell around my neck and I will be the one to lock the door after he has entered.

I opened my eyes to see The Region all around me. I was standing, staff gone from my hand, replaced by a slim torch in my right hand burning with white light and bringing warmth to this wretched land. I had to turn away from this monster and stop his attack. He was killing me.

I felt Station next to me. My Persephone. This is how it used to be. This is what was and the rest was a game to learn. Learn where the toll boxes were. I thought of an old invocation the humans said to force me to appear before them. Little did they know the power they held. "Station, I am the darkness that covers this broken and tortured land. I bring the stillness, the quiet, the pause. I am also the healing, the regeneration, for the new dawn to reveal and I am one with you my Persephone. I'm in you, of you, around you, yes; I am you, and you are me. I am here with you for you are mine, as I am yours, eternally. Wrapped in God's love.

I could feel Station's eyes on me. Her love. I took a step back from the dark man that I knew now to be Satan. The Prince of the Power of the Air. Not my Prince. I could never serve such evil. I'd been made for good. The words formed in my mind. Those very words written by God to help at this moment. I spoke to this evil creature standing in the crossroads.

"God of heaven and earth, God of the angels and archangels, God of the patriarchs and prophets, God of the apostles and martyrs, God of the confessors and virgins, God who has power to bestow life after death and rest after toil; for there is no other God than you, nor can there be another true God beside you, the Creator of all things visible and invisible, whose kingdom is without end; I humbly entreat your glorious majesty to deliver me by your might from every influence of this accursed spirit, from its evil snare and deception, and to keep me from harm." The Prince pulled back from the crossroads and again I felt the pain in my shoulders but this time there was a sudden release then I had wings.

GATE OF THE SEVEN STARS

The Prince of the Power of the Air took on the form of an old man but his eyes weren't old. They pierced me to my soul. I stood motionless looking deeply into those eyes. They were trying to drain the very life from me. It was then I remembered why I wore the old key around my neck. I said, "Not today. Time for you to go."

I took my staff and knew I needed to pull it apart. As each half separated from the other they changed. They both became shorter and they weren't wood any more. They'd become bronze and fire leapt from the end of each making them into two torches. Holding both torches high I yelled at The Prince, "Satan, it is I. Hekate of old. Crossroads are my domain, not yours. I reclaim the power of this place for all time. I promise you it will be I who will one day lock the doors to Hell with the key round my neck and you, no matter what horrors you've created, will be inside locked away for all eternity."

The old man was cast backwards and to the ground. Then he slowly stood and started to change into the image of my Earthly father. He screamed back, "Robin, you are no more than a sick piece of shit. No one deserves to die more than you. You are just a waste of DNA."

His rage was an exact match to my fathers and it started pushing me back into that lonely place where no one cared if I lived or died. I couldn't stop it. The Earthly experience had been so intense that tears started flowing freely down my face. With a chance to vent my rage at my father for the first time, I screamed, "No! It is you that was a waste of DNA. You killed my Mother. Just shot her dead. She never did anything to you except stupidly stand by your side until you had a chance to kill her."

"Your mother was as defective as you were. She couldn't even protect you. Just took the beatings. Never reported nothing after that first time. She left you to run wild around Mason, drinking and drugging. You had a useless life and no one cared if you were alive or dead."

This was too much. Even though I now remembered the whole story, even why I went to Earth in the first place, I was still shattered by it all. Healing from this was going to take more than just remembering. I may not have a chance to heal if my father kept coming at me.

"You know something you bitch, I'm going to correct a mistake I made. I tried once to get rid of your useless life. Today you will die." He produced a short sword from behind his back and started running toward me, blade held high. I was transfixed. The blade looked so odd in my father's hand. The gun fit him better. Thinking this I didn't move. I couldn't move.

Station turned, dropping her sword she lunged, pushing me well away from the oncoming attack. My torches flew from my hands and I fell to the ground. My father reached the spot where I'd stood moments before. Station was there now. I screamed. Station hadn't a chance to move. My father rammed the blade into her back all the way to the hilt. Station dropped to her knees, eyes wide.

From the ground where I lay I could see the point exposed, dripping with the most precious blood I've ever known. The sword had struck her heart. I screamed, "You son of a bitch!" With that, my father lifted Station by the grip of the sword and slammed her face down into the ground, pinning her with the blade.

Station turned her head toward me. Her eyes filled with a mountain of sadness. Then her head dropped to the ground, her eyes closed. I got up and ran to her. My dad was laughing at his handiwork. I pulled the sword from Station's body and turned toward him. A power rose up in me. It was a new mix of Robin of The Region and Robin of Earth. I had to face this monster down. My rage seemed to fill the air around me.

I snapped my head around and said, "I guess you didn't hear me the first time. Crossroads are my domain, not yours. I claim the power of this place and I claim it until the end of time." I threw the sword into the center of the crossroads and pulled out my dagger, my Athame, and reached down to pick up one of my torches. Holding it high I marched toward him. He bent to pick up the short sword.

"It is written in fire. Written in The Shadow Tales: One day I, Hekate, alone of all the angels created by God, will lock the doors of Hell for the rest of time and that I promise. Be warned that when I drive the key home it will be the last time the lock will be turned. In there you will be with all hell, for all of eternity."

My dagger came up as he stood and I planted it

right in his heart. My Athame began to glow with the power of sunlight. I had to cover my eyes it was so bright. A glowing ball engulfed the dark man, The Prince of the Power of the Air. As suddenly as it had come, the light vanished, its work done. Satan was changed from my father back to the dark man and seemed to be growing in size. He spoke with his awful voice, "We will meet again Hekate. You will never pass The Gate of the Seven Stars. No one has and no one will." He kept growing, then began to fade away. My Athame fell to the ground. He was gone.

There was a great silence over The Region. I bent to pick it up my dagger. The handle had changed from white to black and it was warm in my hand. One more mystery to add to my pile. I sheathed it and ran back to Station. She just couldn't be dead. I embraced her, hoping I was still that wellspring she spoke of. I eased her back down and lay next to her on the open road and held her with all my strength. "Station. Please, I pray to God, whom I serve without hesitation, let her heal. To lose her would end my life as well. All we've learned will be lost."

She was too still. I pulled away to look at her and a flood of tears began falling from my eyes, landing on her face. I tried to wipe them away. "Station, wake up. I can't do this without you." I waited what seemed like hours then was struck by the fact the tattoo on her arm was gone. It seemed it had served its purpose. I thought of the tower with the girl trapped inside. That hadn't happened yet. I would have no more chances to study the strange map. I just couldn't move from this spot. I would never wander the night again. I had to stay by Station's side. She was half of me. I lay down next to her and just held her still warm body. I let all my love flow into her. I didn't care if all of me flowed into her. Life without Station Cross was no life at all.

It had been forever and still she didn't move. No breath escaped her lips yet her body remained warm with some life still in it.

I whispered in her ear, "I know the place now. I know where the Palace of Starlight lays. The Queen isn't dead. I'm sure we'll meet her again. I can't fight her alone. I can't be alone. Station, we must go to The Gate of the Seven Stars. Only the Shadow Tales tell of it. It is written that no man or spirit, not even the angels, have crossed through the gate, but you know me and gates. Please, Station. You know, I also have wings. I don't understand, but I'm ready to fly, if you'll only show me how."

Time passed. The night faded into day; Persephone never moved. I pulled away and stood, tears flowing down my cheeks.

"Oh, God, I am lost. Surely I have lost us the war." My stubborn resolve took over. "This Gate dwells on Earth. I feel it's true. Station, I'll find you on the other side. I'll save you." I turned away from her, closed my eyes and whispered, "Go…" Then all went black.

Wood Dickinson

Book Two

DURING THE TIME OF SHADOWS

PART 7

THE ORDER OF ETERNITY

A land…where the light is as darkness.

Job, 10.22

RECLAMATION

A darkness surrounded me and was so complete it felt as if I was trapped inside a felt box intended for a piece of jewelry now closed, stuffed in a drawer and forgotten about. I might as well have been blind for all the good my eyes were doing me these days. I remembered once going to a cave. This was when my personal monster was gone. Lucy and her mom took me and when we were deep inside the guide turned off the lights. That was being blind. The guide said our eyes would never adapt like they do in a dark room. Like my dark bedroom in the house I grew up in. I couldn't remember if there was ever a time when I turned my room light on. Being blind wasn't a bad way of thinking about my life, I think I've been blind from the start. Blind from my birth and life on Earth but even more so when it came to whatever life I was born into and lived in The Region. I've lived through hell and after all my efforts at trying to see, I was still as blind as ever. I noticed there wasn't any wind in the darkness, just a cold that filled the air and felt exactly like the emptiness of the coma I'd once lived in. Was I living inside this darkness, no longer able to walk or even separate the two worlds I inhabited? What I knew to be parts of my memories started to float up from the inky black space that was surrounding me and spun around my head bits and pieces searching for the proper places to insert themselves, filling in my dyslexic-feeling past. Many of these memories felt strange and out of place, like stories I was told when I was a child that now somehow had become true. The more I looked at them I knew they were part of my life. A part that had been kept locked away from me until right now because now was that moment when these memories were to be restored. Memories so strange they made me think about wings. My wings. I mean, I had wings! Then fear erupted with a violence like a long dead volcano returning to life. I hadn't completely remembered all of who or even what I was. I felt as if I was seeing a movie in my head and I was the star. The problem was I could only watch bits and pieces of the film after they'd fallen into place. Some were distant memories filling in gaps I still didn't know I had. If ever there was a time in my life that I should've been committed to an asylum it was now. There would be no way for me to plead a case for sanity with this chaos filling my head. Yup, I was a prime candidate for that dark and horrid psycho ward I feared so much.

I tried to focus on the film clips. Some memories were of the Earth and other memories from The Region. That part of my life in The Region had been locked tight in a filthy mist that's purpose was to scramble everything up. I watched as ages passed. I sensed a mist lifting from my mind and it started to thin out revealing the time I'd spent in the coma. Wow, all my memories came into sharp focus for the first time since all this started. As my memories became clear they revealed the reason why I was in this mess in the first place. How could I have forgotten? My heart beat with urgency. I needed to find The Palace of Starlight. Now. No wonder confusion had become my new normal, I'd lived the life of three different existences but all for the same person. That's the only way I could frame it so I could hold on to these memories without going crazy. Now I saw that these lives weren't separate lives, just separate versions of my one and only life. Everything - memories, images, smells, thoughts - was all folded up inside each other and slipping outside to inside then folding back again. It was like watching an over-used video tape that was holding on to the ghosts of old recordings still embedded on it. The tape in my head had been recorded over too many times. Each recording left its distant echo of my past, dim and fractured, confusing me as to what the true video was supposed to contain. It all seemed too corrupt to be of much use. I had to find the key to sorting them out. My only hope.

I started with a truth I could ground myself with. From the moment of my creation the one who was to be my mate was clear. I was made to love Station Cross as I loved the God of my creation. My purpose for being demanded a mate. I didn't know if I would be able to continue if I'd lost her.

My mind was returning but I was feeling a bit fragmented as I tried to put the pieces in an order that would help me with my current situation. Fragments dropped in place like the six words of pure magic. Words not claimed by any language of man. Words born from the flotsam and jetsam of creation. That very place where ancient gods once dwelled during the Times of Chaos. Those failed gods attempted to rule creation before the Times of Chaos ended. It was in that very place that spurned all notions of magic that the six words were forged.

When the chaos of creation had ended God set about creating mankind and it was then that magic, once pure fantasy of the mind, seeped from the waste left from creation coming like mist into the life of man. During those days fear should have been the only true ruler of man. God sent angels called Watchers. These were the angels who set about the task of watching His most amazing creature of all creation, humans, men and women born as all life on Earth was born. Mankind didn't hold any special powers. Not a single force bent to their will. Man alone was to be enough. He didn't need the gifts given to the angels like the power of the Seraphim or the strength given to a Guardian. Mankind was born without sin but soon sullied himself being snared in the traps set by The Prince of the Power of the Air.

I remembered now how in those ancient days the Watchers of Heaven spent time looking at the daughters of man. They found them to be desirable. These women were young beautiful creatures and presented a great temptation. So, some of the Watchers fell in love. They argued amongst themselves; why should they be forbidden from tasting the pleasures of a human woman? But God had denied this to them. These angels began to live with no thought to what God's will was. It was during the generation of Jared, which means descent, that the angel Shemhazai convinced two hundred of his fellow Watchers to descend from Heaven with him and land on the top of Mount Hermon. Shemhazai named this peak Ardis, then had all the angels swear an oath to keep a pact made between themselves. Ardis means 'cursed' and on that day at the summit of Mount Hermon these Watchers did become cursed by God. They took to themselves human women as wives and mated with them. These women gave birth to a new race fouling the purity of Man. This race was called, the Nephilim. These Nephilim were giants and much stronger than any man. The Nephilim beat man at every turn. They ate human flesh and drank their blood.

These wicked angels taught their wives the ways of roots and herbs, make-up and poisons and showed the men how to make weapons and war. It had been Satan who'd whispered into the Watcher's ears. He's learned these Angel's names and used that power to turn them toward his will. He wanted the angels to teach one last great lie. He told them to teach magic. So, with Satan's beautifully crafted lies in their hearts the Watchers taught the ways of sorcery and incantations of astrology and astronomy. They thought this was the greatest gift that they could give. They were six words of power, the Voces Magicae. Six words that escaped all explanation and few have ever learned the use of. These words, Askion, Kataskion, Lix, Tetrax, Damnameneus, and Aision, once spoken by the angels, were never forgotten. The Nephilim brought corruption and death wherever they went, so a flood was sent to cleanse the whole earth of these abominations. Almost all of Mankind was stained with the blood of the Nephilim. The only exception was Noah's family. But even after this cleansing Noah's son, Ham found tablets covered in inscriptions telling about the use of magic and Noah's other son, Cain, allowed these same sins to continue. So, the words remained in the memory of humanity, waiting to trap any soul who attempted to use them. Station had told me that there was no such thing as magic. She was right. Only the lie.

Before this all began I had created such a perfect

plan. Station worried but I'd promised her I would never lose her. I just had no idea how difficult things would become, how fractured my mind could end up. I felt she had done all she was supposed to do. I was the one who'd failed. I'd lost her.

With an unexpected jolt, my body came to an abrupt stop. No more sensations of spinning so I opened my eyes and found I was no longer trapped in the darkness. I was just lying on my back in what felt like a damp field looking up into a night sky. It looked a lot like Earth's. Now I was fully alone. Not even Sloan to yell at or blame. I wanted to stay far away from this home. The Earth I mean. I should have been happy, at last I thought I knew where my home was. That didn't quell my growing hatred of the fact that there would be no end to the memories of my life on Earth. The pain of a human life had become near unbearable. For the first time, I could step outside my humanity and wonder what kept these human beings going. Lives full of plastic games and make-believe stories. Little if any real connection to the larger reality. I mean, what kept them all from not just committing mass suicide! A subtle breeze moved what sounded like blades of witchgrass. It seemed more like the sound of the ocean. Wait, I could smell the ocean. Then a strange voice spoke, "Robin, it isn't as bad as you think. It's all we know."

I sat up with a start searching around me frantically. "Who's there?"

A calm voice replied, "Just me. You called me, remember? The pain of human life is near to unbearable and you wondered what keeps us going. Why we don't just commit mass suicide? It's all we know, so when we compare it to death it isn't as bad as all that."

I found the voice speaking to me from the gloom. It was a pretty young female dressed all in black. She had rugged looking black work boots on pushing their way up her legs. The boots covered most of her black leggings as they disappeared up under her black double-breasted jacket or maybe a dress. The dress jacket fit tightly. The back of her coat dress was longer than the front and her long black sleeves ran all the way to black lace gloves. Only her face was left uncovered. With short black hair cut more like a man's I had to wonder what it was in her skin that made mine look tanned. I'd seen this girl before. I remembered, it was in Mason on that night that hell decided to pay its first visit. I know now, another life. Not my life.

I turned away and saw I wasn't in a field of witchgrass at all. I'd been lying in damp beach grass near a path that led down to a public beach. It made me feel warm inside. There it was, the boundary I loved so much. A true and ruthless boundary between the world of land and the world of the sea. To me it was a marvelous yet absolutely deadly place. I turned back toward the girl. No, I remembered, Macy. My head felt like I'd had way too much to drink and that was causing this kind of fog-bound thinking. I strained through the blackness, and the leftover mental haze. I remembered I'd tried to use a phone, a pay phone. It needed money. I remembered to dial the operator and ask if I could make a collect call. To who? Oh, to Macy Beas. Who else did I know?

"Macy, right?"

Macy smiled, "Yup." She looked glad to be remembered, "I'm the one and only, girl."

I became overwhelmed with the need to know more. I approached her with loving care and said, "Thank you for coming and I hope you forgive me." She looked confused. With my newly found memories I learned I had certain powers or maybe better, abilities. One was the ability to enter a person's thoughts and seek out any information I needed. The hard part was it was done by touching my tongue to the other person's tongue. In an odd way, it made sense to me. We communicate with our mouths but I wondered if Macy would see it this way. She was at least an inch taller than me so I took her head in my hands and pressed my mouth against hers. I made a real effort to be gentle. Still, she became rigid at first. Then she brought her hands up as if to push me back but something stopped her. Her body relaxed and she let my arms wrap around her waist. Then she gave way to my tongue's gentle probing. She opened her mouth letting my tongue explore deeper in a quest to just touch her tongue to mine. When we did touch a sudden flash blinded me and there were explosions. She'd answered her cell and it was me calling from some dive called Mulligan's Bar and Grill. I guess I can't stay away from those dives. It was located on Route 28 going into Orleans, Massachusetts. I thanked God I was no place near Texas. Macy's arms intensified their grip on my body. It was as if she was afraid I'd let go. I hoped I wasn't hurting her. She was different. I think maybe, with a little help she could see through the Veil.

Before Orleans Macy had been near

Quonochontaug, in Rhode Island. It was some kind of building. No, it was a huge mansion. I faltered, then saw the name, Norwood House and it sat on the shores of Mercy Lake. She said she'd pick me up. When she arrived, I asked if she wouldn't mind a drive up to the public beach in Chatham? It was night and so I stumbled down the long-twisted staircase and found a place where I could lie down in the seagrass.

It was at that moment the haze around me lifted. I could see Macy was worried about me and my actions had frightened her. That made me sad. This kind of kiss was always meant as a gift. I gently pulled my mouth away and stroking her face I wondered at the softness of her skin. I gazed into her large blue eyes. I couldn't see any of Macy's secrets. Her eyes dwelled in a darkness that completely filled them. They were like wells pushing deep down into her soul. I could almost make out what was there, then it was gone. I could tell she was hiding something, but she was also searching just as deeply into my dark green eyes. I felt her arms go slack and she let out a sigh. Her hands slipped down coming to rest on my hips. She couldn't break contact. That was nice. I stole the moment and continued searching in her eyes and then I caught the edges of some unspoken pain. The kind of pain that hides deep inside but for an instant I'd brought her a moment of joy. I hadn't hurt her. I smiled.

Macy exclaimed, "You are the first girl I've ever kissed! I've never thought about, and I do mean never at all, thought about kissing a girl."

I turned away from her, "Macy, you of all people, know I'm not just a girl."

She took my shoulder and turned me back to face her. With true conviction she said, "I know. You must be what, an angel!" Silence. Then she started to laugh, "Okay then, to make you happy, I've never ever thought about kissing an angel, not even once in my entire life. And most of all I never thought of doing it full on French style!"

That had us both laughing hard. Too little laughing anymore. This felt good. I said, "I didn't mean to shock you. By touching my tongue to yours I can see inside your memories. It's kind of a shorthand way we talk. I just knew it would be the fastest way to learn what'd happened to me."

She faltered, "Robin, I saw your memories too. I didn't mean to. I'm so sorry. My God, the pain you've suffered. Robin. I mean, with Station Cross and all of it. I'm so sorry." She reached out and offered a true embrace. This time my mind was present in the moment. I could feel the warmth of her breasts, her smell of spring flowers, waking bird songs sung to attract a mate. Life. Seemed backwards when I knew how she spent her time.

"Macy, you know it's odd, you shouldn't have been able to see into my memories. I'll wonder about that later. Macy know this, you are a special woman worthy of love. It's funny yet fitting, that if you should fall in love you should fall for an angel. I mean, given the work you do. I mean you are a demon hunter." We both shared another good laugh.

Macy said, "Robin, I'll have you know I work hard avoiding complications in my personal life. My professional life's bad enough."

"I know the feeling. Macy, you are a peculiar

human." I thought about what I'd learned about her life. I decided to drop a hint, "That's if you are all human."

Her eyes widened, "Last time I checked I thought I was. Maybe. It all changed, my life changed when…"

"You turned eighteen," I interrupted. "I saw that. It was such a horrible event. Such a trauma in a human life. A break from what seems like our reality." I was saying too much.

"A break, yeah. That's putting it politely. I mean, it was just the freakin' end of all I'd ever known. I went crazy. What came after was lost in a cloud of psychiatric drugs making a black fog, or maybe better just a black hole. I can't remember any of it. There's one thing I can say with conviction, psychiatric hospitals are shit places to land. My life ended that day." She looked down at her hands, embarrassed, no, shamed. She continued, "Maybe we could talk about it someday; I mean, help me understand or at least reason out the idea of, why me? I mean; that's if you want to." Her mood lifted raising her spirits and deciding to abandon the topic, "You didn't call me for a walk down my memory lane, I'm sure. You said you needed help. Tell me, what's up?"

I just wasn't ready to move on from this topic. I'd seen an image that lived throughout her life. Much more than she imagined. There was a place I think. "Hold it Macy, what's a Norwood? Is it a house?"

Macy fell silent. Strong emotions passed through her soul like wood smoke through a deep forest at midnight. Something you can feel and even smell, but never understand. Such a distant door grafted onto her greatest tragedy. Not even one of her making.

Whatever grew in her, her darkness was born long before she was, but now it dwelled deep within her. No demon of the spirit world, this was a demon made by the evil deeds of man and perhaps magic. She sighed, resigned to the task ahead, "It's just the family home. It's where I grew up. I promise, something haunts the halls of Norwood House but it's a mystery to me. No one knows I still live there. It's become my freakin' secret retreat. A mansion old as dirt. Well, maybe a bit older. If you want, someday we could go there but I mean it, there's bad mojo working there for sure. It's something I can't get a grip on and stop it or even contain it." She fell silent.

I'd dug too deep. Macy said, "I know it's not for me to end. I don't have the skills. But somehow it must end. A horror lives in the silence of the halls and empty rooms just waiting for the day I pass from this earth so it can strike out. Another must come and fight it."

I looked up, "Do you know who that person is? Are you afraid to pass the baton to them? Listen, we all have a destiny that belongs only to us. Even the angels."

Macy paused, "I think I'm supposed to leave it to Emma Swift. I don't know. Christ, Emma Swift was my best friend. She was my anchor the whole time I was growing up. She filled my heart with the only fond memories to survive my childhood. I can't do this to her."

"I think you must Macy. You must give her this Norwood House."

Macy said, "I'm afraid to."

"Do you think Emma's strong enough? Macy, she

will have her Guardian to help her. I think if you trust her then do it. Just leave her any journals you might have."

An awkward silence followed. This wasn't going to be decided right now. I said, "Time to move, I feel vulnerable here. I'm sure another time of trouble is on its way."

We started toward her car. Macy took my hand in hers and said, "Robin, trouble is all I know. Every day I take on some freakin' demon or another. I mean that's what a demon hunter does. I get a call, meet a client then hunt for the demon so I can send it back to where ever it is they come from. I don't know. I know that each time I hunt it might just be my last day on Earth." She shrugged, "Still I do it. It's a death wish, I guess. So, don't you worry about trouble. I'm very good at making my own." She opened the passenger car door for me and was reluctant to drop my hand. I'd become a deeper part of her than I'd meant to. No going back now. As I climbed into her car I noticed it was a restored 1970 Dodge Dart. Black over red. Seemed an odd choice for Macy. Macy was far from a typical human. I felt sadness in my heart. I knew I'd never get that chance to explore this issue with her. She needed the help of her angel. Her Guardian. But I could see that that'd become a complicated relationship. I could see it but how could I tell her?

Macy climbed in and closed her door.

I looked at her as she sat behind the wheel. I said, "I'm not completely sure about things so I'm kind of guessing here. I need to find this gate. It's called The Gate of the Seven Stars to be exact. At first, I assumed it was where I was. A place called The Region. But now I think I was wrong. I think it must be here on Earth."

Macy said, "You think?" Then laughed as she started up the car. She pulled out onto Shore Drive and headed back into Chatham.

I gazed out my window as the flickering lights of this small city passed me by. Whatever kind of life I'm now living, it's for the purpose of freeing the toll boxes. I had not a single clue how I was to do that. Things like this seemed to be the only constant in my life. At least I know the mission but I still don't know how to complete it. I thought that I was near a place called The Crossing. It's the place people see when they think they've died and then come back to life. The truth is that if you pass through The Crossing there's no coming back. It isn't a line between here and there nor a bridge. It's like a land unto itself. No one is meant to live there. Wow. It's the Shadow Tales. I was on my own right now. I started to shake. No more help would be coming to get me out of this jam. Some Storm Bringer.

"There are stories called the Shadow Tales. They're about events that have and will take place in the shadows of the Vail. You know, that place that goes unseen in both the Earth and The Region."

I looked back out the window and noticed we were passing through downtown Chatham now—a small town in a crowded land. Macy headed on toward US 6 and off the Cape. That was right. West was where I was bound. As much as I didn't want to go. How completely amazing! Here I was once again riding in a car with a total stranger, putting my faith in her. Once again, I was living in the night, and heading into a place only God knew about. My fear of this unknown place was pointless. I had no doubt that I was the player in the Shadow Tales. Things were coming to an end. I didn't know exactly how I was to play this but I prayed that whatever was coming meant reunion with Station and not my end. Macy kept silent and drove but after about twenty minutes she became fidgety. She said, "Look Robin I don't mean to pry but you've got to explain yourself. How can you know how I can help you if you don't tell me everything that's going on? Please."

I felt she was right. I had to explain myself, "Across the Veil in The Region there are these stories. Stories from times so old that they feel like myth. Some of the stories haven't happened yet. They aren't scary tales like ghost stories here on Earth but tales that are meant to help you when the time is right. Now I'm sure the time is right." Then Macy asked a question I wasn't ready for.

Macy asked, "Do angels have mothers?"

Now the hell that had become my life started to wind around my mind and squeeze. I said, "Well, really, we don't. How do I explain this? Macy, I mean no offense by saying this, but I don't know how much of all this you're supposed to know. I've never had to think about that before. I've always been with others that I'm sure knew more than me. This sucks."

I sat silent staring out the windshield. What was I supposed to do? It seemed that every step of my journey had been planned with roadblocks set in place. I had to decide. It seemed that if I was trusted enough to be on this quest. I should be able to make up my own mind about what to tell, not tell and to whom. I was, The Storm Bringer, right? That should count for something. I mean who's going to believe Macy anyway? I'm sure no one thinks what she does is real, until they need her.

I continued, "I had a mother here on Earth. I was put inside her then she gave birth to me. I also had a mother in The Region but she adopted me. So, I was born there too but my father feared for my life. My birth mother was in a rage over my being, so he was sure she would kill me when I was just a baby. My birth father hid me away with my adopted parents. That's where I grew up." I was just thinking having my Earth memories combined with my creation memories would bring my real self, back. I knew now for the very first time, it wouldn't be enough. I knew I wasn't done yet. I had no idea where I needed to go so I could settle all this. I kept waiting for a sign. "Macy, what's important for you to understand is both of those births weren't my true creation. I will always remember that special moment. I mean, how could you forget creation? Oh Macy, it was amazing to see. It was too much to see. It was before all of time. There was no Earth, only heaven and there were the waters that flowed above and below. That's when I was made."

Macy jumped in, "You aren't getting out of here until you tell me what you saw. Robin, I have to know. I need to know there's more wonder and love than the evil I fight every day."

I felt Macy wasn't going to take a no for an answer. I couldn't blame her, "Okay, first God created time with a single word. Don't ask me, I don't know what the word was He said. My guess is that it's a forbidden word only for God, but believe me it was from this one word that the universe began to take form. Then the Earth was formed and the waters flowed into it and under it and above. Then God created all of the Gates. I don't know the names of all of them but I do know some that were formed like the Gates of Heaven, and the Gates of the Spirits. It was also when He made the Gate of Seven Stars along with the Gate to Hell. It was during the second moment that He created the angels. You'd say the second day I guess. It was so chaotic coming into being right when all of space and time were being born. Everything from the highest heaven to the lowest hell. None of us understood all of it, but Macy, I will never forget creation."

Macy was in a stunned silence. It's not like she hadn't heard this story before, but I guess talking to an eye witness brings it all home. She said, "This all did happen like the stories say." She fell silent again.

I continued, "There was a terror created of fire and made from lightning. Fires burned in all the rivers and as the rivers flowed with this fire, earthquakes shook the foundations of Hell. This caused the rivers to break into seas and the seas were burning with the same fire. All from that one word spoken by God. It was that word that made the lightning and fire."

"I remember how we angels cowered in fear of the power of God. I could barely watch as the fiery oceans became water and the land rose from its depths because in the chaos I could see the horrors. These monstrous creatures showed a glimpse of what was to come as they fought to become gods themselves. It was the Time of Chaos. That was when the Gates of the Spirits were opened. We retreated behind this gate and as it closed the chaos of creation was lost to me. Inside the gates were wheels within wheels and they turned in all kinds of different directions. They were stacked one upon another, extending into the heights of heaven. It was all so confusing at first. I mean it looked like three immense rings and each ring contained three smaller rings inside, all turning in some form of harmony but it went on far beyond where the eye could see. I think it was by some instinct I flew to a lesser gate where I would enter one of the rings. I knew that's where I would live."

"This all seemed to happen in mere moments. It went so fast that my memory of these events will never be completely resolved. What I do remember were all the types of angels. There were the Seraphim who remained at the throne of God. They were covered with eyes, watching always. They were the greatest angels of all. Then came the Cherubim who were charged with protecting the throne of God. Each Cherubim had four faces and their wings covered their eyes. It was clear to me that no angel could assail the throne of God without first overcoming the power of these angels. It seemed an impossibility. These angels were workers of wonder and full of that very power firing creation. I remember that they too burned of fire, so we called them The Burning Ones. The last wheel held the Thrones. We called them Ophanim because they were like wheels themselves but wheels within wheels all covered with eyes. I still don't know their purpose."

"Behind the second gate turned a second ring. A large wheel with three shining wheels inside. This is where the Dominions ruled and the Virtues watched over the planets and the stars. The last wheel held the Powers who were the angels who formed the connection between us below to those above. The last large ring contained three smaller wheels filled first with the Principalities who are angels that commanded our ring. There were the Archangels. These shining ones set us about the work for which we were created. There were only eight but they kept order in the part of heaven below them. Macy no one could help but yield to their will. They were a wonder to look upon; they extended into us the very love of God. That love He has for all of His creation. Their names were Michael, Raphael, Uriel, Selaphiel, Jegudiel, Lucifer and Brachial. Michael and Gabriel would come to me often but Lucifer, who was the most powerful and was loved by all the angels below, did not. We called him the Morning Star and sought his guarded companionship. How could we know of the Great War that was looming and the part Lucifer would play? I didn't know then that one day I'd have to face him. Only now he's known as The Prince of the Power of the Air."

I fell silent. Macy did too. I knew I sounded crazy. I said, "Macy, I'm sorry, but there's a mission I'm on and I know that this all sounds so fractured and totally impossible. I mean you must think I'm completely certifiable and past ready for the insane asylum. I mean, here's Robin Randle secret agent from The Region on a mission to save the Earth and hey, things didn't go according to plan, so now she's living with three lives in her head and can't separate them. She can't even remember growing up in The Region but hey, she's still supposed to complete her mission and save the day. I'll tell you one thing I do remember, I volunteered for this if you can believe that!"

Macy said, "You know, I can. There seems to be some of us, I guess, human or angel, that just stand ready to give everything to a cause no matter the cost. You just feel the outcome of your quest is worth the sacrifice." I'd never stopped to think about things in those terms. Macy was wiser than her years. Damn the cost, someone had to do this so it might as well be me! Boy. I'd gotten myself deep in the shit for sure.

"Ok," I said, "I lived here on Earth but something went wrong and when I went back to The Region I wasn't dead. Maybe I was supposed to be but I wasn't, just in a damn coma. I was told later that I was brain dead but with no advance directive they couldn't turn the machines off. When I fell into The Region I didn't remember anything about my quest. I just wanted out and back here. So, I did that and when I woke up back on Earth my mind was a shattered mess. Memories all mixed up from all these lives I didn't know I had. I thought I was crazy and I was so afraid someone would put me in a mental hospital."

Macy said, "Been there, Robin. Good choice to stay out. I still don't know for sure how I got out but I'm never going back." Macy looked disturbed, "Demons are my thing but I've never fought anything close to your prince. I call him Wormwood."

I sighed, "I've heard that name used. He wants to stop me. I don't know if he ever will but for now he holds all the souls of all mankind ransom. I have to find the Gate of the Seven Stars. Beyond it is a place called the Palace of Starlight. It's overseen by my wonderful mother in The Region. She's called the Queen of Starlight and somehow, she stole all these things we call toll boxes and brought them to her palace. They're really not boxes. They're more like glowing glass-like globes filled with all the good things a person has done in their life. I sound just like the crazy person my dad wanted me to be."

Macy drove on in silence. Finally, she said, "Toll boxes. Palace of Starlight. Boy, there's a lot we humans don't know." With that Macy fell silent and the night swallowed us. I wasn't afraid of the night anymore. I'm the one who walks two worlds, I'm the Storm Bringer. I am the only one who will travel The Crossing. There was one thing I knew in my gut and that's to never go near the Binding Place. The Binding Place was the far edges of Hell. But somehow, I knew that that place was mixed up with what I'm doing now. It must be close to The Crossing. If I fell into the Binding Place I'm not sure I could ever get out. It's not a place for angels. I couldn't figure out why I would ever go there. Where was this fear coming from? Something was missing. Something I still didn't know and that made me feel sick. Always it comes down to what I don't know. I reached under my dirt-stained t-shirt and produced this small key. The handle was shaped like a Star of David with a golden tassel hanging from it. I held it up so Macy could see, "Macy, here is the key I wear around my neck. Entrusted to me by God. I'm the angel who at the end of time, will lock the Gate to Hell. I'm serious. The lock this little key turns is mounted in the door to Hell. The hordes of demons and Satan himself will not be able to break it." I studied the key a moment longer then returned it under my shirt. At times, it seemed to weigh a million tons and it felt like it was trying to pull me down. Other times, I didn't even remember it was around my neck. I bet that was a problem. I bet it was a reflection of my ability to handle the task before me. I let out a sigh. All I could do for the moment was sit silently as Macy's old Dodge Dart rattled down US 6 into the darkness of the night. The darkness I loved. It was the darkness of my mind I hated.

Macy was silent for a bit then thankfully changed the subject, "What have you been up to since I last saw you in Mason?" Wow, an innocent enough question but one I didn't know how to answer.

"Not sure where to begin. See, I didn't know I was an angel when I lived in Mason. I thought I was just a girl. Then these monsters came and they wanted to kill me. Can't imagine that's changed much. I'm putting you at risk."

"Don't sweat it, Robin. Risk has become all I know. Maybe you will be the one to pull me from my own personal darkness. I'm just sayin'. I'm so freakin' tired of it all. Hey, so you know God?"

I took a minute to form my answer. Here we were, back at that place of knowing. I just blurted out, "Yes, I do. I've walked with Jesus. He was the one who told me the stories of The Shadow Tales." There it was. All out in the open. A sadness overwhelmed me. "There's so much more. I just can't talk about it right now. It's not because I don't trust you or anything. It just hurts too much."

"Wow, now that gives one a new perspective. So, tell me, why did you call me?"

Finally, a question I knew I could answer. "I left The Region willfully so now I have to find a way to return and help Station. I fear she's hurt. Hey, I know, pull over a sec. I need to try something." Macy eased off the highway onto the narrow breakdown lane then put her car in park. I opened my door and stepped out into the cool night air. A breeze had come up. It was blowing from the North. There it was, that feeling of silk caressing my face. The air smelled old and tired like the end of time as it was bringing slow death to all living things in the world. I thought for a moment, "Macy, what's the date?"

I didn't even listen to her answer. I knew it was the first day of October, my time of endings. No. The time of endings. I knew that same cutting feeling that was present in the air the night all this nightmare had started. It created this feeling of life and death with me caught in the middle, unable to control my fate. Fate. Was there even such a thing as fate? Was all this part of a master plan carved out of creation before I was born? Doubt filled my soul. Doubt about my place in things. Doubt that I would be enough to accomplish this enormous task. I had to wonder why such an important mission would be given to the likes of me, angel or not? It didn't matter anymore, I guessed. I was here and things were what they were. Looking up into the midnight blackness of space I closed my eyes and reached back into my relaxation exercises then let the cutting night air engulf me. It trapped me in this place unsure of my own sanity. Reaching back into my memories for just a small sound or smell from The Region I willed myself to GO. Nothing changed. All the smells surrounding me remained the same so I opened my eyes to find what I feared. I was still standing next to Macy's car.

Confused, I had to wonder what powers did I have? Did I even have powers? Shit, trapped all by myself on Earth and now seemingly powerless. No hope of ever returning to Station to bring the help I'd promised.

"I'm trapped. I can't believe this. They gave me two names and don't ask me who the they are because I don't know. The first was the one who walks two worlds but I can't remember how to do it anymore. I can't do anything." I broke down and started crying, "I'm useless. If I can't even travel the worlds how could I even hope to be the Storm Bringer?" Macy walked around her car and wrapped me in her arms. I knew this wasn't a comfortable place for her to be but she held me like a mother holds the lost child who was just found. I managed, "I'm so tired of my life. I'm so damn tired of being out of control. No, maybe I'm flat weary of just being." I said, "It's like living life inside a jigsaw puzzle but there's no box top. No reference point or place to grab ahold and get control. Macy, I'm exhausted. She squeezed me and said, "I'm tired too. It's time to find a motel for the night." Macy's arms eased then let go. I looked up into her face and I could see tears resting on her cheeks. Wow. All I knew to do was to return to the car and let the silence engulf me.

We drove, my forehead resting against the door window as I looked outside at the lights of Providence, Rhode Island flickering past. I should've been amazed. I'd never seen a city this large before but now it was just a stream of colors and light that obscured my night. Macy stayed on Highway 6 as we left that city behind. She drove twenty more minutes then broke the silence, "There's as good a place as any." She turned off the road into the parking lot of the Sky View Motor Inn. It looked like it'd been here for a hundred years. Maybe it was built when this highway was constructed. The car shuttered with each pothole that littered the once pristine asphalt blacktop smooth and inviting in those days but now riddled with cracks and pieces splitting apart by inches and falling away creating potholes to be dodged. Not inviting anymore.

Macy pulled up to a flickering neon sign that said lobby and disappeared inside. When she returned she had a key in her hand and pulled the car around the side of the motel and parked in front of room 113. I didn't know what to do. I didn't know my place. So, I asked, "Is it okay, I mean, can I sleep in your car? I mean if you do mind I understand if you do. I can..."

Macy looked puzzled and interrupted, "Of course you may but Robin, I got a room for the both of us. Is that okay?"

More tears, "Macy, I'm so sorry; I don't have any money."

Macy smiled a soft and loving smile. I marveled she still had it in her. She reached out and touched my shoulder. There was kindness in her smile despite all her efforts to maintain that hard exterior, "Robin, I've made enough money for two lifetimes. I don't want anything except answers that can't be bought. I'll become your patron. Is that ok? It would be my honor." I smiled back and could only manage a nod.

We entered the room and a king bed sat covered with a garish gold bedspread. The bed filled almost the whole room. I dropped my pack to the floor and Macy followed suit.

There was a mirror over the dresser at the end of the bed. I caught my reflection. Wow, my hair, usually a wreck on a good day, had gone nuclear. My skin was so dirty. It was the first time I'd noticed how bad I smelled. I was in need of a makeover. How could Macy stand to look at me not to mention tolerate my smell sleeping in the same bed? This needed attention.

I said, "I need a shower, maybe tomorrow I can get a razor and shaving cream. Maybe even shampoo. I need to clean myself up. I'm sorry Macy." I looked at Macy and she looked wonderful. I mean, her hair neat and styled and what I could see of her body was clean. I sighed, feeling like one of the lost boys, and plodded off toward the shower to see if I could regain at least a small piece of myself, but Macy stopped me.

"Here." She handed me a small bag. "This should help." I took it and not knowing what to say, said nothing and entered the bathroom. I reached down grasping the stained and ragged hem of my sweatshirt and pulled it off over my head dropping it to the floor. I dropped my grease-stained jeans along with my panties and realized for the first time since returning to Earth that I was dressed like the old Robin of Mason, Texas. My dress replaced by my old clothes that I'd left at the ruins of the manor house in The Region. I hated that.

I turned on the water and got it hot. Opening Macy's bag and I found a razor, shaving cream and shampoo. I stepped into the hot stream of water and let it carry away the grime of The Region. I fidgeted with the tiny bar of motel soap, dropping it twice. I covered myself in the odorless slime and let the water wash away my travel-worn dirt. Then I washed my hair. I shaved my legs and armpits, and then I turned the water off, taking the ragged bath towel off the rack, blotting myself dry.

I flipped the bathroom light off and walked back out into the dimly lit motel room and pulled the covers down. I climbed in bed under cold sheets and managed a weak, "Good night." She was already asleep. As I closed my eyes once again, I fell. Fell into somewhere in my void and I wondered: Do I ever sleep anymore?

THE BINDING PLACE

I dreamed. It looked as if I'd fallen back into what I now think of as my world. The Region. I was looking down into a valley and saw a lake. It looked more like an enormous piece of black glass rather than the still water it was. Not a ripple showed on the water's surface. The lack of wind left the water even blacker than the night that surrounded it. I thought how things always seemed to come back to October. It seemed right but I couldn't figure out why. A cycle maybe. A cycle that was unfolding. This wasn't The Region at all. This was Earth. The air smelled of burnt flesh. There wasn't any wind but there was cold. An unnatural cold. I could feel a presence under the black surface of the water. An evil as old as the Ancient Ones. An evil created before time. Before the Great War. It had no name I knew but it was part of the unknowing. It emanated all that was bad in my life. No, that's not right. It was all of life. Memories rose up like a viper in my mind. I could see the shadows of the monsters, and the air now stunk of ancient fires burning the wonders of creation. It was my father. I'd forgotten this.

On the day before he tried to kill me he'd come home drunk but it was late and the house was dark. I'd just slipped in through the back door as I'd done countless times before hoping he'd passed out. On this night, I was wrong. He came in the front door as I was entering through the back. I stepped out of the kitchen heading to the living room right as the front door opened. This was the worst possible timing on my part. He saw me in the darkness of the house and screamed, "You little shit! What're you doing out this late? Haven't I warned you to never be out past ten?"

The violence in his voice caused me to stumble backward a few feet. This was going to escalate. I wished I could just melt away. Be someplace safe and warm. My next choice might have brought on the murderous rage that was to come on the following night. He started coming at me. I held up my hands and yelled, "Stop, Dad! Don't you touch me!" My feeble attempt to control his violence just escalated his rage. He came on fast and tripped on the living room rug falling into a drunken heap on the floor right at my feet.

He moaned and started to get up mumbling, "I'm going to beat the shit out of you, then maybe you'll mind. I'll beat you till your face isn't even recognizable."

Truth was if he hit me he'd probably kill me. I'm small and weak but on this night, I found the rare courage to fight back. I retreated into the kitchen thinking maybe I could run out the back door but even as drunk as he was, I knew he was too fast. I didn't think. I just acted. Picking up a kitchen chair I swung. I had to hit him before he stood up. I got lucky and struck him over the head. He went right back down and stayed there. I put the chair down and slid it back under the table and weighed my options. If he woke up in the night he'd kill me. I wasn't safe. Lucy was gone but I thought of our secret cave. I was too scared of the night to try and make it there. There wasn't an option so I went to my room and locked the door. I pulled my dresser over to block it. At least he couldn't surprise me. I unlocked my window and loosened the screen so I could run if I had too. I called out to God broken and alone, "Please." He didn't answer. I climbed into bed and cried myself to sleep.

On that far edge of what felt like falling asleep my memory shifted away from this and to Redding's Mill. I could see it, this memory as vivid as a movie. I thought I'd finished with this but a final veil lifted. I still hadn't remembered events right.

I'd thought before, how could it be Lucy was dead? She was my best friend. My only friend. I liked Jim but would never let him close. Lucy always felt right. Her mom introduced us after my dad raped me. I was nine. My dad was gone for a few years and that gave me a chance to have Lucy over and I was welcome at her house. We'd talk about nonsense to keep memories in their place. I'd seen bits and pieces – her mother's love. The father gone from her life. Different from my experiences after my own rape. Her mom loved her and she had made sure the monster was gone forever. I saw that Lucy was still hurting from that event to this day. Now unknown to her, this was a common bond between us. Lucy didn't know that I'd been raped. Her mom had kept Lucy safe. She'd protected her as much as a mom can from the horrors in this world. Now in my case, no one had protected me. I'd been left to my own nightmares, my mind molested just like my body had been, but now looking for a way to lessen the pain.

The final clarity of events came into my mind. It wasn't Lucy. Lucy didn't die at Redding's Mill. Jim had. It was Lucy and I that swam to the pool's edge while Jim screamed in horror. We both shot out of the pool without regard for our nude bodies. Mr. Beam hadn't noticed and he blasted the monster with his shotgun. The pool house came down and I grabbed Lucy's hand and ran to our little secret cave. Naked, filthy and cold, we crammed into the back of the cave and held on to each other all night.

I remembered saying to her, "We're safe, Lucy. Trust me." Fitful sleep filled the darkness and with the first light of dawn we crawled out into the forest and made our way to Lucy's home. We were quiet as we showered, dried and slipped into Lucy's bed. She was crying in such a soft and fearful way. I held on to her letting all my love flow into her. I wondered, was this the first time I was a wellspring? Could be it's the first time I remembered

This memory brought the pain of loss. Where was my Station Cross? I felt as if a deep part of me had been torn from my being and lost to the efforts of searching for what is the unfindable.

Jim was the one who went missing and the pool was destroyed. Howard Beam was missing as well but no one suspected we'd been there. Now I understood. This event was no dream. Somehow one of the horrors of The Region had crossed onto Earth looking for me. It wanted to destroy me utterly. Then I wouldn't be able to die and land in The Region. It was so out of place, so unbelievable, I'd blocked it from my memories. Events that became condemned to my dream world. All this before the coma. I recognized this horror now. It was that very creature that plagued my dreams night after night in the days prior to Sloan's arrival.

After the events at Redding's Mill a sad thing happened. Lucy's mom got a chance at a great job in

Austin, Texas. Within a month they were gone. Just before they moved Lucy's mom came into Lucy's bedroom and sat on her bed so she could talk to me. She was crying, "Robin, I hate leaving you. I could try and get custody and you could come with me?"

I said, "Mrs. Jones, my dad wouldn't let that happen. He enjoys his power. Don't worry. I'm gone all the time. I'll be fine." She didn't look convinced but she knew I was right. My dad was a veritable demon.

A week later they were gone and I was alone. It was October 1st when they'd moved. On this same date the following year I met the Dust Witch and went to my doom. After that I had no more family to worry about. I was just lost returning from The Region needing healing for my fractured mind.

I looked at the black, still water. Now I recognized this valley. It had been ages since I visited this place. I used to love sitting on the quiet shores of this lake. Once this valley had been called Isfinias but no more. Now it was named the Valley of Dying Stars. Yes, I knew this place. I knew this lake. I knew it wasn't in The Region but on Earth. Oh, now things were getting strange. Below me, in this valley, lay a lake not only filled with silent black water but filled with an evil beyond my imagination. This lake was filled with that which has no name. A thing of the unknowing. I had glimpsed a page from the Shadow Tales. The name of this lake came into my mind like a silent breeze. In those ancient days when I walked the Earth I'd named this lake. I couldn't believe this. I'd never realized it was in reality the Gate of the Seven Stars. I'd named the lake Amaramtiam Phasis, the Lake of Murders.

Maybe more dangerous than the evil things dwelling

in this dark water were the seven dying stars. They were scattered about the valley hidden from my view and keeping secrets, even from the Queen of Starlight. I'd been the one who named this valley as well. I had named it Isfinias. A word thought to be nonsense to the great magical thinkers of Earth. So, this was the Gate of the Seven Stars. Were these stars the same? I'm sure that this is the gate I needed to find. This was my final destination and with that thought I was shot with the pain of Station's absence. I had no idea what her fate was. Was she alive or dead? Or maybe lost in a hidden place. A place I would never know. Maybe this place. Too much. Tears started to well up in my eyes but I took a deep breath and stopped them.

A voice pierced the night air. It sounded as if it was far away. I closed my eyes so I could let all of me listen. It was a girl's voice. Someone who was familiar to me. She was yelling, "I'm locked away. Away in the tower. Help me." A tower. That brought back the image tattooed on Station's arm. The image that scared me. I knew the voice. Lucy? How could that be? Then she spoke in broken angelic, "Solpeth, telco train knothole salman. Ze oela dosig au vivq. Oi pommel train unpin do telco a au monons."

I understood her words. She was saying, "Listen, death shall be midst wonder. They make night this nest. This palace shall be wrath and death of this heart."

What did this mean? Was the wonder my love for Station? It felt as if this was a message that had been sent to kill my heart or more importantly, stop my quest. The Prince of the Power of the Air was using everything I held dear both here and in The Region to torture me. Anger welled up inside me. There was not going to be any heart dying on my watch. The human part of me took over my mind. I had to stop this. Stop it all. I had to head west. The valley, this lake was in what is called today the Muir Woods. It was there that I'd find the hidden door. In The Shadow Tales, this door was called Ohobantia. There I must create or break a boundary. Cross it somehow. Exercise my liminal rights. This was the only place where I could go with any hope of saving Station Cross. If I died trying to save her I would do so with no fear and the truth of the love we hold between us.

I woke with a start. It felt as if I'd fallen from the place in my dreams through the air and back into the motel room. Macy had been shaking me and I guessed it had taken her a minute to rouse me to consciousness. Seeing the old motel room, its stained and ancient walls all around me, I remembered stopping last night. Macy said, "Are you okay? I thought I was going to have to call 911."

I shook my head trying to clear the cobwebs away. "I'm here Macy. I'm okay." I sat up with a jolt.

"The hell you are! Robin, you have to tell me what's going on. I told you I'd help any way I could, but you're making things impossible." I sighed. She was right. I was in a very dark and dangerous place. It was only fair Macy should know what I'm dealing with.

"I'm sorry. I shouldn't have involved you…"

Macy cut me off, "Robin, I'm here. I told you to call me if you needed help. I'm a freakin' big girl. If I didn't want to be involved I'd be gone. Stop the excuses and tell me. Tell me what's going on."

I had to stop fooling myself and accept the truth.

I knew somehow that when I'd signed on for this mission I fully well knew anything could happen. There are few secrets on my side of the veil. The Crossing was one. I was getting dangerously close to the Binding Place.

I said, "It's The Crossing. The Crossing isn't like a bridge crossing a river it's like a space you cross between life and death. You've heard the stories about people who have died then were revived? These people tell tales of their journey to another place. The stories vary only slightly but it seems the visions are of a heaven-like place or sometimes, hell. The truth is they aren't in either one. They have entered The Crossing and that's as far as a human can go and return. When you enter The Region you don't, well, you can't return. What I mean is, your earthly body is dead. Angels never have a reason to enter The Crossing. What's there is as much a mystery to me as it is for you. Macy, I know this is confusing, but say you are dead. In your journey to The Region from life here on Earth you would pass through The Crossing. You'd only spend moments there but there is a power there that can turn back those who aren't ready for death."

I paused, looking at my hands. For an angel, I felt small both in size and in strength. I looked up into Macy's blazing blue eyes, "Macy, I don't know when I'm asleep or awake. I don't even know if there's a difference for me anymore. My heart is searching for a way, a way back to a person I love. Her name is Station Cross. The last time I left The Region she was there with me but seemingly lifeless. I have to find some way, no matter how impossible, to help her or at least know she's still alive. Not knowing is throwing my ability to focus way off. Everything seems to be pointing toward a simple fact. The way back to her is my way forward, through The Crossing and opening the Gate of the Seven Stars. In some unimaginable fashion, I think I'm living in both The Region and Earth at the same time. No more dreams. No more sleep. Only ors. Ors means darkness in my language."

I dressed in a silent room, no longer worried about the mundane things of life like shampoo and shaving cream. I knew with all my heart that the only way back to The Region, and Station, was through the horrors of the Gate of the Seven Stars. I knew that passing through the gate would bring me close to the Binding Place but I couldn't see another way. If I failed, the Binding Place would end me. I'd be trapped in hell along with those creatures I'd come to hate. That's The Prince's plan. He was going to try and trap me in that very place he never wanted to go. I needed to accept that as a fact. I wasn't sure I could. We left the golden bedspread of the Sky View Motor Hotel and headed out to Macy's car.

As I opened my car door Macy broke the silence, "I studied Angelic but never thought of angels speaking their own language. I mean I should have. Some of the words I use, some of words the sigils use are in that language."

I managed a smile, "It's funny. Why I'd never remembered that I knew how to speak another language. I don't change from one to the other when I speak. It just works out." I know. This is another one for the Robin Randle Unsolved Mysteries list. "Somewhere on earth a man was taught Angelic and he wrote it down in a book. I don't know, maybe that happened." The morning sun was well above the horizon. It was a bit disorienting not being my normal awake time. It was pushing me deeper into my confusion. I felt something. It came over me like that scratching in your throat predicting an oncoming cold. This was something that wasn't there a moment ago. My tattoos began to throb. That was new. Shit, everything I feared was coming true. When I thought about the Binding Place all I could see was cold black steel. Steel so frozen it would shatter into fragments at the slightest touch. It was the same cold I'd felt on that first night of this odyssey all the way back in Mason. What was then a thing of imagination now had become real. The difference in this cold was it shot through me like a bullet erupting through my whole body. This bullet tore through my heart leaving a dead empty place in its wake. I wasn't ready for this but it had come as sure as the sunrise. I stepped away from Macy's car as I closed the car door.

"Macy," I faltered, "Something bad is coming. A monster. No, a demon I think. I can't tell yet but if it's a demon it will be one of the ancient Fallen Ones." I didn't even stop to think if Macy would understand. This monster had been coming for me from the start. It'd been waiting for the exact proper time when I'd be too weak, no, more frail and full of self-doubt. I didn't know what kind of help I needed. All I wanted was someone to intercede for me, but that wasn't happening. I was too far down this rabbit hole. I knew this was a creature from the Binding Place sent to Earth to try and finally claim me for its own. This was the end of all things. I'd begun to cry knowing

I'd failed in my task. It was too late. I'd never free the toll boxes. I'd never save Station from the fate of destruction. I was going to fall into eternity through The Crossing and into the Binding Place as if it were a black hole in space.

I wiped tears from my eyes and looking over at Macy she'd climbed back out of her car and gone to the trunk. She popped it open and took out a soft black grip and a staff. My staff. Returning to me she dropped the case on the ground and handed the staff to me. She said, "I almost forgot," then she kneeled on the broken asphalt and opened her grip. I'd guessed it was where she kept her tools. She pulled out a handful of sigils cast in different metals and covered in symbols, words written in the books of time. Some were only slips of old parchment She reached in again, pulling out pieces of different colored chalk and some dusty old books filled with more sigils. She dropped it all on the ground and grabbed a big piece of white sidewalk chalk and began to draw a circle around the both of us.

Macy said, "I don't know how you fight demons in The Region but here on Earth we use circles, symbols and words. I'm sorry, I forgot. I was given that staff and told it's yours."

It was my staff. I asked, "How...no, who gave this to you?"

"It was this old guy. He called on me one day when I was back at Norwood. It was about a month ago. He never gave me his name. Wouldn't come inside the house. He handed it to me and said, 'Give this to Robin when you see her.' Honestly, I didn't even know I was going to see you again! He was an odd fellow dressed in dark colors and wearing a black duster with a flat brimmed cowboy hat. His name will remain forever a mystery, I fear. I tried to fix him but it felt like I wasn't looking at someone, like he wasn't there. How he'd found me and in Norwood House will always remain a mystery. I mean that place is a secret. No one knows about it."

I looked at my ancient staff. It felt so familiar in my hands. My heart strengthened. Here was a piece of the real me I could hold on to. I'd lost it in The Region somehow when I was confronted by The Prince of the Power of the Air. I was capable of doing some amazing things with this staff. In The Region. I searched my memory as to how I might use it on Earth. Sloan must have found it somehow then given it to Macy, but he'd told me he couldn't cross into The Region anymore. Then there was the how of the fact he'd known Macy would see me again. It wasn't like I'd told anyone we'd ever met. How did he get it in the first place? Another one for the Robin Randle Unsolved Mysteries list. I was the girl without answers. It was only my life for crying out loud. That wasn't true, I thought. This current life wasn't my real life. It was a ploy to obtain a goal. The problem was I felt as real as any human must feel. I wasn't feeling angelic at all. Whatever power I'd had I'd left in The Region. It was like I'd been split in two. I felt overwhelming loss. Disconnection from life, from Station, hopeless in all my efforts to return to her.

The ground started to shake same as an earthquake. I stumbled forward and fell to the asphalt. This wasn't good. This monster had picked the perfect time to attack me. I was at my weakest but struggled up on all fours and looked back at Macy. She was still drawing on her circle. I'd fallen outside its safety. It was then that the sky opened up. It tore open like a sheet of old paper and behind the sky was another sky full of darkness and foreboding. Clouds were swirling, lit by a familiar full moon. Maybe my home. I should have felt some comfort in that but in actual fact it'd become a no man's land. A land laced with fear and loss. I rose, stumbled and tried again getting to my feet while holding onto my staff and then the Earth was gone. I whirled back toward Macy but she was gone. Amazingly, the circle she was making was still there. It wasn't made out of white chalk anymore. Now it was a brilliant glowing circle of gold. Markings kept appearing as Macy kept drawing. Maybe there was hope I thought. I needed to get inside it. Stumbling toward it I fell again as a roar erupted from the sky. It was like the sound was carried in a wind that pushed me toward the ground. Now the roar's pitch changed causing it to become more of a scream and so loud I didn't think my hearing would ever recover. Shocked by the realization I knew this sound. I forced myself to a standing position and made a break for Macy's circle. It was then that the creature unleashed a new horror. A brilliant flash of pure white light came out of the blackness. Lightning struck the ground all around me. Thunder rocked me and I fell again. This was the horror from my dreams. Not dreams, I thought. This was the monster from The Region that was to be my undoing. I stood and stumbled into the circle and sat down with conviction. Looking all around me, I searched for the source of all this chaos. Pure night had replaced what had been the morning.

Even the full moon was no longer overhead, making it hard to see. It seemed that the land around me had become flat and lifeless. No trees or houses. No roads either. It was a vast emptiness. I could feel a wicked cold in the emptiness filling my heart with echoes of hopelessness.

I remembered how Station tried to get me to move away from the meadow where my parents, my home in The Region, lay burning to the ground. That was when Station had told me that I was the one that created the tattoo that covered her arm. I couldn't have. I mean I didn't remember how I'd done it. My thoughts were broken by another cry from the creature hiding in the darkness surrounding me. The flashes of lightning followed and were so bright I couldn't even see the creature as an after image from the lightning, then I was deafened again by a thunder as loud as creation itself.

Chaos rained down on me as the beast screamed again preparing to shatter me with more lightning and thunder. This time I closed my eyes, shielding them from the horrific light then covered my ears in an attempt to block some of the explosive thunder. I opened my eyes and I could see a post set in the ground, with chains hanging from it. As my sight cleared I saw that there were hundreds of these posts. No, there were thousands and each one had a man or woman chained to it. Only the one before me was empty. Waiting for me. I stood looking all around me as the horrific sound of inhuman torture filled the air. Screams woven into weeping and moaning; endless cycles of torment enacted on lost souls caught in the Binding Place. I shouldn't have been here. I couldn't be here. An eternity of pain and suffering foisted on those souls that'd rejected all belief in God. People lost now to the truth that there is life after death regardless of their beliefs while living on Earth. The monster was quiet now and looking down at me. It had hundreds of tentacle-like arms flowing from a gaping hole torn in the creature's face. The arms were twisting and turning and reaching for me. I sat still inside Macy's golden circle and could only wonder if her chalk and symbols could protect anyone from such a monster as this.

The creature kept trying to reach for me but the power Macy had imparted into her circle was holding the arms back. I could only imagine what Macy was dealing with on the other side of this creature. I was still holding my staff and just grabbed it in the middle and pulled parting the two torches held within. The firelight from my torches blinded the monster and it moved away from me and then stopped. With a sudden burst the monster struck out at me and I was flung into the air losing both torches and falling to the ground well outside the safety of Macy's circle.

If this was to be my end then I must stand to face this horror with the determination of Station Cross. She would have wanted it that way. I yelled, "You will not so easily bind an angel to your posts! Within me dwells the power of God!" Then darkness covered me and my senses fled, saving me from any awareness of suffering at the hands of this creature.

I had no sense of time, only darkness. I was still standing and no chains were attached to my body. A blast of air, no, blasting winds, had blown me out of the Binding Place. The Winds of Heaven. I'd never felt this wind and, I guessed, never needed its protection. I'd heard of these winds but never thought they would ever come to my aid. I'd been blown by the Winds of Heaven away from the binding post and now I lay on a forest floor. The day was ending, the sky growing darker as night consumed the light. Somehow, I thought I'd heard Macy calling my name. Struggling up from the ground I yelled out, "Macy. Help me!" That was all I had. With those words, I fell back to the forest floor and waited to see if I would be found. Maybe I was still alive.

It seemed to me like I was back in time, living inside my coma, struggling to be free of its icy grip. I heard thunder in the distance and rain pelted my face. Unable to open my eyes I felt arms reach under me, lifting me to a dry place where the warmth of another human body seemed to dwell. The warmth was close, holding me and I floated up from the coma and back into life. My eyes flickered open and I could still hear the sounds of the thunderstorm. Next to me was a girl. I couldn't place her but I knew she was a long way from home. Here just for me. I struggled awake and recognized the smell of Macy Beas. I tried again to open my eyes and this time I could clearly see that I was under a makeshift lean-to that was keeping the storm off me as Macy warmed my body with hers.

THE WIND OF TERROR

When I woke, I was alone. The rain had stopped but it had left the air with a heavy scent of pine. It was a dark odor. A pungent stink reminiscent of some Christmas buried deep in my retched Earthly past. I didn't need to recall all the failed Christmases I'd lived on Earth so I sat up and rolled out from under the lean-to Macy had built then struggled to my feet. Now that my mind was clear I was shocked to find that I was standing next to a giant Redwood tree. I stumbled backwards then caught myself and looked up at a tree that towered at least 280 feet above my head. This tree was at least 1,000 years old. Nothing compared to my life. Just a tick of the clock but to this world, it was ancient like the lake I was seeking. I could only look up and feel just how tiny I was. I turned my head and looked all around me. This had to be my final destination. The Muir Woods. I turned around and noticed a steep rise ahead of me. I could feel it pulling me. The lake. My lake. I guess I should know because I was the one who'd named it long ago. In those days angels walked the Earth. I know we'd tried to help mankind. It was during that time that I'd named this lake Amaramtiam Phasis or in English, the Lake of Murders. I used to love coming to this place to rest. Find moments of peace and time to be alone with Station. Then those 200 Watchers of Heaven were corrupted by Satan and all that was, was lost.

I turned away from the rise and looked for Macy. She was standing among the low ferns gracing the forest floor. Hand on the lean-to just watching me. A sadness crossed my heart. I walked over to her.

I knew it. I knew that here was another time of endings. My life was cluttered with them now. It seemed funny, well not funny, more like strange in a coincidence kind of way. I just couldn't remember enough beginnings to match up with all the endings. I walked up to her and Macy just stood there in fettered silence. Seemed she just had no frame of reference to start from. I couldn't imagine this girl unable to speak. I understood though. I was having that effect on people these days. Even on myself. Things happen to us that no matter how much we've learned; or experiences we'd lived we couldn't find the proper place to file them away. This landing, I guess I'll call it that, was now one such event in Macy's life. I said, "I don't remember much. I mean like even how we got here."

Macy stood straight looking into my eyes, "How do you think? We drove. Or rather, I drove. You weren't in any shape to take the wheel. Can you even drive a car?" She shook her head, "Never mind. Took us two and a half days cross country. A record for me. I was surprised the old Dart had it in her. Macy turned away and looked out into the forest. "At the motel parking lot, you just kind of faded in and out. I've seen weird shit but that was real block buster movie effects type stuff. There was some kind of demon or maybe just a freakin' monster, I don't know. It never totally came into this world. I don't know if I stopped it or if it was something you did." She turned back toward me, her eyes burning. She was scared. "You faded back in and I grabbed you. Things settled to just a ragging thunder storm so I pulled you into my car. You were mumbling that you had to get to the Muir Woods. Get to some lake named Amaramtiam Phasis. Personally, you should know that that lake isn't on any maps. Not here anyway. But we're here. Exactly where you wanted to go." She paused and looked at her hands like she didn't know what else to say.

I said, "Macy, the lake is here." I pointed over my shoulder, "Right over that rise. It's a place meant only for me." I walked up to her then stopped. I took her shoulders in my hands and looked deeply into her stark blue eyes, "I can't even begin to thank you for all you've done for me." Didn't that just feel lame?

She stood there in silence staring into my green eyes then she turned and looked out into this ancient redwood forest. The sun's light was beginning to falter. Night was coming. Maybe my last night. Then she said in a rather flat and lifeless tone, "I've changed my mind. Robin, I think, and I mean for the very first time, that there really are some good reasons why we humans operate on a need to know basis. Some very good reasons in fact. Robin, I just didn't need to know that monsters existed. I mean sure, I've seen glimpses of things I didn't understand while working on demons but shoot, I never had time to focus directly on them. I mean in the movies, sure, I get it. Real life, not so much." She shook herself as if shaking off a dusty old coat.

I said, "Maybe, this particular memory would best be left here, Macy. I can help."

Her head snapped around, her eyes flashed an even starker blue looking as if they could drill holes right through me. "And just how do you suggest I do that

Robin? How do I choose to forget the events of my life? No, I'll keep them, thank you very much." Her anger shook me. Tears immediately welled up in my eyes. I knew she was right but it still hurt. Why on earth should I believe my mission, quest, or whatever my life had become was so important? More important than a single human life. How was it I could ask this poor girl to do what she'd just done for me knowing well the long-term effects she would suffer would last the rest of her life? And all just so I could learn more about my enemy. Maybe win this hopeless fight.

My chin quivered as I started whimpering, "I'm sorry Macy. I had no right to put you or anyone for that matter through the danger of something like this." I broke down into a full-blown cry, "I'm, I'm… hell, this sucks. I know it's just not enough, saying these things. I know but it's just all I have. I'm sorry."

Macy's eyes cleared. She looked at me with gentleness more like that of a human mother. The mother I'd never had. Then put her arms around me and held me tight. I sobbed. She stroked my hair with slow deliberate strokes meant to comfort, "Don't cry Robin. You will always be my angel. How could you have known?" I sucked air in and gasps stifling tears.

I stuttered, "How…"

Macy interrupted, "Don't cry Robin. Just don't. You see, my part is done. Now I get to go home and put my feet up by a warm fire. I get to leave all the rest of this up to you. See, you are the one who has to trudge up that rise to Amaramtiam Phasis and face whatever horror awaits. A horror I can only guess at. One I'm not strong enough to even see. So, knowing what you're about to face is beyond me I should be the one in tears, not you. Tears for your sacrifice." I couldn't answer. My mind tried to wrap around her words.

There it was. That word, home. Would I ever go home again, I thought? Would I even know my true home if I saw it? It was getting darker. The time had come to end this and let Macy go. I just had to leave her with something other than this image full of monsters and a broken angel. I wasn't sure anymore how I could help her or if I could ever help anyone. So, I decided on telling her something that might help her in the future. I said, "Macy, listen, that evil living inside Norwood House isn't from demons, but it will reach out to hurt all it can. I'm sure it killed your mom and dad and then worked as hard as it could to drive you insane. When the attack came your Guardian, an angel that was created to be only your protector tried to protect you from the attack and to do that she literally merged herself into your soul. I've heard of that happening. That did save you but I just don't think she meant to merge with you." Macy opened her mouth then shut it again.

"How could she?"

"I don't know how but I do know this, she can't separate from you until your death comes. Then she will be free to help another human. If you do nothing else please, leave Norwood House to your friend Emma Swift. This is not a problem you can fix. Your Guardian has given you unique abilities to bind demons but trust me on this, it doesn't extend to malevolent spirits born of this world. From Earth."

Macy shouted back, "So that's it? That's all answers you got? You can't even tell me how to leave the house to Emma can you? I mean how do I just leave that horror for Emma to sort out? Don't you get it? I love her."

"I'm sure Emma knows you love her. She will understand why you left her the house. She'll know that she was the only one that you trusted with your darkest secrets. I'm sure she'll figure out what needs to be done to rid the world of that horror. I do know this, I can promise you, her Guardian will give her knowledge and protect her."

"Sure, like mine did for me?" Macy fell silent for a moment then said, "So, tell me, is this what we do? Just leave our messes for the ones we love to clean up?"

I wrapped my arms around her and held tight. After a moment, I kissed her cheek then pulled away. Time to end this.

"You know better than that. Thank you, Macy. You've done more than you'll ever know. I've got to go. I'm onto my last call. I know I've probably said too much as it is."

I shrugged my shoulders, turned and started walking up the rise ahead of me. Time to face The Valley of Dying Stars. Macy was in another world. When I reached the top of the rise I turned one last time and she was already gone. My destiny was to meet my fate alone. I turned back and looked down into the valley. There it was just like in my dream, well, more like my nightmare; that black still water of the lake just resting there in the place I'd once called Isfinias. Now it was a place called the Valley of Dying Stars. To be honest, I had loved this place once. In the ancient times, it was the lake where I'd love to come and rest. I had named it Amaramtiam Phasis, the Lake of Murders. In those days, I don't think it was here. Not in this exact location. It seemed as if it had drifted like so many things in my life had done. I thought that over ages that I'd been gone from Earth this lake had become filled with that which has no name. A thing of the unknowing. I wondered, had those things always been in the lake? Things hidden from me? Maybe I'd loved this lake because it held an amazing gate not even I was meant to cross. Maybe somehow, I'd felt it.

All the storms were silent now. The sky was clear and the stars of this world blazed among the giant Redwood trees. The world seemed silent, a relief from before, but then a single voice pierced the night air. Not too far away now. I studied the valley below. It looked just as I'd dreamed it.

A girl's voice cried out, "Please help me. I'm locked away. Away in the tower. You know how to save me, so please, just come and help me."

I could see it now. A darkness deeper than the dark of the valley floor below. No doubt remained. It was the tower tattooed on Station's arm. That image that had filled me with such abject hopelessness. Fear seeped into every fiber of my being. This had all become too much, I thought. Alone and lost in a wilderness now unknown to me. I didn't even have a compass. How was I to move forward? I thought maybe I should just run away. Who'd blame me? Right? Maybe I could still catch Macy. I shook my head. What was I thinking? All that I'd done. All that has been suffered by my friends like Macy, and what about Station? And who knows who else I'd affected. Who else had helped me on this quest. Running was my norm when I was just an Earth girl. Now I know I'm an angel. Inside me dwells the power of that angel and now I had to dig deep and push forward and end this. What was that that Macy had said? She had told me that there seems to be some of us, human or angel, that just stand ready to give everything to a cause no matter the cost. That's right. This is my mission. My duty to perform. No one else is coming to do what needs doing.

I thought all this just as the girl's voice called out again and it was filled with a hopelessness unlike any I'd ever heard, "Solpeth, telco train knothole salman. Ze oela dosig au vivq. Oi pommel train unpin do telco a au monons."

The words were clear to me now. She was speaking these words for my ears only. I knew I was the only living creature left on Earth that could speak Angelic. She'd said, "Listen to me. Death shall always be midst the wonder. He's made a nest, a place where wrath and death can rule your heart."

That was it. I couldn't take any more of this taunting. I had to stop it. Stop it all. I could tell that it was here that I would find a hidden door. I could feel its power. I am the one who could open any door. I could cross any boundry. That was one of my greatest gifts. This door was a door called Ohobantia. It waited on the black and cold dead surface of that wretched lake. Now it was my time. Maybe even the reason for my creation. I will break this boundary, cross it somehow by exercising my liminal rights. I knew this was the only place where I could hope to find the Palace of Starlight and just maybe save my Station Cross. Even if I died trying to save her I would do so knowing the truth in the love we held. I studied the valley before me. I could see that the black tower was close. A trail had opened at my feet, inviting me, so I started down toward the tall black form. With every step, a coldness was growing in the air. Wind was gathering for the fight. This cold air was unnatural, something ancient was woven deep into this mystic wind. The source of this arctic air seemed to be the tower itself. With each step, I thought back to that day so long ago. Mason, Texas. The last time I'd walked home or at least what I use to think of as home. I remembered the way the wind had blown on that night. It blew like there was a living thing with another kind of wind buried deep inside it. A foul-smelling wind full of evil, monsters and daggers. On that night, the wind had cut through me with the same dull and painful knives that I'd felt on the night I'd walked home from Mel's. That night that I'd thought all this had started. Now I realized that the first time I'd felt this wind had been before my coma. Before my trip to The Region. I understood now how connected all these pieces really were. This cutting wind was made just for me. For these kinds of moments. Just like it was doing now. So that was it. The forces that have been fighting against me have been doing so since I'd started this mission, not just since my coma induced vacation in The Region. And now I'd learned that it was this wretched tower that was the true source of the arctic tempest I'd experienced and had so casually blamed on the Snow Queen.

The waning moon had finally risen enough to cast its tattered yellow light over the tower that stood ahead of me. This tower was something old and yet something new at the same time. The growing moonlight had revealed symbols that looked as if they had simply grown across its shiny black surface like vines; somehow it reminded me of the trail of tattoos I'd set with ink on Station Cross' beautiful arm. The tower's symbols were twisting and curling out then turning back on themselves, until they enveloped the entire tower's surface with contours that looked as if dug into its obsidian-like surface. I thought that this must be writing. Could they be words scribed from its base to its crown? As I got closer I could tell that they were indeed words. I couldn't read them but they felt like words of demarcation, wait, no, more like words of delineation, liminal words that wrapped the tower creating both the power to imprison like a cage and the power to keep rescuers constrained, unable to enter. I could finally see that these words had been formed using the ancient words that were lost before Earth's creation. I had known these symbols once. They were part of what we'd simply called, the old language. It was the language used by angels in the days before the Great War. That war that would give birth to The Prince of the Power of the Air and his legion. We were told to forget this old language. It had become cursed by the demon. So, I could no longer read the true meaning of these words. This writing confirmed what I suspected. This obscene structure was the invention of The Prince of the Power of the Air. No work of God carried these idolatrous markings that were only meant to force this tower to exert and create an unhallowed space. This tower occupied just a moment of temporal shifting, holding a pure yet transitory power that forced The Crossing to remain open connecting the Earth to The Region so the energy to power it could pass at will. That's why its power was so strong in both the worlds. Whatever or more likely whoever was trapped inside this tower was done so by using powers that are wicked from without and transient from within. Using these words forgotten in the mist of time assured the absolute dominance of this prison. I mean, think about it. Just where and when had this tower been created? It had to have been someplace well-hidden I'm sure and before the real time had started. I wondered, how did The Prince even know he'd need this prison and need it right here and right now? Another one of those Robin Randle mysteries to file in my mysteries without answers closet inside my brain. I laughed at that thought. I knew in my heart all these answers didn't really matter anymore.

The cold, dagger-laced wind brought terror to my soul. A dead emptiness that was gouging out my life with each step I took toward this tower. Here it was, more of the unknowing. More of that which should not be.

PART 8

IN THE VALLEY OF DYING STARS

It is the time when crimson stars
Weary of heaven's cold delight…

-Dream-Time
Ella Higginson

THE BLACK TOWER

The trail I had been following played out right at the base of the tower. It was round with a pointed roof cap that rose a good hundred feet above me. It was completely black, not like dirty stone, streaked with ages of dust storm erosion and polluted air. No, it shined in the tepid moonlight reminding me of obsidian. I stepped closer and touched the stone. It was obsidian and it felt as if it was frozen by icy winds. The surface was covered with ancient words. As hard as it was for me to believe, the tower looked to be one single piece of stone carved into this shape. No mortar lines where stone met stone were visible as it loomed overhead shining black like the natural glass it was. This tower had been forged in the heart of a volcano and born perfectly formed just for this purpose. The writing had been etched with painstaking accuracy onto the tower's glass-like surface, and then fused with a power that made the words glow with a dim light that changed color as it passed through the letters giving life to these words. This language was born deep in the mists of time. It was when the ancient monsters of the chaos were laying their plans to hold dominion over all creation. These words were as old as the wretched seven words of pure magic. As the evil energy streaked around the tower it started out the color of white lightning then faded to a deep blood red giving way at last to a pale blue glow. These sparks of light grew ever stronger as they went up the tower's surface until finally they shattered the night as they wove the wicked north wind that could travel all the way to Mason. The stone was starting to leave my hand numb. All my senses told me I wanted to keep my distance from this wretched tower but that wasn't happening. I couldn't imagine entering this horror. I found myself in awe of the hopelessness held by this monstrous bit of Wormwood's handy work. The winds being spun around me had taken on the smell of bitter almonds and the frigid air ripped at my skin. It was all around me like vines on a plant, crushing me with the power of a language I could no longer understand. It was spinning the terror of the unknowing. The terror of this tower's unknowing. This tower should not be on Earth, yet here it was. I felt I had to do something to get away from this freakish, malformed cold but there was nowhere to hide. I could only hope this chaos wasn't living inside the tower as well. I found it hard to take a step so I screwed up my strength and forced my feet into an awkward kind of stumble making my way around the tower's base only to fall face first onto the forest floor. As I spit dirt and pine needles from my mouth, I struggled to get myself up off the lichen covered ground. It was then I saw it. A problem designed to pull the last bit of hope from my heart. The doorless opening for the tower was a good fifteen feet above ground level. I just had to be short, right?

I thought the only way I was going to get into this forsaken place was by trying to fly. The notion of flying felt foreign to me. Not enough time had passed for me to process all that had happened. It was then, while contemplating removing my sweatshirt, that I realized I was now wearing my dress from The Region. I mean why should I be surprised? It seemed things adjusted around me depending upon need. I didn't like that. Out of control was how my entire existence felt. Nothing more than a fractured person that wasn't a person but an angel. I hoped with all my heart that things would start to feel a little under my control.

I had no idea how to do this so, I just concentrated on the idea of unfolding my wings. I thought that maybe through sheer will I could get them to unfold but nothing was happening. I relaxed and started my silly breathing exercises. Still unsure of how I should do this, I pushed deeper into myself and just breathed. I created a vision in my mind of my wings unfolding. I imagined folds forming on the skin on my back. Folds that split open exposing new arms. A different kind of arms covered with feathers and without any hands. I could feel odd changes in my back. I pushed a bit harder with my mind and kept the vision of wings unfolding in the center of my thought. I took a slow and steady breath deep into my lungs. I let it expel and with that my wings unfolded. I looked to either side of me in total disbelief. I really did have wings. It just drove home the feeling of not belonging to this world. To Earth. I wasn't supposed to be here, on Earth I mean, yet I had to be if I was going to pass through this forsaken gate. I felt my wings and they felt like another set of arms. I knew I could control them just the same as any other part of my body so I leaned into them to make them beat and I slowly rose into the air. When I was level with a ledge at the opening, I leaned toward it and that brought my feet to rest on the landing that lead to the base of the stairs heading up to whatever creature waited for me at the top. Pulling back on my wings I was able to fold them back into my body. I stepped forward and looking up the staircase I saw that the writing was here. Winding away up and covering the interior walls just the same as it had the exterior. From down the circular staircase blew that frozen wind. That's what was making the tower so cold. Wow. This wind could travel anywhere on Earth. I guessed the true source of that wind was in the chamber at the top of these stairs. The black obsidian stone shined making the surface of the stairwell look as if it were made of glass and the streams of light marked and flowed up the same kind of writing until it disappeared around the curve in the stairs.

I mounted the first step and was met by a scream. A scream born out of the agony of some monstrous physical torture. In my mind, I could see the image of the girl above me lying on the dirty floor of her cell, creatures large and small climbing over her body. Some had many legs each with a sharp claw protruding at the tip. Others were larger and looked like crabs the size of a Labrador Retriever, claws grabbing and ripping at her clothes, its complex mouth opening and closing as it ripped flesh from bone. My heart raced now. Each step filled me with terror and physical pain was growing in my body. With every step, I felt the same ripping at my flesh that I imagined this girl was suffering. I had to hurry but the pain-laced fear slowed me down. If my vision was true, I didn't know if I could ever stand before this suffering creature to try and lend aid. The smell of putrid and decaying flesh filled the icy wind that was racing down from the chamber above. The screams racked me to my soul. Gasps and crying out, "No, please stop. Let me just die." The terror this poor creature felt as she screamed had to have been born from unimaginable pain. Pain beyond any I'd ever known.

I steadied myself and kept making slow but balanced progress up the steps of the tower. The closer I got to the top the louder and more pleading the cries had become. The icy wind was blowing with gale force now. I felt as if I was in a hurricane. That was until I turned the final corner and took that last step so I could finally see who or what dwelled in this cell at the top of this prison. I stepped into the cell and I was met by a sudden silence. The wind just stopped like it had never been. The glowing letters had played out at the last step leaving the interior of the cell colorless and dark. I could see that the floor was flat and a large semicircular window opened to the outside world. This window was more the size of a shed door opening but without any door or a window to seal it up. No bars or railings protected this opening, it was filled with just the emptiness of the night.

On the floor sat a small girl, her back to me as she gazed out the opening. She wore a dirty tattered dress and had long unkempt red hair. She was still and looked to be without injury. The screams, the smells, had all been part of the binding etched into the walls of this God forsaken place. The moonlight had grown strong here, lighting some of the interior of the cell. It looked as if there was nothing else here. No cot or table. No sign of food or water. No chain holding her to the wall. I had to say something. I wasn't even sure I could get her out of this place. I used a soft voice not to scare her, "Hello. I'm Robin and I'm here to help you."

The girl replied in a scratchy and hoarse voice much like one who had been screaming endlessly at the walls of the cell, "A bit too late for that, you bitch." She stood and turned toward me. What I saw couldn't be yet I knew it was real. It was a monster of my own creation. I faltered, leaning back against the wall. I started feeling light-headed like you do when met with an unexpected shock. You know, like getting a cast off your arm. But this was far worse. I couldn't pass out. Not now. Not here, while I faced this horror. I couldn't hold on in my mind so I screamed.

THE UNFOLDING

My screams echoed inside this unholy tower, fading like a warm breath cast upon a frigid window. Before me stood the one creature I'd never imagined. The worst of all this, all that's happened to me, seemed to wash away with this one revelation. Nothing could have or would have prepared me for the prisoner I'd found locked away in this tower. Now I knew why fear was all I could feel when I looked at this place on Station's tattooed arm except now I was here and the feelings of dread consumed me. I'd become filled with the fear that the day would come in all of this when I stood before this unavoidable horror. A day when I would have to stand fearless before this creature who'd been locked away in this tower. A creature who was now lost to all of time and space, forgotten by everyone but most horribly forgotten by me. How could I have done this? This creature's fate was my doing. She was a victim of my own agony spread over mistaken places and time lost to all of creation itself. Before me stood Robin Randle. Not a ghost or reflection of myself but the Robin who'd been born of The Region. The Robin who'd had twenty wonderful years of life growing up with parents who'd loved her followed by this endless hell of entrapment by The Prince of the Power of the Air.

Her eyes flashed red with hate as she said, "You! How long I've been waiting for this day. The day the wretched bitch would return all self-righteous and holy." Her voice sounded as if it'd been torn from her throat, cast into a fire's flames and planted back inside her. It bore no real resemblance to my own. "I was told by my jailer that one day you'd return from The Region and set me free."

I said, "I'm so sorry. Everything has been so confusing …"

She interrupted screaming, "I waited for you! You were supposed to come and save me, but I guess you forgot! I've been waiting 300 years. Three hundred fucking years locked away in this hell!"

I stuttered, "But it couldn't have been, I mean I'm only eighteen years old." I knew I wasn't right about my age but had no reference anymore.

She laughed but her laugh turned to coughing so hard she spat blood on the ground at my feet. "Shit. You stupid whore. Just tell me how long you wandered around The Region trying to escape back into your other life, your earthly life?" I stood silent. I didn't have a clue how long it'd taken me to travel The Region. I'd spent seven months in a coma on Earth but maybe that'd been a long time in The Region. Maybe she was right.

"I didn't know about you then," I couldn't help myself. I started to cry. Not for me but for all of those I'd failed. It seemed that there was much more failure in my life than I could have ever imagined.

My other self laughed, "Go on and shed your worthless tears. You know what? I hope Station Cross is dead. And I mean forever dead! I hope you die trying to cross that Gate of the Seven Stars or drown in Amaramtiam Phasis. I will hate you until the day I'm released from this hell."

I said, "I'll get you out of here. Give me a chance. There must be a way." I noticed she wasn't held by chains. Her bindings were the wretched words scratched into the walls of this tower. Not a tower, a prison. I was confused by her outrage, making me unsure of what if anything I could do to help her. I said, "Robin, I have great power over boundaries. I am the one who can open any gate, work any lock or cross any threshold." I stepped forward reaching out and grasping her frail shoulders. I was shocked by the bony feel that was in my hands. I gazed into her hate-filled eyes and gasped, "You are free of this prison now. Leave here as you please."

She said, "That's it? That's all you had to do to free me from this hell?" She backed away, eyes still flashing hate then she turned toward the opening in the wall. She looked back at me, "I know you just want things to be okay, but I promise you, they won't ever be okay. Not for me at least."

She turned away and stepped off the window's ledge and into the air. I hadn't imagined she would ever do this. I would never do this. I screamed and lunged for her but missed, hitting the floor and sliding forward toward the window and ending up teetering on the ledge of the opening. All I could do was watch as she fell. She flipped over and over, finally landing with her face looking up toward me, her eyes empty now.

I looked as her lifeless body turned into a cloud of black dust and started whirling around like a tornado. It got larger growing up toward the window where I stood. I slid back from the ledge so I wouldn't fall myself and watched as the black dust tornado grew, then seeped in through the window. It was accompanied by a low rumble. It spun around the cell with me in its vortex. Then the dust cloud just stopped. With that, the dust blew apart, back into tiny almost invisible fragments and the cold October wind that had filled this tower rose and blew her remains back out the window and into the empty night. All but her memories now lost forever from existence. I scooted further back into the chamber and felt dizzy as the weight, the desperation of her memories blew their way into my mind. They were coming as pictures. These images formed memories in my head and now I knew first hand, the horror of her capture followed by the years of lonely waiting in this tower. Waiting for me to come. Waiting for me to set her free. As the years slipped by, they had become filled with a hopelessness that lead to a hopeless hate. That hate fixated on me. It felt so wrong. It felt as if my head was being pressed together to its bursting point. Pain replaced feelings blinding my eyes. This wasn't me. Or maybe it was more that she wasn't me. Now I understood. She had only been a shadow. A shadow I had created from myself. To me, at least until now, she'd just been a backup plan. An idea I'd had at the outset of this mission. I remembered thinking if I failed to find the Palace of Starlight then maybe a shadow creature, one that was made from my spirit, might be able to locate it in The Region. It seemed a harmless idea at the time. I'd simply merge the shadow back into my spirit and then I'd know the location as well. Now I saw what I'd done. I'd just carelessly dropped her into The Region as part of this plan I was living, then forgot about her.

The pain in my head stopped and for the first time since I'd started this quest, I knew I'd found my mind and it was whole. There wasn't a doubt in my head that this plan of using a shadow of myself, a shadow to be born into The Region had been pure recklessness. By using this shadow I'd hurt a lot of people. Sloan. I understood now that he'd thought I, the Robin of Earth, was really his shadow. His Robin. He was just trying to help me. Keep me safe. I'd hurt Station too. She'd rescued this hopeless creature after demons had attacked her home. Then Station tried to protect her from The Prince of the Power of the Air himself. My shadow hadn't even recognized her and didn't trust her. That's what lead to my shadow's capture and imprisonment. I stood. I couldn't believe this. I'd played right into a finely crafted trap that The Prince had set for me. He'd planned that I would be unable to escape from this tower once I'd entered it to save the only thing I couldn't resist saving. Me.

THE LAKE OF MURDERS

I t was then that everything changed. I reeled back and fell to the floor. Thoughts formed in my head. They felt like smoke at first. I thought that there had been many times in my life when I believed I was insane, despite all my fear about being locked away in an asylum. A fear of being locked away and left to die. Now I found myself sitting on the filthy floor of a cell that had been built just for me. My own personal asylum. No sharing. No need to. Maybe there wasn't much reason to share anything at all when your mind had cracked into hundreds of unidentifiable pieces with no way to sort things out and make it better. In my cell, there were no drugs to dull my senses or therapy protocol to fill my days. There had been so many days when I'd wondered how I could ever hope to reassemble a fractured mind like mine? I looked into my memories and saw things that I'd only recently learned. Things I'd never known had existed. I faltered. How was I to know for certain that I wasn't a lunatic. Just look at how I'd grown up on Earth. Constant fear of being hit too hard, or too many times. No mother who cared. Very few friends over the years. I mean all this should qualify me for a private room at the local lunatic asylum. Right? No, not right. This place I was in wasn't a room, it was a cell. It felt like a jail cell. One without bars but still locked like you see on the TV shows. In my dreams, I had imagined that my cell was always filthy and without light. I could smell the excrement that I'd passed. There was no toilet in my cell. The only sounds I'd ever heard in my dreams were disembodied screams followed by hopeless moans. It felt like the constant background music of my life. I knew that really it was me. I was the one screaming. I was the one lying on the floor moaning as I rocked back and forth. Then I know that I'm the only one in this lunatic asylum. It was being kept open just for me. The world didn't know what else to do with Robin Randle.

But I thought, this wasn't right. This picture of my reality was wrong. I pushed in my mind and fought to block out these images. A distant thought was trying to emerge. Something about a tower. I wasn't in a cell? What was this about a tower? I thought I saw a window but then things just got dark. I tried to stand but my legs felt like rubber and I fell back onto the floor. It was how I'd felt after a night out soaking my brain with booze. What was I doing thinking about a tower? Sure, towers filled with angels right! To ever think that I was an angel. Not a day in my life had I been an angel.

Complete darkness pressed in on me. I couldn't even form a thought. Then a tiny light emerged before me. It glowed with the soft silver light of the stars and I was being pulled toward it. I struggled to get closer but kept slipping away. Things felt like they do when you'd been dreaming but now you realize you're on the edge of sleep and start struggling to wake up. Part of you wants to stay in that dream space but you know you have to wake up. Waking up is the only way to escape. I thought I needed to escape. Then suddenly I smelled the ocean. A boundary. I love boundaries. Those places that mark the end of something along with the beginning of something else. At the ocean, the beach can serve as the boundary. The very surface of the water is a boundary as well. Water serves as a literal boundary between life and death. Those creatures of the air drown in the very water loved by the creatures of the ocean. Those creatures of the ocean gasp for the oxygen that surrounds them unable to extract it from the air. Why did I love boundaries I wondered? My thinking faltered. The light before me flickered then suddenly grew bright turning from silver to the golden burning colors of a sunset. I could see the cell I was in. There was a large open window before me. I was in a tower. I understood now. The tower itself was a boundary. I stood and this time my legs didn't fail. My vision cleared.

I remembered. Robin of The Region was free and I felt that my entire being had started to change. The truth was becoming clearer. I wasn't from either Earth or The Region. I really was an angel like everyone kept telling me. I've always been an angel. The fragments of memories, the hallucinations and voices it just stopped and for the first time in what seemed like eternity my mind became quiet. I walked toward the window and looked out onto the lake. The Storm Bringer. That's right. But I felt I wasn't the storm. The storm I was to bring was Station Cross. I felt only she could end this horror created by The Prince of the Power of the Air. It wasn't the Queen of Starlight at all. She was just being used. I wondered about how I was going to do all this now? Station was surely dead to all creation. I just had to accept that and find my way forward, alone.

It didn't matter anymore. I'd lived the sin of the flesh. Human sin. For me there would be no forgiveness. That was reserved for mankind alone. Angels who sinned only had the depths of hell to embrace them at the end of time. That would surely be my fate as well. I reached for the tiny key I wore around my neck. It was still there waiting for the day I'd lock the door to hell now with me behind it. That didn't make sense, but it had to be true.

Below me near the shore of the lake burned a campfire, no a watch fire set by some unseen hand. There was no one tending it because that was my place, my fire to tend, alone.

The Prince of the Power of the Air had almost succeeded with his trap. No stronger boundary had I ever felt than the one blazed in ancient words on the walls of this tower. But, in the end he'd failed. No boundary could hold me. I spread my wings and enjoyed what now felt natural to me. Stepping out the towers window I floated down to the firelight's edge and softly landed on the forest floor. I breathed in that wonderful smell of wood smoke and listened to the gentle noises of the night that surrounded me. I stepped into the fire's brightness. I had to do one more thing before I was finished.

PART 9

IN THE PLACE OF THE UNKNOWING

(THE PLACE THAT SHOULD NOT BE)

Mary was greatly troubled at his words and wondered what kind of greeting this might be. But the angel said to her, "Do not be afraid, Mary; you have found favor with God."

Luke 1:29-30

THE ENDING TO ALL THINGS

For the first time in my life, or maybe better, for the first time since I'd started this quest, I'd felt a measure of stillness. What was once my fractured mind now seemed calm and complete. There was a knowing who I was, what I was capable of. What I needed to do. What I couldn't rid myself of was the guilt I felt. Guilt for how I'd lived my life on Earth. This guilt shot through me like the lightning and thunder it was. The sins I committed were still there and they made me feel as if I was a lost soul. In truth that didn't matter anymore. I wasn't seeking any redemption for what I was about to do. I only wanted to tell God how sorry I was.

I walked out of the firelight and stood close to the edge of the lake. I gazed down into the water. I could see through the water's surface. It looked more like glass than water. There below the lakes surface were the seven stars of this gate. Now I could see that they weren't really stars at all. Each star like point of light was actually an enormous volcano with horrific fires belching upward toward the lakes surface. It was this fire that produced the star-like image at the volcano's peak. These seven volcanoes surrounded an immense plain. In the center, I could see a structure that must have been the Palace of Starlight. The Shadow Tales told of a place that was at the end of Heaven and Earth. Its name was Beit Ha Dudo. It was a place where mountains of fire burned with eternal madness. A prison for the Watchers of Heaven. I now know what that story meant. The two hundred Watchers, those evil angels who had been led by Shemhazai. These are the angels who had landed on the summit of Mount Hermon. Shemhazai had named that place Ardis which means cursed. These were the angels who'd taken wives of human women. These are the angels who created the Nephilim. Below me I could see all of these evil angels and they were black with burns from the seven stars. I could also see the Nephilim. Giant monsters seemed to be asleep. Next to them were the women who'd given birth to these horrors.

Finally, I'd found it. My goal. This was a place of legend. A place only told about in whispers, its existence woven deeply into the fabric of the Shadow Tales. This was a forbidden place. I'd always thought that legend had told us that this place was beyond Heaven and Earth more as a metaphor for the fact that it was supposed to be unreachable. Unreachable from anywhere in all of creation. Yet here it was. Just standing beyond this gate. The Gate of the Seven Stars. Those creatures would dwell in this prison until God unmade creation. There would be no judgment for them. No hope. What a perfect place to hide the Palace of Starlight. I wondered, like the tower I'd conquered how had The Prince of the Power of the Air done this? A pointless question. As they say, the answer was well above my paygrade.

I turned away and fell to my knees before my watch fire. The last thing I wanted to do before I crossed this gate was say I'm sorry. I knew what my fate would be. I was to join these monsters forever. I would be for all eternity separated from my God and my love Station. I yelled out to God and said, "It's true Lord, I'm no better than the creatures who dwell below the surface of this lake. I too have sinned of the flesh. I failed you, my God. I failed to remain pure. I ran away from my responsibility. I sought only to gain that which was of benefit to me. I forgot You as I forgot Station Cross." Tears streaked my face and I sobbed, "I know that forgiveness is something you created for humankind. It's not for the angels. This very prison below proves it's so." I stopped. I couldn't go on.

Then there was a silence much like a cold winter night when snow had covered the land leaving a hush over God's creation. I noticed that the trees had become still as if the winds had frozen in their pathways. I looked into the fire and even its flames had been stilled in their dance. Somehow time itself had come to a stop. I felt that I was now standing outside of myself waiting for something. Then I heard a gentle voice come from the edge of the darkness just beyond the reach of the fire's flames.

It was a voice that came to me as a whisper. But in this whisper was immense power. I'd talked with Jesus and this wasn't Him. But still I knew it was Him but in the form of the Holy Spirit. This was a part of God I'd never experienced. It felt it was a part of God not meant for the angels. The voice whispered, "My strong and brave angel. You took the mantle of humanity. Something the angels are not meant to do. Yet you willingly stepped into this world. Did you think that while you were in human form, you'd be any less able to avoid the failures and sins than the humans themselves? Forgiveness is a grace imparted to those who walk by faith while knowing perfection is beyond their reach. You, my Robin, have walked by that very faith. You may have felt lost but I promise you, you never were. You have always been living for this moment. I tell you, forgiveness from your sin is a gift that I give you. You will share this with mankind. Be at peace my angel. Go now about your task and sin no more."

A gentle breeze returned, blowing and stirring up the campfire making the flames jump as the tree branches began to wave. The moment was over yet it had felt like eternity. I couldn't believe it but I was still loved. I felt deeply cleansed. A feeling like I hadn't had since before this all started. I turned back toward the lake, I thought I saw a tall figure standing near the water's edge. I gasped, "Station?" But there was nothing. No reply. It was just shadows playing against even deeper shadows that surrounded the lake. I saw a lone black bird flying in the night. A raven maybe. I smiled. I knew better than to hope but I would gladly take a sign of good luck. I knew it was all on me now. I approached the black still water and another raven flew out of the darkness of the lake. I flinched thinking it was heading right at me but it turned away and circled back into the darkness. I heard its call as it reappeared out over the water and impossibly turned white. I'd only seen a white raven once in my life. It was when the ravens entered the Hall of Stars. They came to save me from an attack. That was when the Queen of Starlight wanted to kill me. That had been so long ago. I knew now that I had no real idea of how long ago that had been. How long have I been doing this? I don't think I'll ever know.

That thought made me long for Station. The raven was her symbol. She had told me that once. She had said that it was a symbol of freedom. It seemed so natural to me. I could stand before the city gates and keep them locked or I could make them fall open. I was the guard at the crossroads. The limits imposed on all living things didn't apply to me. I could fly into the air then dive into the ocean without fear of death. Station told me once that the raven was a symbol of eternal life. That ravens also bore some of my liminal powers. She'd told me that ravens could open any door. Just like me. I wondered now, was that true? Oh, if that were only true. I sighed. That had been another life. My only love had taken that hateful blade meant for me. Her last act was to save my life. How I wished that I could've saved hers instead. I watched as the white raven slowed and circling the lake's surface seemed to disappear. That was it. Now it was time. Time for me to open the gate that can't be opened. It was time for me to go where no angel was meant to tread.

CROSSING THE GATES OF DUSK AND DAWN

I approached the lake's edge and pondered the stillness of its waters. I could see clearly now that what I'd thought was water, always thought was water wasn't water at all. There had never been any water in this lake. It had been an illusion created to hide this gate. I could tell that the name I'd given this lake only helped hide the truth about the secret realm below its surface. Makes sense. This is a place no one was ever to go. I smiled. And who would have ever thought that the gate to a place that was beyond Heaven and Earth would be on Earth and in the Muir Woods no less. I had to see the truth of this place if I was ever to enter this realm. I let my mind drift as I gazed into the water. I let my eyes drift focus as well. I reached out with my liminal powers and probed what looked like the water's surface. That surface disappeared the space just filled with darkness then a blaze formed and I saw them. The Gate of the Seven Stars was actually made up of two gates. Each had its own name. They were the Gates of Dusk and Dawn. They were used as a single way in and a single way out. The best way to keep someone from just crashing through a door was to make it so the door disappeared once you came through. If you knew you couldn't go back out the way you'd just come in maybe you wouldn't try to enter through that door at all.

I stood still centering myself then raised my hands holding my staff in my right, my Athame in my belt. I said, "I will open these gates and enter this wicked place." I recited the ancient words told only in the Shadow Tales. Words crafted in the distant past. When I'd first heard them, I had no idea that they'd been created just for me to use. I continued, "At the Gate of Dusk I stand, I pray God guard me with your right Hand. Guide me through the crossing blight, deep into this wicked night. Then once done I beg You Lord, guide me from this forsaken land to Your Gate of Dawn, from the beauty of my night into the Glory of Your Light."

As I finished these words the glass-like surface of the lake turned to sand and wind came from below the sand and blew it up into the air before me. The wind blew the sand into itself shrinking the sand as it blew harder. Then a flash blazed across the valley floor blinding me for a moment. As my vision returned the surface of the lake was gone. Now there was an impossible hole in the earth before me. I gazed down into this hole at the valley floor spiraling what must have been tens of thousands of feet below me. The stench of sulfur and the heat from the volcanos assailed me. I turned away and looked one last time at the magnificent trees that spread through the valley and into the darkness. I enjoyed the cool night air as it caressed my skin. With a slight effort, I pushed and spread my wings then I stepped off what had been the shore of the Lake of Murders. For just a moment I passed through the gates. This was a place that didn't belong to either where I'd been or where I was going. A liminal space locked and unpassable unless you had an angel to guide you. I know now that I am that angel. My liminal powers allow me to be the helper to others needing to pass from one place to another.

In The Region there are thousands, maybe millions of angels that guide the human's soul from their death to a place in Heaven. My liminal powers extended far beyond that. I had to let that moment go as I started to glide down into this forbidden land. It looked as if I had to descend a million miles before I would reach the valley floor.

When I entered this realm everything around me changed. A tepid wind blasted by me as I descended. All vestiges of that horror-filled and frozen wind that had been created inside the heart of the black tower were gone. Now there was only the stink of hidden dying things and the heat from the seven volcanoes. A heat sent from a hell that would never open its gates for the wretched creatures of this realm. The stink grew as I glided nearer to the ground. It reminded me of the dumpster back of Mel's All Night Diner. What a strange thought. I flew in arcs gliding back and forth studying the land below searching for the best place to land. There was a dread that came over me. There was something here that was a part of me. How could that be? I feared the touch of the ground but I knew there would be no avoiding it. I looked up into this new sky and found a full moon shedding its lifeless light into the air and soaking the land below in a silver that seemed old like tarnished candle stick holders. I could see the Palace of Starlight. It was sitting in a huge meadow separated from all the hopeless creatures of this realm. I aimed for that meadow but didn't want to land in the open. I quickly slipped down in the air picking a spot of darkness on the meadows edge then slowed my descent and gently stepped out of the air landing on what felt like sticky yet solid ground. I silently folded my wings back into my body. Then I jerked my staff apart and created my two torches. I held them up high so I could see what hid in the horrid darkness that now surrounded me.

It appeared that my good fortune was still traveling with me. I'd landed right next to one of the wicked giants. A Nephilim. The smell was that of vomit mixed with blood - a mixture that could never be cleaned up. I looked at this giant. He seemed to be sleeping. I spoke with my best commanding type voice, "Wicked creature spawned from sin, I command you to tell me your name."

At first, I was only met with silence. I wondered if this creature had been rendered unconscious by some unseen force. I stepped closer my feet sticking to what felt like blood soaked ground. Then the giant stirred, looking as if every movement caused him great pain. "I am Og."

I asked, "Do you mean to harm me Og?"

The giant groaned and rolled away from me. The ground shook with his movement. In a voice that sounded more like scraping stones than what I'd expected from a living creature, Og said, "No harm could I do even if I wanted to. My life is spent and now I rest in the horrid torment of this prison for my sins. Be off, angel. No creature from this land can harm you. We are the forsaken. We are the ones beyond hope."

I was shocked by his words. The creatures of this realm provided no resistance to my quest. I knew that not far from where I stood was The Palace of Starlight. How did The Prince move this structure into this forbidden land? One more mystery to add to my never-ending list. All around me I could hear the keening of these wicked creatures. They suffered in this prison. I thought that this would be their home forever. Even with the evil they'd brought to humanity, I still felt pity for them.

Knowing what Og had just told me I thought I should be safe yet there was a terrible fear building inside of me. I was repulsed by these misshapen creatures and worried they might still have enough hatred deep in their hearts to take action against one very small angel. I felt the need to be careful as I picked my way through the littered bodies.

Then there was a violent suddenness in the air around me. The sky had changed above my head. I looked up to see that it was now late in the afternoon on a cloudless day. I stepped from behind the last giant that blocked my progress and found that I now stood on the open meadow leading down toward the Palace of Starlight. I could see the tips of its towers. A warm summer-like breeze started blowing my hair into my face. It stung my eyes. I reached up and pushed my hair back into some semblance of order. Now I'd learned that it wasn't the creatures of this prison I needed to fear. I wasn't the only one that held a key to this gate. I heard this awful scream. It was followed by a shattering blast of lightning that struck the ground all around me. I tried to cover my ears before the thunder exploded but it never came. I walked forward and found myself standing in a meadow that was sloping down and away from me. I knew this place. I remembered that I'd never seen a meadow like this before. I looked around now seeing it for the first time with my waking eyes. It was filled with waist-high grass as green as new spring leaves and as the wind blew this grass started swaying like hula girls at a late afternoon luau on Waikiki. This was my horrid dream from before this all had started. Before I'd left Mason. That recurring nightmare. It hadn't been a nightmare at all but a vision. A vision of my future sent to help me face the coming monster and maybe live. In my nightmare, I never lived. I search my mind thinking. How was I to use this.

Looking up I knew what I would see. Storm clouds were rolling in from off the horizon, spinning and tumbling like a wicked ocean reaching out a warning just ahead of its hurricane. The clouds were changing color from a steel-like gray to a boiling black with lightning flashing highlights into their creases. This storm carried an evil. Maybe I'd been wrong in thinking the angels could conquer this evil. Now I thought only God could fight this coming monster. I felt fear as it rode on the tips of the wind. This storm looked as if it was fighting inside itself. Tearing itself apart then reforming darker and more violent than ever. I knew it was bringing something powerful and wicked and it was coming on fast. The lightning flashed budding from the clouds like small flowers then exploding into blossoms that grew across the length of the entire sky casting a searing white light that blinded me. Then finally, there was the thunder. It was a thunder that could only have been born at the center of the earth. Everything shook. I stumbled backwards as the grass around me was blown as flat as a dirt road then I was shaken to the ground.

I had hated this damn nightmare. I used to have it every night before Sloan came. Then it had stopped.

I hadn't even thought about it since then. Now I needed to search my memory for a clue to how to survive this. I knew without a doubt that this storm was bringing a horror left over from the ancient times before the chaos had ended. These were ages I could not remember because I hadn't been created yet. I'd been told the stories but I felt they weren't going to have done this creature justice. I'd been told that there was a time when these monsters fought for their right to be a god but now they exist only as echoes in the imagination of man. I was on my back. I opened my eyes and my vision cleared. I scrambled to my feet and looked up into this raging storm and saw what I feared was coming. A horror torn from the pages of some ancient and forgotten manuscript not meant for the eyes of man. It had a bulbous-shaped head that seemed to stretch out for miles across the sky as it pressed down out from the boiling clouds. A black face formed on the surface of the creature's head and what began to grow and hang from it looked like a hundred wild black snakes whipping around with a mass uncontrolled purpose. I looked for some kind of shelter but I knew there wouldn't be any. The top of the towers of the Palace were visible to me but the Palace was too far away. I knew I wouldn't make it. I'm sure other traps waited for me there anyway. Not an option, so I just stood there frozen in my terror. Then looking back up into the sky I saw the coming snakes and knew it was me who was to become their purpose. These wild black snakes began to resolve themselves into tentacle like appendages dripping with some kind of heavy black oil that was beginning to rain down on me. Where this oil landed, it burned through my clothes and started to burn my skin as well. It burned my arm like I'd just held it over an open flame. The tentacles reached up toward the heavens, then turn falling back toward the ground, and me. They dropped from the sky like lightning. Just like in my dream There wouldn't have been time for me to hide even if I could have found shelter. These tentacles were just there and reaching out toward me. They looked like long broken fingers bending in impossible and horrid ways. They reached out and stroked my face then each probing finger split in two and created even more dripping black fingers for this monster to use. It began to caress my waist. The tentacles tightened and held me captive so I could be painted by its sticky black oil. They ranged all over my entire body. Everywhere they touched there was pain like hot grease. The black oil penetrated into my skin causing blisters to rise and erupt oozing more of the black oil from my own body. It smelled like a hundred dead and decomposing rats left in the walls of an old house long abandoned.

The creature's face began to grow a deep-set pair of eyes that ignited and burned a red as red as a setting summer sun. I think that they longed to burn holes right through me with the power blazing from their black distorted sockets. These eyes spewed hate. That hate was all I could feel. A hate just because I was here and still alive to witness this monsters' birth. A hate that let me know that when I'd been a human girl I just should have died when my dad had tried to beat me to death. I couldn't believe this but I actually began to feel remorse. I thought I really should have let myself die at the hospital. I shouldn't have slept in that brain-dead coma. If I'd just died then this monster wouldn't have had to waste its time coming here today to kill me.

It was just when I'd thought this that a deeper darkness opened in the monster's face right below its eyes. Inside this new and growing darkness, I could see stars. Midnight had come to that one spot. An evil midnight for sure, full of dark matter and black star dust filling the space between all the dead angels and dying suns all of this born in a distant age. It was the age when creation had only happened a moment ago. I know this sounds crazy but it did seem as if these stars had been waiting for me. Waiting for me to see them since their birth just so I would know all was out of whack with both space and time. I felt these stars. They were watching me, knew me and now they had learned the truth. I was the one who'd cheated death once. Now I was being called upon to settle that debt. The tentacles encased my body and reached up and tightened around my throat choking me with their oily stench. I gasped for air but found I could no longer breathe. A sadness passed through me. I thought, I would never know the wonder of drawing a breath again. The light faded from my eyes and I could feel a distant pain somewhere in my body but I could no longer tell where it was coming from. My life was slipping away. I had only moments left. I wondered at how a life was nothing more than a collection of these moments and now mine were done.

The creature lifted its head and looked toward the sky vomiting lightning that arched upward then turned back toward the ground. With that lightning came a horrible scream followed by deafening thunder. The world around me was growing darker but not from its own darkness, this was a darkness from within me. It was my life force, my angelic being slipping into death. Amidst the pain from the burning oil I smiled. Now I understood why I had to be the Storm Bringer. I knew Station could have handled this creature. But for me, I felt helpless. Again, it raised its head and looking toward the sky lightning screamed out, it arched into the sky and curved back toward the ground almost striking me. I thought that lightning wasn't supposed to do that. After it hit near me the ground shook with such force the creature released its grip on my body. I fell backwards onto my butt burning with the pain from the black oil painted all over me. Holes were burned in my dress. I writhed back and forth hoping somehow to put out the fire that was ripping into me. I saw the two unlit torches of my staff on the ground next to me. I realized I still had my Athame but what good would that small dagger do against such an abomination? To have come all this way, to have suffered so much, to have lost so much, only to fail. I could just hear my Earth dad yelling at me about how I was a wretched waste of DNA. Maybe it was true. I was good for nothing now. Dad would have been proud.

I looked up at the monster and above his head at the edge of the sky I saw that white raven again. Maybe it had followed me through the gate when it was open. The raven was being trailed by what looked like hundreds or maybe thousands of black creatures whirling and twisting their way down toward me. I couldn't make out what they were. What was this next horror to be? The ancient monster that had been attacking me seemed transfixed by the spiraling cloud of black so I stumbled to my feet fighting through the pain that enveloped my body. I could tell that the cloud was coming closer to me and it wasn't really a cloud at all. It was an enormous flock of black birds. They were ravens. Station had told me that the raven holds mystery and contradictions. A portent of death and a powerful symbol of war. Over the endless ages, the raven had been part of the mythology of the Celts and the Norse. Even to this day people remember the name Morrígan. She was thought to be a Celtic goddess but I knew better. The Irish called her Mór-ríoghain, The Great Queen borrowing on my own three form reality.

The ravens swirled and descended closer to the monster. They spun around in great circles creating a living storm. They were calling out together their intrepid "Kaw, kaw, kaw." The sound became deafening and brought the horrid monster before me to a standstill. He'd become silent, just watching as the ravens flew into a circle around his head. They drew their circle tighter like a noose. The white raven dove into the mass of black birds and was gone.

The ravens stopped and drew together like one animal then exploded, no longer were they birds, now they looked more like leaves as they fell to the ground. Like the fall leaves shed from the trees at the coming of winter. They swirled in the air and then engulfed me bringing with them that distant smell of a fall that seemed a lifetime ago when dusty leaves haunted the streets of Mason back when all this had begun. Some of these black leaves came to rest on the ground around me and a few had stuck to my body. Where the leaves touched me the oil and the burns it had created disappeared. More leaves covered me until I felt I'd become buried in them. Then they dropped away from me and all the black leaves around me turned to dust and blew away on the wind. I stood stunned. The pain was gone. I had been healed. Given a second chance. I had to use it. I grabbed the parts of my staff and snapped them back together. Looking back up into the sky I could see what had been revealed with the passing of the black cloud. It was an angel, wings spread and a mighty sword in her hand. She tried to thrust the sword into the monster's neck but she wasn't able to get close enough to do it. Now that the ring of ravens was gone the monster became focused on his attacker. The creature seemed to be directing its lightning to create a shield that it held between the angel and itself. I looked around. I had to help somehow. Then I noticed that the sun was beginning to set. What a wonderful gift.

I hold power over all liminal places. A powerful place that most humans never thought of was the very dusk and dawn used to build the gates I'd utilized to enter this land. At dusk, you are neither in day nor in night. It is in that space a boundary can be made. I needed to put this creature in its own space then seal it off from me. Right as the sun sets, I can do that. I stood still breathing deeply relaxing my body, I closed my eyes and centered my spirit. It was fortunate the angel above me was keeping this monster occupied so I could do this but that wouldn't last much longer. I opened my eyes and watched as the sun touched the horizon. This was my moment. I sunk my spirit into the dusk that surrounded me. The liminal powers flooding through me felt like a raging river bounded by steep canyon walls. Amazing. I had a deep sense of control over everything that existed around me. I could feel the connections. I was connected to the grass in the meadow and the soil it grew in. I was connected to all the prisoners held in this realm. I could feel the trees and even the clouds in the sky. I could even sense the toll boxes trapped in the Palace of Starlight but the Palace felt strange like it was something that was out of place. I found the monster before me and I raised my staff and took from the power of the dusk and spun it up like a cocoon encasing the monster. I looked up and saw that the angel hadn't been trapped in this cocoon. I closed my eyes again and lifted this creature that had been sent to kill me into the dusk itself and there it will be trapped until time is undone. I slumped, exhausted. The angel above me slowly descended and it was then that I could see beyond my wildest dreams that precious smile that could only belong to Station Cross. I was dumb struck. Words just wouldn't form in my head.

Station looked at me then laughed. She said, "Did you think I would sit out a chance to bring all this to an end?"

I stuttered, "But how? I thought I'd lost you. That you were gone beyond my reach."

Station walked toward me and turned serious. "Long story. We have a mission to finish." I knew she was right. Mystery or not, she had returned to me, a miracle I'd never anticipated. I had to accept it. I walked up to her and lightly kissed her lips. "As always, you're right. Then let's end this." I took her hand and with my staff in the other started toward the Palace of Starlight. It was night again. That liminal moment of dusk now gone until dawn takes its place. A moon was back in the sky painting the meadow in ghostly silver light. Enough light to easily see our way to the Palace. As we approached it, I noticed there were no roads leading in or out. No liminal spaces of any kind. If the Palace had a boundary, I couldn't see it or feel it.

Then we came to a stop. Before me loomed a place I thought I'd never see again. The last time I'd visited here I'd barely escaped with my life. And that was my human life. Before us stood the Palace of Starlight. It wasn't the glittering wonder that I'd seen before. Now it was dark. It was filled with the memories of all ambitions lost. The Palace was abandoned with hopelessness circling it like a spell of protection. I knew it really wasn't abandoned. There had to be at least one creature lurking inside. Its caretaker. The Queen of Starlight. Station said, "Here we are once more. Now let's end this. Ready?"

I replied, "This time, yes!"

We entered the Palace. I was stunned. The last time I was here the interior shined with brilliance. The Hall of Stars seemed to lift up miles above my head. This place wasn't built using human geometry. Wormwood had spun more of his tricks making a palace that grew as space was needed. Now the only light afforded us was the soft silver light emitted from the globes that were deeply trapped within its walls. Station called out a challenge, "Queen of Starlight! If you still exist, we've come to end you and your

Prince's plans. Speak!"

I heard something stir in the air before me. It looked as if each individual piece of dust in this immense chamber had begun to glow with a faint blue light. Millions of pinprick points of light filled the air raising up hundreds of feet into the unknown reaches of this place. They spread across the hall from where I stood to the far wall maybe fifty yards away. I said to Station, "What is this?"

Station drew her sword and moved away from me circling toward the far wall. "I have no idea. Whatever it is Robin, it's not good." She silently disappeared into the gloom. I could only watch and wait as the points of light started a slow spin inside the hall pulling together in a mass that looked like a spiral galaxy floating in the vast reaches of the universe. Then sound began to invade the hall. The sound of the ocean. That recurrent sound of the ocean lifting itself up towards the boundaries of land. Always lapping at the rocks and beaches that guard these boundaries trying to gain some purchase. Erode the liminal space between them. This made me wonder again just how The Prince had brought this palace into this forbidden realm. When we'd approached the Palace, I hadn't noticed any of the typical markers that are always left behind to define what is the Palace and what is not. Stones circling the building or a road. A foot path even. I thought how Macy had used salt to make a circle around herself in an attempt to define her space safe from the demons. There had to be something to define where we were except the Palace's walls.

I turned and walked back out of the Palace and onto

the land surrounding it. I looked for any telltale signs of demarcation. The massive stone walls looked as if they had been placed into the ground not set upon a foundation. I couldn't find any trace of a sign that this building truly sat in this realm beyond Heaven and Earth. Maybe that was why I couldn't sense any connection to it when I'd opened the liminal space before. What trick was The Prince using here. I went back into the Palace and was greeted by a fifty-foot-tall image of a person that looked vaguely like the Queen of Starlight. Her body was composed entirely of the pinpoint bits of blue light. When I'd entered this entity turned to greet me. It spoke. "Robin. I have been waiting so long to see you again. She gestured to the room. You can see things aren't as beautiful as they were last time you were here. I blame Station Cross for that. Anger filled her visage as she swept her arms around the room yet she didn't move from its center.

I said, "Station Cross was doing her duty. She ended you the day I left."

The Queen cackled, "It looks to me like she didn't do a very good job. Stick with the task until it's done, I always say. That bitch didn't even return here with you. How pathetic." She didn't know Station had already entered the Palace. I was sure she waited ready to leap into action.

I said, "I'm here to unbind this place. Release the toll boxes back to their owners."

She said, "Oh daughter of mine, I think you'll find that quite an impossible task. This Palace of Starlight is anchored well in its place. What's left of my tattered spirit being bound to it."

Anger flared inside me, "The last time I was in this place I was broken. An angel bound in human form that had lost all memory of her life or mission. Today I'm far from that." I paused then said, "Listen well you shade of a creature. I am not your daughter any more than you were ever a Queen. You have been lied to and manipulated in everything you've done. You have never been anything more than a shadow. The child you had was only a shadow as well. On the other hand, I am a very real angel. I'm not afraid of you or your Prince. Now that I am whole, I am a very powerful angel, despite my size. All liminal places belong to me including those of this forsaken realm. You've lost but I will do you a favor. I will end you for all time."

The Queen seemed to summon power from the space surrounding me. I could feel a prickling of the hairs on the back of my neck. The hazy image before me pulled together becoming dark then it emitted a flash that felt like looking into the sun. It was so sudden I was blinded by her actions. A screaming sound filled the air that was so loud that covering my ears had no impact. I dropped my staff and stumbled to my knees. This was too much. I could feel blood coming from my nose then tasted its coppery flavor as it had made its way into my mouth. I wasn't going to lose to this monster. I grabbed my staff and used it to stumble to my feet. I turned away from her and opened my eyes clearing the brightness from them. I'd had it. This had all gone on too long. I turned back toward the Queen and raised my staff. I yelled into the screams from the Queen, "May the fires of God dispel you!" A bright golden flame grew above my staff. It was the firelight of my God and it leapt from the tip of my staff toward the dark mass before me. The Queen burst into blue flames that rose with sudden violence toward the infinite ceiling then vanished. The screaming sounds stopped. It was silent. As the fire died, she turned into the same black dust that her daughter had become and the dust rose into the air on a tornado wind cold with ice and death. It blew through the Palace, taking with it the ashes of her shadow's life. She was gone. I thought, wow, I was the Storm Bringer. Death did ride at my heels. I'd been the one to finally put an end to this desperation. I wiped the blood from my face and moved toward the center of the Palace and pulled my staff into its two torches. Both leapt to life bringing a true white light to the darkness of this place.

Station appeared from across the hall, "That was impressive. Guess you finally got your mojo back."

I laughed then said, "Station, I don't think this building is even here. I think it's all an illusion created to trick me. If I were to try and move this structure back into The Region I might actually die in the effort. I bet the real Palace is still back in The Region. I feel the walls of this place are only illusions built in the liminal space surrounding the toll boxes. I can feel the toll boxes. It must be the humanness in me. I guess that's something I'll carry forever. I want to do that. The toll boxes are here only the Palace is not." I turned toward the great Hall of Starlight and said, "Palace of Starlight, be gone. Free these toll boxes and never again return."

The walls of the Palace faded to mist and millions upon millions of beautiful globes pulsing with bright white light streamed together following each other into the air and spreading wide like a river then waited. I could see that where they waited an opening in the sky had formed. It was an opening in the fabric of this horrid realm. All that was needed was a guide to show the way.

Station and I held hands and spread our wings. We rose into the air and flew toward the head of this living river. I had to lead it to freedom. As I took my place, I could feel all the hope that had been freed. It washed over me like a healing bath full of love. Soon we came to the opening in the sky above the valley floor. It was a hole being held open for us by Gabriel and Michael. They smiled at us as we passed from that place that stood beyond Earth and Heaven back into The Region. We landed at the edge of the Southern Ocean, the very place where I had started my journey through The Region. I took in a deep breath of the salt sea air and fell to my knees touching the sand to make sure it was real. Station reached out to me, helping me back to my feet. Looking up I saw the river of toll boxes returning to The Region.

Station said, "My love, my Robin, do you think maybe we've earned a little time of respite?"

We both laughed. It was a moment of true wonder. A moment of peace. For the first time, I knew I was finally home.

ASK FIRST THE HOLY

THE JOURNALS OF MACY BEAS

NOVEMBER 31ST, 2010 - 12:00 Z

I don't know why I keep writing in this stinking journal but it sure has become a habit. I start every journal entry with 'My name is Macy Beas.' Silly. Stupid really. I think I'm afraid pages will get torn out or something or the journal will get freakin' destroyed. If at least a few pages remain they will have my name on them. A little evidence I once existed. That's probably it. I need people to know I was here. Don't we all? When I die I want proof I lived a life no matter how freakin' strange. Any day could be my last and I know that. I should stop this but I can't. Shit, I sure live an unusual life. Probably most would say I need to be locked up in an institution. That's because they don't understand what the fuck is going on in the world. They're ignorant of spiritual things that don't fit neatly into their freakin' faith. I'm just sayin'.

That makes me think of when I was nineteen and found out for myself, and boy, that was a hell of a shock. That's a different story for another time so I'll write it later someday. Shit, maybe it'll just leak out. Who knows.

Today is the first day of October. This will be my busiest month. Always is. I think that's because people are more freakin' open to what's real. Halloween or the coming of Halloween or something scares them. I don't blame them for being scared. I'm scared too. Every single day I'm scared. That's why I write this journal. I have this odd idea that if I write it down maybe somehow that will help me forget and be more at peace. Honestly, it doesn't at all but shit it's such a habit I can't help it. Here's a secret. I think if I write every day I won't die. It's the day I don't write that will be my last. Boy how fucked up is that? I guess I'm paranoid and that's enough of a reason to see a doctor. After what I've seen; what I've done, I think I have every reason to be paranoid. There ain't no doc who could help Miss Macy Beas.

I just rolled into to Mason, Texas. Stopping for lunch at the Willow Creek Cafe. I picked It for a reason. It's right next door to the Chamber of Commerce Visitor Center and I figure they'll have a free city map. Then you know what? Oh yah, time to kill me a demon. I've said this a million times. No one thinks demons are real until they meet themselves one. Then they get the freakin' shit scared out of them. "Oh, I understand now." Then somehow, they find me. I think mostly by Web search. Isn't that where everyone goes when they need a demon hunter. That's it, Macy Beas—Demon Hunter—really, I should get business cards.

I don't know. Demon hunter does sound strange, but I call it as it is. Seeing that vail all around me that divides our world from whatever that other world is creeps me out at times. Mostly things stay on their proper side, but today in Mason there's a creature I call a demon that has crossed that line and needs to go the fuck back. I always tell the client, "I felt the monster move under me. Demons when they die have nothing else to lose and that's the truth all plain and simple." Like shit. Morons don't ever understand you can't kill the dead and the demons. Yea the freakin' lies I have to tell.

I don't think that's completely true but I sure know the people I help don't want to hear the truth. Wow, today is going to be bad. Going to see Mrs. Elvira

Mullins to cast out or bind a class four demon. Maybe it's the fourth Mansion. I don't know but I keep trying to learn more. The great mystics have written book after book, grimoires they call them, full of bullshit. People think it's all true. Boy do those fuckers have something to learn. They have about ten percent and that's it. All I know is the ruler of this demon is Stolas and he is one very freakin' wicked dude, but I have a long-standing grudge to settle with him.

This will be my third go at Stolas but I think I'm ready this time. I have his binding sigil. Just so I have a record, what I need to do is call up Stolas then banish him beyond the gates of Hell. Sounds simple enough. Wish it was. I'm going to earn my $15,000 today. I have some fish's liver and fish's heart so I should be good to go. What I know for sure, is things never work out the way they are freakin' supposed to. Oh shit, I bet this will be just the most freakin' greatest time of my life. One thing I know, this time Stolas goes down. I've been hunting him to settle my score and today he will meet the true Macy Beas. He'll wish he killed me when he had the chance. - Δ

NOVEMBER 31ST, 2010 - 13:00 Z

My name is Macy Beas. I'm sitting outside Mrs. Mullins' house in Mason, Texas. Went to the visitor center and they did have maps. I also found out Fred Gipson was from Mason. I loved Old Yeller. I'll have to find a copy when I get home and reread it. I have my kit ready. I'm supposed to purify myself. This journal is part of that process. You know, when you meet me you'll find I don't talk like I write. I mean I don't curse around people and it's a bad idea around demons too. So, I get it all out here. Need to someplace. Cleans my soul. God, I just want to be done with this. I guess if that's going happen I have to get going. I Just want whoever reads this, that's if anyone ever does read this, to know I got this far. Now I'll see if I make it back. - Δ

NOVEMBER 31ˢᵀ, 2010 - 16:23 Z

My name is Macy Beas. I met Mrs. Mullins. She looks like everyone's grandmother. Short and a little bit round she had a flowery house dress on and her gray hair was held together with bobby pins. Really the only thing we shared in common were horned rimmed glasses. Hers kind of brown and mine thick and black. Mine fit my goth nature. What else can I be? With the life I live and job I do being a goth is just part of the package. Shit, just give me crap and you can keep the demon.

Today I'm wearing black leggings with a very short lacy kind of black skirt and a very tight black t-shirt. You can get away with that when you have tiny tits. I think it all goes well with my jet-black hair; all natural. No black lipstick today just deep deep red. Oh and my glasses. Black horned rimmed of course. All the black is a real contrast to my pale skin. The T is long sleeved so almost all my pasty pale skin is covered. Except my face.

Yup Mrs. Mullins and I make a great pair. Tonight, I spent the time eating one of her home cooked meals.

Funny. I never cook. I don't know how so this is like the first home cooked meal I've had in months. This was the best kind of home cooking too, fried chicken! You'd think with all the crap I eat I wouldn't be thin, but genes are on my side.

Mrs. Mullins described the problems she's having. There seems to be something trolling around that's literally wrecking the house. It also is suspected to have killed her little poodle Ellie. Ellie was just a year old and one day she suddenly became listless. She wouldn't eat or drink, just whimpers in the corner of the kitchen. Ellie was declining so rapidly Mrs. Mullins grabbed her up and drove her over to the vet but Ellie was dead before she got there.

"Did the vet determine the cause of death?"

Mrs. Mullins said, "He said he'd never seen anything like it. I mean the dog got sick at about ten in the morning and by one she was dead. The vet said maybe some rapid progressing parasite but after he did an autopsy there wasn't anything. He said she looked like she just aged fourteen years in a few hours."

"They autopsy dogs?" Boy that's a new one on me.

"The vet said because of the possibility of a dangerous parasite he had to."

You see, the way to handle a demon is with circles, seals, and what is known as Angel Magic. The last is the best but nobody can make it work. Except me of course. Now learning Angel Magic that's another whole story. It sounded like Mrs. Mullins had a freakin' demon around. For sure. That calls for my bag of tricks.

"Mrs. Mullins would you mind leaving for a couple of hours?"

"I'm not sure dear. I don't mean to be rude but I just met you."

There's always that freakin' excuse to deal with. I dangled my car keys and said, "Take my car. Then we each have something to lose." Fastest way to trust. "This is going to get messy and I don't want you to get hurt."

She considered the offer for a moment and decided I could be trusted! Really what she's decided was, she wants rid of the demon. She took my keys and grabbed her purse. Stopping at the front door she turned and said, "Be careful, dear." With that she was gone. Now to find this demon.

Just for the record, that's if someone is reading this, the whole exorcism things is way overrated. Works on people pretty well but that's about it. No worry. I never worry. This is what I was made for. If my numbers up it's freakin' up.

First, I have to flush this demon out. Then I have to bind him so he can't hurt me. With that done I send him back to where ever demons live. Now when this guy shows up he's supposed to be a raven or something probably funny looking. I mean will this thing even look scary? That's why I get lazy. I know better. Never skip a step. I always say that. I should have put the fish heart on the stove and boiled it. But do I follow my own rules? Freakin' bet I don't and that's going to end this all one day. So, I start, "In nomine Patris, et Filii, et Spiritus Sancti." I cross myself and continue, "GLORIA Patri, et Filio, et Spiritui Sancto. Sicut erat in principio, et nunc, et semper, et in saecula saeculorum. Amen."

I opened my kit and took out my bottle of Holy

Water. Placing a small amount in my hand I flicked water in all directions. That's when the trouble started. The Holy Water is scattered to prepare the area. I mean these are the freakin' things they left out of the damn grimoires. At least the ones that I have.

Right before me this black smoke begins to just form out of the air. It was getting thicker and darker with a kind of swirl to it. I freakin' didn't like this! Nothing supposed to be happening yet. The black cloud reeked of burning flesh. I stumbled backward and couldn't help but throw up. Mrs. Mullins is going to be so happy about that! I steadied myself and reached into my jean's pocket and pulled out my trusty protection amulet. It's like a silver dollar except when I made it I inscribed the Grand Pentacle of Solomon on both sides. It's supposed to fend off evil spirits and draw good ones. I just love all these symbols and markings. I always wonder who made them up? I'm sure not Solomon. I tossed the amulet just in front of me and the smoke solidified into a raven as big as me.

Wow one freakin' big bird and mean looking. Not at all like my drawing. It proceeded making raven sounds and stepped toward me but stopped short of the amulet. Stolas was very upset at me. His wings were flapping all over and I just knew he was gonna break something and Mrs. Mullins would be pissed. I needed my protection amulet but I'd left it in my bag. I wasn't sure if the Solomon sigil would work where my bag was. There wasn't much choice. Boy I'm stupid. I always put my John Dee Amulet around my neck just in case and now it was just in case and it's in my bag.

I started inching toward my kit and the Raven kept a tight bead on me. Every time I'd move he'd start the squawking again. The noise was unnerving but the gashes in the wood floors were much worse. That was a clear sign this freakin' demon wanted to kill me. I got on my knees and started leaning toward my kit trying to catch it by its handle. I leaned a little too far and my balance faltered. I fell flat on my face. Suddenly I had an enormous beak slam down almost hitting my head. I mean I freakin' felt my hair move.

Panicked I scrambled back toward the protection of my amulet then noticed somewhere in all that I'd grabbed my kit. I plopped down on my butt and pulled out my Dr. Dee amulet and put it on then pulled out my case that held my full set of sigils. I opened it and grabbed a Key of Solomon amulet made for the 1st pentacle of the Moon. This one opens doors and I needed a door bad. No binding sigil would do. I placed it on the sacred floor in front of me. I know the words by heart.

I said, "Gohol Odzamrah." That sort of means, "I say appear." The raven became still and the dark shape kind of melted into a manlike looking monster. All black except his fire red eyes. He was trying to pierce me with them. I could tell he hated me with every fabric of his demon being. He did want me dead.

I got to say I was scared this time. This was a real mean dude. He spoke in that velvety speech demons always use, "You have become known Macy Beas. You should be more careful. There are ones who want to eat your soul." I didn't like this but I couldn't show this fucker I was scared. Fear is the mind killer.

I simply answered, "Stolas, today is my turn to live and your turn to die. For my parents I say, Gohol Ipamis Oisalam Gohon Lad Caiman." The effect was immediate. He screamed loud enough to break the windows. Then my door opened and he was gone. I stayed very still. I don't trust any of this magic type stuff. The words are Angelic and mean something like, "I say you cannot be in this house. I have spoken in the name of God forever." I think it's not so much the word choice or order but just the fact it's Angelic. That scares them.

I heaved a sigh and picked up my amulets and put the Holy Water away. This was a close one. I'm just getting sloppy. I needed to burn the sigil of Stolas in the house so I took the one I'd drawn on virgin parchment and burned it in the fireplace. I didn't know what to do about the two shattered windows and damaged floor. I'll just give Mrs. Mullins a discount. $10K; full warranty never to return.

I'd learned very early on that there isn't anything like magic. There's just here and there and some symbols act as keys and open doors or forces the demon into some action. The real driver was the Angelic language. Learning it was a bitch. You know they didn't have like Spanish, French, and Angelic classes in school. I don't even know where the language came from. I've never seen an angel. Not a single one. - Δ

OCTOBER 3RD 2010 - 20:04 Z

My name is Macy Beas. I thought the weirdness was over for me for this day but it wasn't. I see demons when they are on this side and I can see the vale that divides the worlds but the one thing I've never seen is an angel. I wasn't sure they even were real except these damn demons are supposed to be angels who went bad.

Tonight, I stopped at a dump to eat some "real" Texas food before I hit the road for Temple. My plan is to spend the night there and tomorrow be long gone from Texas. This dive I'm currently in is a bar named Mel's. I don't think one beer and some bar food will keep me from reaching Temple. It's not that far.

I'm sitting at a two top and reading the menu that was on the table when my waitress walked up and asked me if I wanted something to drink. I didn't even look up. I said, "Beer please. Your best draft."

She said, "OK. Name's Robin if you need anything. I'll be right back with your beer." I spotted the chicken fried steak and decided to go for the cholesterol. It was then that I looked up and saw Robin walking back to the table with my beer. She's rather short but a shapely girl with ginger hair and her skin makes mine looked tanned. When I saw her, the look on my face must have given away my amazement.

"Is everything ok? You look like you've seen a ghost."

"You know, I'm not ok by a long shot." To my surprise Robin sat down across from me. Looking around there weren't many people in the place.

"Me neither. Passing through?"

"Uh yea. I had a job here and it's finished up so I'm going back home. I'm sure I won't make it. I'll get another call before I get there."

"So, where do you live?"

Now this is one of those freakin' questions that I won't answer. Never. I have a set of cardinal rules. One is, no one knows my phone number or my address. It's just a thing I have but I answered her anyway, "Saint Louis Missouri. At least for now."

Robin looked around the bar to see if anyone needed anything, "Big city. I've never been outside of Mason."

I looked her right in the eyes, "Now that's a lie. You've been somewhere. Somewhere beyond the vail."

Robin had a look of shock on her face. "How could you know that? I've never told anyone and I mean no one about that. Who are you?" She was scared.

"It's ok Robin. I won't tell anyone. I promise. I don't tell anyone what I do or where I live. I don't even give out my phone number. Doesn't matter, I travel so much I don't have any friends anyway."

Robin said, "I know how that is. The friend thing I mean." Then I had a thought. She doesn't know she's an angel. Something must have gone wrong someplace.

Robin looked like she was going to get up so I reached out and touched her hand. Another one of my rules broken. Don't touch people. She didn't pull away but sat back down. She said, "I'm sorry. I'm rude." She took a moment to gather her thoughts. "See, my dad beat me and I spent seven months in a coma. It seemed like I was living in another place trying to get back here. I know I sound certifiable."

"Not really," I said. "I hunt demons for a living. Now that's freakin' certifiable," I paused thinking how I could frame this. I'd never explained it to anyone so the words stuttered, "I can see things no one else can. It's like I see a vail or hazy wall all around us. It's a boundary between here and somewhere else. On the other side are demons for sure. They cross that boundary when they find a soft spot."

Robin was looking into my eyes with so much intensity I blinked. Looking down at the open menu in front of me. She said, "You've never seen anything else? I think maybe I was in that place. I was someplace."

I looked up, "No. Nothing else. But...," I couldn't go on.

Robin said, "But what? I know something about me isn't right. My dreams are so scary and I think maybe they aren't just dreams."

"I was going to say that you have a glow about you. It's a beautiful glow and I just know, like with the demons. I know you are an angel or something."

Robin started laughing. "I think you are not seeing too clearly today. I'm anything but an angel. I'm just a broken-down waitress living in Mason pushing drinks all night at Mel's." She stood. Not rude but in a friendly way. "Gonna eat?"

"Sure. Chicken fried steak. That'll do it." She wrote that down on a ticket then smiled at me. It was such a lonely smile. I just chucked my rulebook out the window.

"I'll get that right out. Thanks for talking. It was nice. What's your name?"

"Macy Beas." I fished in my kit and found a very old card with my info on it. Handing it to her I said, "Here. You can always call me." She took the card and looked at it like she'd never had anyone even care enough to reach out the hand of friendship.

"Thanks. I might." She smiled and walked back to the kitchen to put my order in. I didn't see her again.

So that's it. My one time seeing an angel and the angel didn't even know she was an angel. There has to be one strange story there. - Δ

NOTES ON REAL MYTHOLOGY AND RELIGION

I know that some people will be confused by the interweaving of myth with religion but I'm ok with that. I upset people on a regular basis. To give you perspective, I'm a Roman Catholic. The idea of ariel toll booths and demons manning them is taken from a tradition found in the Eastern Orthodox Church. It is an idea not widely excepted but I found it to be fascinating and almost unknown to westerners. Of course, there aren't any real toll booths that's just a metaphor. The idea is one dies and what we think of as the "near death experience" is just a time of transition from here to there. Once we are there we travel up through the air to Heaven.

Satan has power over the air so the notion it is full of demons waiting to stop you on your journey seems very logical. They will point out failures and attempt to convince you how you are not worthy to pass and head on to Heaven. Two angels will be with you and they will defend you. They will carry your toll box full of the good things you have done and at each challenge take an event of your life out of the toll box and use it as proof you have earned passage.

You either make it to Heaven or you fail and go to Hell. The Orthodox idea is this isn't a permanent placement. You still could get out of Hell before the door is locked. Now I say again, this is a concept that is not accepted by the mainstream Orthodox Church. Note my bibliography for references. Father

Seraphim Rose has written extensively on this subject and I refer you to his work.

This model may fly in the face of some Christians because it looks like you "earn" your way to Heaven but the more you study this material the more you understand that's not true. Now I believe all stories have a basis in fact somewhere. Noah and the flood are documented by several cultures. The same is true of the Olympic and Pre-Olympic gods. Many of them had the same aspect but changed names from culture to culture. There must have been something the people were referring to. Not the gods of Olympus because if so where did they go? Reading the Bible, you see man had a lot more interaction with angels than we hear of today. Angels are mentioned around 225 times in the Bible.

I feel it is one possibility that mankind viewed these angels as gods and goddesses when they had no frame of reference in which to put them. There is a lot written about angel's interaction with humans some good some very bad. It brought in wars and eventually the great flood.

Maybe goddesses like Hekate were angels doing the will of God in a world not yet familiar with the one true God. If so after the flood all names would have to be changed and a different way of interacting with humans found. What we do in creating fiction is ask, what if? That's all this is. That's why I teach, Be Curious, because you never know when you'll find a fascinating trail to follow. Look at the bibliography for reference books used to help create this story and this reality.

INTERESTING BOOKS

Many books were referenced during the writing of this novel. Here are a few I used. I read and referenced many more. Some are fascinating volumes recounting a hidden history, some are religious texts, some are questionable as to their history and worth. There were many books written during the first few hundred years of the Christian Church. Many of these books are not included in the current Bible. They were either redundant, texts tainted by other philosophical ideas or heretical teachings not in keeping with the core Gospels of the Bible. Some Old Testament books referenced were not part of the traditional Jewish Faith either.

There is value in many of these sources but mostly the books I relied upon were the Bible (both east and west) The Soul After Death by Fr. Seraphim Rose and Dr. John Dee's works that came from the era of Elizabeth I. If you go to these source materials use good judgement in what you take as truth and what is myth.

Rose, Fr. Seraphim. The Soul After Death. City: St. Herman of Alaska Brotherhood. 2009.

Saint Nikodimos of the Holy Mountain and Saint Makarios of Corinth. The Orthodox Study Bible Philokalia: Farrar, Straus and Giroux, 1986.

Fox, Matthew. The Physics of Angels: Exploring the Realm Where Science and Spirit Meet San Francisco:

Harper. 1996

Hauck, Rex: Angels: The Mysterious Messengers City: Ballantine Books. 1994

Mythology

Brines, M. E. Of Myth and Magic. City: Smash Words Edition. 2011

Coulter, Charles, Russell Turner, Patricia. Dictionary of Ancient Deities CITY: Oxford University Press. 2001

Rankine, David; D'Este, Sorita. Hekate Liminal Rites. city: Avalonia. 2009

Digitalis, Raven; D'Este, Sorita; Bramshaw, Vikki. Hekate Her Sacred Fires. city: Avalonia. 2010

Turner, Patricia; Coulter, Charles Russell. Dictionary of Ancient Deities. city: Oxford University Press. 2001

Meyer, Marvin W.; Mirecki, Paul Allan. Ancient Magic and Ritual Power. (Religions in the Graeco-Roman World (Reprint), V. 129) (Religions in the Graeco-Roman World (Reprint), V. 129) Brill Academic Publishers. 2001

Wassermann, James. The Mystery Traditions: Secret Symbols and Sacred Art: Destiny Books, 2005.

APOCRYPHAL TEXT NOT INCLUDED IN THE BIBLE

Apocryphal books include suppressed Gospels and Epistles not included in the New Testament of Jesus Christ or any other portion of the Ancient Holy Scriptures. Some of these books were venerated by the primitive Christian Church during the first four centuries.

Nylons, Dr. A. The Book of Jubilees -The Little Genesis. The Apocalypse of Moses Old Testament. Apocrypha. Pseudepigrapha. city: publisher. 2010.

Rutherford H. Pratt translated by E. C. Marsh and R. H. Charles editor J. B. Lightfoot. The Lost Books of the Bible and The Forgotten Books of Eden. City: Collins-Wood 2010.

Friedman, Richard E. The Hidden Book in the Bible city: HarperOne. 1998

The Book of Enoch - Anonymous

The Forbidden Gospels and Epistles - Archbishop Wake 2004 eBook #6516

OCCULT TEXT

Donald Ryles PhD and Johann Scheibel. The Sixth and Seventh Books of Moses. Lulu.com. 2011.

Peterson, Joseph H. Arbatel: Concerning the Magic of Ancients city: Ibis. 2009.

Harms, Daniel, Clark, James R., Peterson, Joseph H. The Book of Oberon. city: Llewellyn Publications. 2015.

Peterson, Joseph H. Grimorium Verum. CreateSpace. 2007.

Skinner, Stephen; Rankine, David. Veritable Key of Solomon. city: Llewellyn Publications. 2008.

Oribello, William. The Sealed Magical Book of Moses. city: Inner Light - Global Communications. 1991.

Grimoires - A History of Magic Books - Owen Davies

Summoning the Solomonic Archangels and Demon -Stephen Skinner & David Rankine

Princes - Stephen Skinner & David Rankine

The Sealed Magical Books of Moses - William Alexander Oribello

Wassermann, James. The Mystery Traditions: Secret Symbols and Sacred Art. city: Destiny Books. 2005.

Davies, Owen. <u>Grimoires</u>. city: Oxford University Press. 2010.

<u>The Key of Solomon the King</u> (Clavicula Salomonis) Solomon, King of Israel. city: Weiser Books. 2000.

Barbiero, Flavio translated by Steve Smith Inner Traditions Rochester. <u>The Secret Society of Moses: the mosaic bloodline and a conspiracy spanning three millennia</u> by VT & Toronto, Ontario Includes bibliographical references

Blavatsky, H. P. <u>Studies in Occultism.</u> iBooks.

Skinner, Stephen and Rankine, David. <u>Solomonic Archangels and Demon Princes.</u> city:

Golden Hoard Press. 2011.

<u>Secret Symbols of the Rosicrucian</u> - Vondel Park 2006 http://www.lulu.com/qabalah

Heindel, Max. <u>The Rosicrucian Mysteries.</u> ebook #29855. 2009.

ANGEL LANGUAGE AND MAGIC

The Private Diary of Dr. John Dee and The Catalogue of His Library of Manuscripts Edited James Orchard Halliwell B&R Samizdat Express. iBooks.

DeSalvo, John A. Decoding the Enochian Secrets Inner Traditions. & Bear & Co. 2010.

Rankine, Stephen Skinner & David. Practical Angel Magic of Dr John Dee's Enochian Table. LLEWELLYN WORLDWIDE, LT. 2010.

Joseph H. Peterson Editor. John Dee's Five Books of Mystery

The Angelical Language, Volume I. Based on the journals of Dr. John Dee and Mr. Edward Kelly. Aaron Leitch. 1555.

The Angelical Language, Volume II. Based on the journals of Dr. John Dee and Mr. Edward Kelly. Aaron Leitch. 1555.

Adam McLean, Editor. A Treatise on Angel Magic

Savedow, Steve. Sepher Rezial Hemelach: The Book of the Angel Rezial. Weiser Books. 2000.

Johnson, Ken, PhD. Fallen Angels self-published. 2013.

Douglas Van Dorn. <u>Giants Sons of the Gods.</u> Waters of Creation Publishing. 2013.

JEWISH TEXTS

Berg, Michael. The Secret History of the Zohar. Kabbalah Publishing. 2009.

The Essential Zohar: The Source of Kabbalistic Wisdom - Berg, And.

Zetter, Kim. Simple Kabbalah. Conari Press. 2000

Berg, Yehuda. The Power of Kabbalah: Technology for the Soul. Kabbalah Publishing. 2004.

The Zohar - Matt 2003 Stanford University Press

Cohen, Shoshanna. 10-Minute Kabbalah. Fair Winds. 2003.

Henning, W. B. The Book of Giants. Forgotten Books. 2007.

ABOUT THE AUTHOR

Wood Dickinson is a writer and producer of award-winning feature films. He is also a fine art photographer and published poet. Wood is a graduate of Texas Christian University with both BFA and MA degrees in communications. He lives in Kansas City with his wife, Patti, and cat, Patrick.

WOOD DICKINSON'S WEBSITES AND BLOG

WEBSITE - www.wooddickinson.com
BLOG - www.10pastmidnight.com
FACEBOOK - www.facebook.com/wood.dickinson
TWITTER - @wooddickinson
PORTFOLIO - wooddickinson.myportfolio.com

-COMING NEXT-
LEGENDS OF THE END

Book Two in the Robin Randle Series (late 2019)

JOIN the Robin Randle Community at
www.robinrandle.com or on Facebook at
www.facebook.com/TheRobinRandleStories/

If you enjoyed this book, please leave a review on Amazon or Goodreads.

51823191R00174

Made in the USA
Columbia, SC
26 February 2019